CRASHING TIDES

CRASHING TIDES

By Gwendolyn Marie

Independently Published

Book design by Cristina Tănase

ISBN-13: 9781674905891

Printed in the United States of America

First Edition

For Nicholas

Crashing Tides

"When beholding the tranquil beauty and brilliancy of the ocean's skin, one forgets the tiger heart that pants beneath it; and would not willingly remember, that this velvet paw but conceals a remorseless fang."
—Herman Melville, 'Moby Dick'.

"Yet on through moors and tree-clad mountainsides, over crags and cliffs and trackless wastes I ran. The sun was at our backs: I saw in front—or it was fear that saw—a giant shadow. For sure I heard his frightful footfalls, fled his panting breath upon my braided hair."
—Ovid, 'Metamorphoses'. On the Nymph Arethusa.

Prologue

She lived behind walls all of her life. Caged like a wild animal, regarded as such. Yet fortune came and she escaped her prison. But where did this bring her, she wondered, as she looked down to the stranger transforming in her arms, and then up to the madman staring at them both.

"What did you do?" she said to the madman named Triton. She tried to help the stranger, pushing him to his side to make sure he did not suffocate on his own blood. Triton had referred to him as the Pathfinder, though she knew nothing else about him. No matter how she tried to save him, she knew it was too late. She felt tremors in his body. Blood dripped as tears from his eyes and in those eyes she saw chaos. He tried to reach towards her, though not in reflex nor in desiring help, but in a blind struggle to retain his hold on life.

His arms seemed paralyzed though, preventing his intent to grab and claw at her. She knew that if she kept trying to rescue him, she would be trapped and both would be damned. And so she stepped away and took one last look pass the stranger and at Triton.

He did not move to stop her. Did not start a chase. Just watched and let the scene play out as if for his amusement.

She ran. Through the hallways, through the doors, she ran until one finally opened to the outside. However, neither grass nor concrete met her bare feet. Forests and cities did not come to view. Only steel under her stance. Only the ocean came to her sight.

Snow fell in the night sky. Water rose in waves, crashing against the hull of the ship. The wind tore against her skin as if to stop her, but still she ran. She spared one more glance behind her. Everything was shades of grey in the nightscape, but she saw the outlines of her captors. Their shadows were visible through the snowfall.

Triton. Several other forms flanked him.

Terror surged from the sight, but still she would not be subdued. Yet deep inside she knew the ship trapped her and deemed any escape pointless before she even had the chance.

All her life she wanted to get away. All her life she desired to escape, to fight, and then to live. And now she was faced with that life-long wish. She could jump and find freedom. The problem was that she would die as well, the cold sea swallowing her whole.

One wish came true: her escape. Perhaps if she tried for another.

To wish upon a star.

When did humankind find the belief that its troubles, hopes, and dreams can all be fulfilled by looking up above. By picking out that one shimmer of shining light and whispering the words that we can tell no other.

Did anyone truly presume that their dreams would be answered, she wondered. That their fears would be torn apart by starlight, leaving only our desires that could come true.

Still she looked to a star in the snowy night sky.

And even though the stars were hidden by the clouds, she murmured the words of longings that went unanswered for so long before.

Unlike all the other wishes she once made, this wish was different. This wish she had the sky above to wish upon rather than a ceiling. She needed it to come true, and with all her soul she had to believe that her voice would be heard in the cosmos above. That the star would answer, that her words did not fall upon deaf ears.

"Free me."

Free from all, a slave to eternity.

A gloved hand came from behind to restrain her. One of her captors pushed her down and she fell on the steel deck as he put his weight on her. She tried to fight back, but he folded her arms behind her in restraint, pressing his knee into the small of her back.

She would not plead, nor beg for his mercy. Instead as he pulled her to face him, she thrusted her knee between his legs. As he leaned over, racked in pain, she shoved her forehead into his.

Blood.

Hers. Not his. She had not met flesh when she had struck him in the head, but instead a mask and respirator. She grasped to stay conscious. Darkness descended upon her vision and soon she could not tell the dark of night from the dark of her subconscious.

One thing remained. The star she had wished upon, the light fading in and out amidst the overcast winter skies. She had to focus on it, to ward off unconsciousness, if she wanted to end this nightmare.

Though it did not wound him as expected, the guard loosened his grip. She was able to get out from under him and started away. She could only crawl as blood fell from her head in drops below. The red mixing with the white.

Something encircled her leg. She pulled, imagining instead she had found forest and the roots of the trees had come to life, granting her a repose as they pulled her beneath the dirt. But she knew this was not true. The grip tightened and another hold came upon her upper thigh. It was Triton. His hands grasped her.

He pulled her away. He pulled her back to hell.

Chapter One

Wild is the wind. Free is the spirit.

The wanderer walked, without a past, without knowledge of the future, toward a destination yet seen or known.

What was ahead mattered little as she walked along the coasts, spiraling beside the sea. And what lay behind her was forgotten. Yet she did not question why she was there, why she walked, why her past was gone. The answers were beneath a depth greater than the ocean floor, her memories being a blackened thought in her mind. From her perspective she always walked along the shore, always strode alone—without possession or care. Untethered to even the most simple things, she walked nude without as much as a name. But being stripped of all possessions exposed her to a primal freedom. It felt right and for the first time within even a forgotten life she was free.

She could only guess why she started this journey, or why along the way her memories perished as the sun was now to the midnight skies. But does it matter that the waves break with such tenacity to shred shells into sand or that each droplet of water may not succeed to find the ocean again. Does it matter why she walked?

Nature need not be questioned; the aberrant exists even without a place. And she would not search for why she was here, for what was important was neither the past nor future. What holds significance is life, and that is singularly defined by the moment itself. So she walked with each step harmonious with the lawless rumblings of the sea. Her sole companion was that of the animalistic—impromptu and irresistible— rage of nature.

Nothing lasts. Sandy beaches changed to rocky shores. Glistening in the moonlight, a dorsal fin peaked between the waves, indicating she was not alone. A peregrine falcon cried above, interrupting the melody of insentience. And then beyond a doubt, her solitude broke.

Steps, once unbound, faltered as a figure came to her sight. A man, but was he real or imagined?

Her hair, caught in the wind's dance, lashed against her back as if urging her forward. She succumbed and walked closer. The form became clear. He was dressed in a faded shirt and cargo pants rolled up to his thighs. He held a makeshift spear in one hand, composed of a knife tied to a stick. A net was in his other. Still a figment, she wondered, or did clarity come hand in hand with reality.

The man stepped into the waters. An unusual air clung to the enigma before her. Though she was sure that by now he noticed her presence, he did not grant a passing glance. Instead, his gaze remained on the sea. She looked over him, believing him to be one from tales long forgotten: a Fisherman. Even with her memory lost, she remembered the word as she knew the boundless pool of water before her was called an ocean and the fire of the sun, now hidden, would come again.

The waves burst upon the shore in spray as she walked to him. Coming closer, she then stopped at the cusp between the water and the rocks as she heard him speak.

"It is wonderful out here," he said, addressing her with his voice but not with his eyes. The words rang true to her, for no place other than here did she wish to be, no place as wonderful.

"Why are you here?" she asked, not in unkindness but in curiosity. It felt odd to her, for in his presence her spirit no longer soared, but was bound to adhere to the principles of conversation. However, the Fisherman said nothing, breaking her preconceptions. And though silence was his response, she accepted it in answer. The principles did not apply here, it was just the two of them. And so she spoke again, as the Fisherman waded out further, tracking what lay below the surface.

"Predators feed at night beneath the sea," she said, remembering the dorsal fin she had seen moments before. It evoked in her an image of the fin's possessor, though something told her upon sight of the Fisherman that he would accept confrontation without indecision. He would not flee the water as any sane person would do.

That belief was why she did not leave, why she stood still, intrigued.

"And I am one," he responded.

One of the predators. He spoke with such nonchalance that his words hypnotized her, not of meaning but rather of tone. He seemed not to care for anything but confronting one challenge after another; that was what she felt from the self-proclaimed predator.

Her stare danced toward the sea, visually chasing the fish as they darted to and fro between the Fisherman's legs. The shadows were difficult to discern in the night, but the movements were clear as they rippled the water.

Not invited to stay, but still not moving to go, she waited to see if he would succeed in the capture of his dinner. Hunger welled at the sight of him, the net, and his spear.

"Is fishing a challenge, when you have a clear advantage over the fish?" she asked, taking a step closer to the Fisherman. The spear set him above the instinctual fish, she believed, as well as human prowess set by evolution. Hunting had once been an everyday affair in the lives of their ancestors. Not an honored occasion, but rather habitual. Not of challenge, but of survival.

No reply again. An uncomfortable shift arose in the resolution of the Fisherman. Perhaps he did not want her to stay, she thought.

Minutes grew long as the hunt went on. She waited, knowing that it was too late to continue her path. Not in the sense of time, but rather she could not imagine herself turning away from the Fisherman. He threw the spear into the scales, in calculation to bring death and an end to his hunger. She desired to learn the same to satisfy her own hunger. Hunger that grew and grew as her sight lingered on the scene.

Without warning, the Fisherman stopped his hunt and turned to her. He spoke, his words as gutting as she imagined the knife would be. "In the bogs of Maine, surrounding these island shores and outward, life is driven by death and madness. Despite these horrors, there stands one thing. A trace of hope withstands the environment that destroys all else. The orchid Arethusa grows in the devastation and even flourishes in these impenetrable swamps. It is a piece of lasting dignity where no other can be found."

She barely understood what he said. Did the Fisherman even speak to her? Instead, it was as if he said it to the waves, breaking in white chariots, driving their pearl hooves into the shores. She even mused that he was not the one who spoke; rather, the rumblings from the sea itself formed the words. Whatever the origins of the allegorical voice, she listened as if said for her alone as he continued, the waves a crashing chorus to his questions. "Are you the Arethusa? Are you the last shred of hope within humanity, carved from the dragon's mouth to devastate ... but instead you bloom unexpectedly?"

A whimsical smile graced her lips. She did not know what to make of his view of life, entombed by darkness and gloom. All she could do was to interpret his words as a fancy of storytelling threads woven in her mind to create tales to delight in.

"Am I?" she questioned. "You ask, but I do not know. I only know that my stomach growls watching you."

She stepped closer on the rocks to him. Did she see fear pass in him?

"Teach me to fish," she continued, "please Fisherman."

Half of her expected no response, but he nodded in a voiceless tolerance. Without the charisma of a gentleman, the Fisherman stripped himself of his shirt and threw it to her. Still he remained silent as to why she was nude, not that she could explain if asked. She caught the shirt and pulled it over her head, unsure if gratitude or resentment came in wearing it.

It smelled of salt and fish, sweat and him. The shirt fit her as a dress, offering modesty in replace of the wind against her skin. Though even with her confinement in his shirt, she was enticed to begin tutelage under him. His teachings began not of speech, but for her to watch and learn.

She stepped into the water to join him. She delighted in the chill of the waves; they pounded against her as if to bulldoze any infringement standing in their path. Given time, they would have. Now, however, they only offered serenity.

The Fisherman sunk his blade into a fish. Red replaced the translucent blue. Was this the poet of only moments ago, she asked herself. Figurative speeches about orchids now replaced by the unembellished hunt.

As the sign of his kill diluted, she met his gaze. He acknowledged her with a sternness in his face. An inadvertent rejection of her presence dwindled in the stare between them. Why did she sense these emotions —why had she seen fear, she wondered. But instead of focus on this, she chose to see what was beyond his disapproval, a sense of familiarity and perhaps hope.

Or perhaps what she saw was just the moon aglow in his eyes.

"The fish view you as a presence outside their own world," he said, tearing the small fish off of the knife and throwing it into the water. She almost reached in to grab it, wondering for what reason the Fisherman would waste a prospective meal. But watching the body, watching its death soak within the waters, she understood as other, larger fish began to swarm near. He then handed her his spear. "In order to kill them, you must first make them accept your presence. To view you not as an intruder, but as something that was always there to begin with."

She stood still, though at first the fish rushed away. But it was more than the physical stillness she realized she had to obtain, it was from within that she had to focus upon. Lure the rippling of her soul to peace, to calm the creatures into a false hope. She thought of the deep sea predators, the dragonfish in particular considering the shared namesake of the dragon's mouth orchid, the arethusa, the Fisherman had mentioned. She mused that she could draw upon the starlight behind her, having it act as her own photophore, deceiving the prey. Or perhaps she could be fast enough to grab their bodies from below without them slipping through her fingers with ease. However, she suppressed trying to catch them bare handed. She was not the Fisherman. In order to learn one forgoes their instincts and listens to the wiser, at least at first. That was the foundation of civilization after all, to learn and build on the knowledge of others.

Then you can deviate. Then you can create the new.

Each fish scampered between her legs, even becoming brave enough to nibble on her skin with their beaks of fleshy scales. Painless though ticklish, their pecks and hesitant ventures turned more audacious as they became to view her as a humble co-inhabitant.

"It is not enough to be accepted. For one moment out of the ordinary will send them scattering back to the depths, allowing their instincts to overrule," the Fisherman said. "Instead watch them. Predict their movements. Though it seems erratic, even in chaos lies an underlying order. You will find reason within the rhyme."

Understand them, feel them, and see their movements yet to come. As a fish slid pass, she struck out and embedded the spear into the scales. Pulling upward, she smiled. The fish squirmed on the blade's end, her soon to be dinner. The body twitched in a last finality signaling the swimmer's end. The kill reflected in her eyes with a ravenous triumph; soon it would become meat so delicious that it would melt upon her tongue in feast.

Would thoughts of such bring her under the flag of evil—of one whose motto is within destruction? To kill something to appease your hunger: that was not evil, she reasoned, as long as that 'something' was not your own species. But why think of morality now, she wondered.

What would the Fisherman believe, for surely he, more than anyone, would understand the saying: death for life.

"Is it wrong to feel such good spirits in the wake of another's death?" she asked the Fisherman, looking to him for the answers.

In response to her question, the Fisherman opened his mouth as if to say something of grave importance. But nothing came, no words of wisdom or fanciful anecdotes. Instead he shook his head and turned. He had been there too long and had already offered her the only guidance he could. And so he left. He left her standing in the tides, and he walked to the shore and beyond, into the shadows of the night.

Alone once more, only the falcon remained.

Chapter Two

The Reaper's hand brought quiet to the night-lands. In its clutch life was gone: the fish had died and the Fisherman had walked away. Disappearance and death were synonymous to the beholder. But she embraced this solitude, even if in her brief memories she had known solely one. Now every moment that passed marked his departure from her life.

The Fisherman left no trail, though the spear and the shirt she wore offered proof of his existence. The purpose of the shirt was basic: to cover, to shelter, to inhibit. Tied and weighted by its material, she wondered how much this piece of cloth restrained her. The small pleasures, such as feeling the wind caress her skin, were lost and lost not by an uncontrollable force but by her own hand. Certain freedoms were denied in her choice to keep the shirt on, but in a simple way it allowed her to remember the Fisherman and to know he was real.

She spent sometime in the water, teaching herself to swim. Not knowing if she already knew or was learning anew, she moved her arms and legs through the sea. The buoyancy of the salt helped her, but she did not go too far from the beach in order to be able to put her feet down and remain above water when needed. Soon the cold became too much and she walked to the shore to start a fire.

Trees stood alongside the coast, and broken branches were abundant. She took some birch tree branches and several strips of juniper for tinder and searched the rocky shore for quartzite. She created a fire pit, and then struck the rock against the Fisherman's knife, which she had removed from the spear. The sparks lit the birch after several tries.

Survival by fire: was it instinctual or learned, she wondered as she cared for the sparks until they became stronger flames. She then set to readying the fish. Soon the smell of roasted meat filled the salt air. She breathed in, taking joy of her labor in making the fire before her. Perhaps the knowledge of creating fire was innate, and perhaps, she mused, the Greek Titan Prometheus had not only given fire to humans, but had wired it within their biology so even when memories were forgotten, fire never would be.

She held the fish at the end of the stick, cooking it as sparks danced from below. She watched the incandescence of flames pirouetting, watching as they grew and danced in the breeze. The fire seemed alive. Life must exist in the fire, for nothing else could animate it with such wonder.

As she stared at the burning tinder, her thoughts strayed to the whereabouts of any other human.

The Fisherman was the first, could he be the last? She supposed others lived beyond the shores, but now she wondered if society existed at all. The lighthouse she saw in the distance did not shine. The tower stood, stark against the shadows of night, lacking the ray of hope it offered to seafarers. But even if the revolving beacon shone, it would be in vain. Not one ship appeared on the sea. The shore was empty. She did not even see a solitary beachcomber. She saw houses between the trees, but the lights were not on. Were the people all asleep? Or simply not there.

In the sea, the fish swam, the sharks hunted. Nature flourished, as long as the lights were off, as long as the land remained empty of humans.

Grateful for the seclusion, she sat still watching the flames, yet curiosity spun in her mind as to what happened.

Maybe everyone was sleeping. Dreaming, hidden from her sight.

Or maybe they had never existed. Perhaps her presumption of human society was false—that her memory failed in this conjecture. Though, if it had, what other beliefs were false? Would the sun rise or would blackness forever possess the earth?

No. The sun will rise. Society existed.

Her musings became reflective on her own nature. Her blank past, yet her inability to mourn the lost. To basic things such as her name. Had she ever been a child with a mother to name her? The foam from the sea, gave rise to Aphrodite, so it may be with herself. Not that she was godly, she mused knowing that was far from the truth, but rather brought to this earth whole, as an adult. She was one who rose from the shores, and now was in need of a name.

Nyx. For some reason those letters combined in her mind's eye. Maybe it was her previous name, if she even had one. It did not matter, for it felt right.

With a name, came an identity. Wanted or undesired, needed or useless, she could not tell. But being alone, her name was left unspoken, only real to herself.

Shifting the timbers, she moved the fish to outside of the fire and picked off pieces to eat. The flaky white meat vanished in her bites. She saved some and threw it near the tree line, knowing the falcon was still nearby. Her insatiable appetite fed, yet somehow her hunger persisted, being more than a hunger for simply food.

Night turned to dawn. The sun rose at her back as she began to walk, the fire a withering blaze behind her. She did not follow the seashore again. Rather, she started inland, diverging from her journey across the coast. Intentions changed like the direction of the anarchic winds; winds roused by the gods or in her case by the Fisherman.

As she walked further from the coast, she saw a town. Would she find the civilization she had forgotten, she wondered. But she was hesitant to find companionship and answers for she felt like an outsider, and almost stepped away from society's door.

This was not society though. A closer scrutiny proved that to be true as she walked closer.

A broken sign marked the entrance; the town's name was worn on it —not by age but by misuse. She could not make it out, but if the Fisherman was correct, she was on a coastal island in Maine. However, the settlement did not paint a picturesque northeastern summer. Vacationers did not enjoy the sunrise. No cars drove along the roads to arrive to early morning jobs. On the contrary, it appeared to be abandoned. Abandoned not solely by life but by the divine, the town being left to fend for itself but failing profoundly. But to Nyx it promised the enchantment of a forsaken land awaiting an outsider to break its isolated, lonely existence. And in return, it would end her own isolation, her own solitude.

The buildings once swarming in a hive of life now whispered farewells from beyond. They stood to both sides of her, reminiscent of a ghost town. She wondered if she would find someone ... something. The Fisherman perhaps.

Yet no life resided in this forgotten world of abandoned relics. Houses but not homes. Dwellings but no one to dwell within them.

Yet there was something.

The air. The smell.

Rot, death. Humans evolved to abhor such a scent, but alas curiosity overcomes even that. And so she pushed ahead.

But then through the silence, through the smell, came a noise. It cut upon the emptiness and seemed to make all else disappear. Even the smell shriveled, as her hearing peaked above all other senses. She was not by herself. It escalated behind the side of a building, speaking otherwise against her musings that none inhabit this forgotten town.

She heard steps. A rodent? A scavenger? No, she reasoned, it was too regular. Too heavy.

Nyx followed the noise and walked around the corner. Then it came to sight. Her senses pivoted, her mind uncomprehending of what was before her, as if her vision was now compromised due to her reliance on hearing and smell moments before.

Disbelief came. And then belief.

A human figure walked before her. He, or rather *it*, was not the same as the Fisherman, nor as a human should be. A festering emptiness in its eyes echoed what should be found in a corpse. But it was not dead, nor ever had been. It lived. It moved with the desire to quench its thirsts rather than to lie down and accept the end—of the world, of humankind, of civilization, of itself.

It had red hair. It was taller than she. Soiled, tattered clothes hung from it. Sores spotted its flesh: gashes never bandaged, wounds filled with puss, boils. Injuries along its skin, which could have been healed by antibiotics or even care and cleaning, were left to rot. Tissue surrounding the more fragile surfaces of the face and neck had deteriorated, revealing underlying muscle. The nose of the male, both flesh and septum, had been broken away. The nasal passageway underneath lay exposed, like a dark third eye staring upon her.

Hopes of escape turned ill as it lessened the space between them in seconds. As it came close she could see it was not red hair color. Rather, caked blood. Blood that it desired to spill again; its slobbering lips curled back, anticipating quick satisfaction of cravings that seemed to have gone unfilled for too long. It brought its teeth near.

It was human before her, but there was no wisdom behind its stare. No logic or sagacity for what she saw was solely primitive impulse. She stood in awe, unable to register whether it was reality or an illusion.

It reached out and grabbed her, awakening her to its reality.

Snapped out of her shock, she took the Fisherman's knife and pounded it forward and in, embedding it deep between its ribs. She felt a gush beneath the impact, and her strike sent all the air out of this human beast causing it to release its hold on her. She turned and ran, the knife left embedded in the wound. But its tall form swayed as a blade of grass against the wind, and it again took chase. Even as she ran, she heard the trailing breath close behind.

As she turned the corner of the main street, her run from the creature faltered. The smell from earlier should have prepared her for the sight of corpses littering the street. She paused for seconds and then realized she would be dead herself if she hesitated anymore at this sight. It would be through the dead, for her now, where salvation existed.

Nyx ran between the corpses in hopes to escape. What had befallen the lifeless was not something to fear, but it was difficult not to as she saw their lifeless gazes upon her. She ran; the smell of rot danced in the air, filling her nostrils. One could only guess how long they were decomposing. Flies swarmed in delight around some and even inside their banquet. Degenerated lips exposed teeth and painted on the faces was an expression cemented with the horror of the moment before death arrived. Jaws opened, shrieking in their hushed tragedy. They seemed to cry to her, as if to suck her down besides them. But they were of no true threat. The threat came from the creature chasing her; the one making the only sound besides her amidst the silently screaming dead.

The redhead gained on her. Its hand reached for her again; it grasped her shirt and began pulling her toward it. She tried to rip away, tried to pull against this tug of war battle, realizing how the clothes condemned her. If she had been nude, escape would have been hers. But the choice had been made, and the shirt now truly became a prison. As if knowing this, the creature pulled more tenaciously, causing her to lose balance and fall. The human beast drew over her, teeth clenched in a grin as it looked down at Nyx.

The human remnants of this world came full force unto her in the rotting brutality she beheld. Was it always this way, even back when this city flourished? Maybe, but it was not as apparent—the beast not as visible. The blossom deceives. Appearances mislead. Behind the refined smiles of the past civilization, this frightening monstrosity had always been present, hidden in manifestation. Present, even if only behind closed doors. But now it lived unrestrained in the absence of the pretenses and norms of society. Restraint from within and without were gone; what remained was chaos. Its eyes reflected this. Its greedy mouth told the unsaid story as it sought its feast.

This cannot be the end. She pulled herself along on the ground, continuing to fight against the eventual, no matter how seemingly hopeless. But as it hovered, pausing for a second to ready itself for the final attack, a shot sounded. The creature's lips receded further back, the grin stayed though now it reflected one of fear. It fell. First to its knees, then its body went limp, and it fell to the street, the other dead welcoming it home. Dust swept upwards in the wake of the perpetrator and behind stood a stranger holding a weapon.

The gun bearer was a man. Not like the dead scattered in this town, nor the thing that had chased her, but a rational living human. Older than herself, his face depicted a depth carved by the sights of war. He was dressed in a thick grey material that covered most of his body, supplemented by gloves and boots. The clothes held a strange balance between a soldier's field clothing and that of a hazmat suit. A fabric covered his mouth but his eyes were lucid above it as he stared at her.

She looked between the warrior and body of the redhead, a thankful acknowledgment hinted upon her features. He said nothing, however, allowing only his gaze to accept her unspoken thanks. Then he moved his weapon to take aim on her. No shots were fired, not yet at least.

Three others came from behind him: two more men, one woman. Dressed similarly in uniform, the others stood as humans, not creatures. As soldiers. Quizzical expressions painted what she could see of their faces, as if they could not comprehend her existence. They asked no questions and kept their distance from Nyx. It seemed they waited for her to begin, to explain her appearance here ... or to attack them. Rather than fulfill their mindsets either way, she stood and ran.

She ran across the street away from the four. Weeds scattered in the sidewalks, breaking through the cement crevices as nature tried to reclaim its dominion. The human dead lay motionless in her path, no longer the kings of the land, only a part of the landscape. But she ran nonetheless. Were the soldiers good or evil, she wondered, for though one had saved her, he had also took aim on her. They could be the ones responsible for the dead she saw.

Before she could distance herself forever from their presence, another noise rang out from behind her. A needle-like dart pierced her back. It allowed her a few moments of clarity—and dread—and then her body dropped to the ground amidst the town's tragedy. Limbs paralyzed as the chemical of the dart raced throughout her. She began to lose focus, but she still saw a human carcass lying to the left of where she had fallen.

Maggots had made it a home, inching their way across the precipice of the chin to the throat in search of fresh decay. A hole was torn on the cheek; however, the cause was not of bacterial lesions or decomposition. Instead it seemed to be chewed off. Maggots spilled from the tear, finishing the feast that was started by another. That was the last sight before the induced sleep came. The dart's sedative drowned out her movements and thoughts, caging her. But alas even if caged, the wild can never be tamed.

Chapter Three

"Why did you run?"

The voice awakened Nyx from her forced slumber. She tried to get up, to move, but could not. The soldiers had shackled her by ropes; the bondage chafed her wrists. She pulled against them, but to no avail. Panic edged inside her, but instead of allowing it to overwhelm her, she looked to the sky. It was as if the more she stared within the blue abyss, the more likely she would transcend the ropes that contained her. Then once more her spirit would fly. Take me away, she silently prayed, to where the seas thunder to find their forgotten fury.

Clouded visions, which had been induced by the tranquilizer, began to fade. The understanding of her predicament became clearer. She tilted her head and looked around the horizon to the distance, wanting to know her surroundings in hopes it would convey some advantage. The far off trees, visible between the buildings, rustled in the wind. In the past one would never hear the forest's song for it would be lost in the town's commotion. Her focus shifted from the natural sublime to the man-made degradation. Buildings stood that were void of illumination, vacant of life. Every window embellished a dark hue, lacking any light and any movement.

She then looked to the immediate surroundings. They were just outside the buildings in a clearing. It must have served as a park, for rusted swings and slides hid in the overgrown grasses. An age of innocence reflected here; children's laughter rung in her mind superseding the brutal cries of the past. Her captors must have treasured the clearing of the antiquated park, though not because of the lost echoes of mirth and childhood joy, but because it granted the ability to see and kill any attackers before they became a threat.

"I am Leander. Please tell me who you are." The same voice. A different question.

When she had first come upon the soldiers, she assumed the worst; it was why she had run. And her instinct served her right, for here she sat, contained with rope. Outwardly, they were unlike the creature she had come up against, for these humans did not look monstrous. But inwardly, she believed them to be the same. Both had sought to make her their captive. Both threatened her, and though she did not realize why, freedom was everything to her. All hopes and dreams seemed ingrained in being free, for it felt as if all of her life she was not. And so she did not respond, instead she continued to survey her situation.

Out of the four soldiers, two stood in the distance as guards. The other two stood near to her. Both of their masks were off, but they still kept an adequate distance from her. The one who identified himself as Leander kneeled to her right as he questioned her, repeating himself in a fruitless interrogation. The second, the gun-bearer she had first seen, stood close to Leander; a stern, almost emotionless, expression graced his face.

An eerie feeling grasped her: that he was there to guard them from her. Somehow they viewed her as a threat. Not surprising considering her appearance. She wore an over-sized ripped shirt, akin to the indecency of the beast and not of a civilized being. All that they probably wished was for her to enlighten their understanding of who— or what—she was, in order to change the potential foe into a friend. But so far she gave them no reassurance, only silence.

Leander turned to the other soldier, probably seeing her distrust over his weapon.

"Hector, it's okay," he said, motioning to take aim off of her. Then he turned back to her, hope in his voice that she would now answer the questions. "Where are you from?"

The soldiers, the beast, the dead, the Fisherman even: these were what she made them to be. They translated into a mirage of thoughts, a reality that held whatever truth she made of it. It was in the mind where reality existed, transformed as we wish. And she was not sure if these soldiers were good or evil. The only evidence to who they were were her chains.

She turned directly to face the one closest to her—Leander. He seemed to be the captain of the squad, though his age must have been similar to hers. He spoke the inevitable questions of an interrogation, ones she ignored as she studied him. In his face she saw concern—a tale woven in Leander's features of repentance for having to restrain her. Looking closer she saw curiosity that told yet another tale, contrasting with the guilt. He wanted her here; he wanted to decipher her. For in her mystery, he believed clues would be found.

"How did you survive?"

The final question left Leander's lips almost as if he expected no answer. Her presence mystified him, as if she were a mermaid washed up upon the shores. And the last word that resounded confirmed this, holding such fairy-tale stipulation ... *survived*. Survived what, she thought, but did not ask.

He moved his gloved hand close to her, as if to put a wisp of her wild hair back in place. The soldier, the one he had referred to as Hector, almost reached out to cease the movement, but Leander's own sense stopped the gesture before being finalized. He withdrew as if she was not a human but a vile creature, venomous in nature. Not a mermaid, not serene. Rather, a siren whose song lures sailors to their death. Their song first sounds amorous, harmless, possessing promises of love. Most dive into the rocky waters in hopes to obtain such rapture. A few are not enticed, standing safe on their vessel. But then the lullaby turns tenacious in the siren's mouth, offering wisdom and knowledge beyond the divine. None can refuse the second calling; their deaths woven in the siren's tapestry as they abandon the ship, looking overboard for their answer. Seeking everything, but finding solely death.

And now here she sat, she appeared as the siren who emerged in the aftermath of the destruction of many, holding the wisdom Leander begged for. He was the sailor, escaping death in the first storm, only to be dragged along the ocean bottom in his quest for knowledge.

But what knowledge did she contain, she thought. None, for she could not even offer him her real name or how she came to be here. If she did answer their questions, they would not believe her, and then what would happen?

A sharp breath, breaking his trance, brought Leander back to reality. It seemed to her that he shook off the tales of sirens. After all, she would not lure him to death. She was not what he feared.

"Talk to me," Leander said, his voice carried a concern of what would become of her if she should not comply.

Though if she did, she wondered, what would become of him.

"I will, but release me," Nyx said.

Surprised to hear her at last respond, his fears of her being a fiend appeared to dissipate and warmth replaced his hardened features. It seemed the human monsters, like the redhead, could not speak. In her silence, indisposed to the governing social cues, she realized she had left them no choice but to believe the worst. Now her speech demonstrated otherwise. The five words halted her impending death sentence and proved to the soldiers she was human. But even with Leander's eased disposition, Hector remained solid in his stance, viewing her statement as in-compliance.

Reaching up again, this time Leander lassoed the piece of hair awry and pulled it back from her face. He tried to offer amity in his action, as if he cared for her well being, and did not wish her harm. She did not flinch from the curious gesture but rather skewed her head to again unbound the strand of hair.

"I cannot," Leander said, his voice containing dislike for his position. But for the sake of civilization, for the hope of humanity's redemption, he had to find answers. "Not yet at least, but the more you cooperate the sooner I can get you out of the binds. Tell me: who are you? Why did you run from us?"

She took in everything: from the shake of his head to the intriguing frown that crossed his face. However, the frown reflected no sorrow. Instead it reflected the ambiguity of one placed in a position of undesired authority far before his time.

"We do not wish to keep you in custody," he continued. "You must understand what is out there and our puzzlement over how you are here. How you even survived is beyond us."

Placing his hand up against the playground's slide, Leander paused. Nyx had forgotten if she had ever slid down the metal slope as a child. Nothing came in recollection. Nothing of her past.

"You are able to speak, so you are not infected. I see it in your eyes," he said. "But then who are you? Where are you from? Please ..."

"Please free me," she said. She knew the answers she would give would not satisfy them, and her only hope of living would be to get away.

He walked toward her and revealed a military knife in his hand. The action caused the warrior who had initially saved her, the one named Hector, to react. He had been unreadable during the questioning, standing wordlessly to the side. But now he advanced. Whether he moved forth to assist in her execution—or to stop it—she could not be certain. But Leander did not use the knife to end her life. The blade sheared down to seek rope and not flesh, cutting the strands and leaving her to the independence she so desired.

Her gaze flashed to Hector, intrigued to see whether relief or disappointment would fill the inscrutable stare due to her release. But he stood, still unreadable to her.

Leander's decision illustrated that the soldiers were not mindless killers like the one she crossed in the town. To detain her without reason was making them such in her mind. Maybe Leander saw this, that though humanity was on the verge of collapse, they should not hold someone if they were guiltless.

"There you go; you are free. Now answer the questions."

She stood, about to leave. But not yet, for she mused over his questions of whom she was. Even she did not know that answer, if there even was an answer to tell.

"I am what stands before you. Nothing more, nothing less. I come from the foam of the sea, to the shore from below," she said, recalling her previous analogy explaining where she came from. It was enough for her, and she hoped it would ebb Leander's constant questions.

He did not step toward her, giving her an acceptable periphery. Still, he did not find her answer sufficient. She saw that in him. The soldier continued to go against the tide no matter how strong the current, wanting answers even if she had none to give, for his questions were not just about her. The way that he looked at the abandoned playground, the town's collapse. It was as if it was new to the soldiers ... and they were but foreigners to the travesties.

"A name then?" he asked.

To give a name contained the same indomitable limitations as the binds that had kept her. To give a name would be even more severe than the rope, for the restraint was intangible and not easily cut by the corporeal knife. Still, he had shown her compromise. Therefore she spoke the name that she had given herself in the fellowship of the fire, out loud for the first time.

"Nyx Arethusa."

The Fisherman's words now came to her. Arethusa—the orchid, which she had made her surname. The percipient warning of the Dragon's mouth remembered. The Fisherman's unyielding whisper spoke in her mind even though the illusion of the weathered guardian did not come to sight. She only saw Leander.

"As said, I am Leander—captain aboard the Thalassic."

He spoke with a sincerity shining through his previous demeanor. For him the tides changed, and the first breakthrough was met. He continued, introducing the rest of his squad, first motioning in the distance to the two that secured the outer area.

"Megaira and Diomedes."

As Leander spoke their names, Diomedes called out with a smile, "Just call me Dio!"

Nyx looked toward them. The two looked like opposite ends of the spectrum. Dio was large, both in height and width. He was not fat per se but the pounds of muscle he carried were not rigid and cut as one would expect from a soldier. Features caramel and broad, his ancestry must have been American Indian. His face had an everlasting cheer to it; he probably saw a bright side to everything, taking life as it came.

She smiled at him from the distance, and he returned her greeting with a genial wave and grin before returning his attention to surveillance of the area. The other soldier, Megaira, had a slender form, chiseled and probably not an ounce of fat on her. Golden hair outlined fair skin. Her face the stark opposite of Dio—looking for a fight even where none existed. One glance at her, and you knew to beware. She paid no mind to Nyx, regarding her as one would an inanimate object.

"I owe much to them," Leander continued, "as you now do to Hector."

As he spoke the last name, he referred to how Hector had saved her life from the redhead. But she wondered otherwise: did Hector really save her, or just damn himself.

She focused upon Hector. His face was unchanging. The body epitomizing what is expected of a soldier. His expression showed nothing more than it needed to.

Leander continued and she looked at him again, wondering what he expected from her now that introductions had been exchanged.

"We can offer you protection," he said. "I would not recommend you venture forth alone. That Chaot is far from the last. They are everywhere, the land is theirs. Where we travel is not much safer, but at least you would not have to walk through hell alone, lest you become it."

He said these harsh words meaning no animus. He said it as if it had become the jarring truth of the age—an age absent of the civilized.

"Chaot?" she questioned. Even with her amnesia, she knew the meaning of the sky, the birds, humans, cars. But not Chaot.

"Yes, like that thing in the street you came across," Leander explained, his surprise clear as to why she would not know of them. "You do not know of the term ... or of them?"

She could lie and say it was just the term she did not know, for what would happen if she admitted the truth? Clearly she had missed some event that had shaped humanity, and that had become the world these soldiers now lived in. Nyx couldn't remember things from before, or how it used to be, other than assumptions. Was it even an event she had missed, or was this the world as it always has been.

"Did you come from a place without these?" Leander continued, taking her silence as the latter. An edge of hope in his voice, or incredibility, for perhaps he thought it was impossible that one could live without knowledge of and free from these things.

"I do not remember."

Leander nodded, accepting her answer for that was probable, more so than a fairytale of a land not touched by the pandemic. "I will check you over, you may have suffered head trauma resulting in some memory loss fighting with the Chaot. But until your memory returns, know to be wary of the Chaots. A bite, saliva shared, even a substantial scratch from one of those things would make you susceptible to the disease they carry. Any direct form of bodily fluid contact. Once infected you will suffer the same fate of the Chaots."

Leander studied her for a reaction, surely wondering about her lack of knowledge surrounding the Chaots and if it was in fact due to a hit.

She registered no terror, only a stark realization of what the world was now: life and love definitively cut short, making once comrades into enemies as the contagion transformed its victims. A disease so strong it could break the minds of the most dedicated warriors with but a wisp of its tendrils.

"Come with us. After our operations, we will go back to our base, the Thalassic. You should be safe there."

At the corner of her vision, she could not help but see Hector's gaze. He looked at Leander with what she believed to be objection but he remained silent, too restrained by duty to misstep authority. It was evident, she believed, that Hector did not wish to compromise the safety of their homestead, the Thalassic, nor did he desire having the extra weight of her hindering their operation. Not only could she be a liability in such a hostile environment but also an anchor to their movements and mission.

She, however, did not want to accept Leander's offer. She was puzzled over the proposed safety granted by the Thalassic. If the Chaots now roamed as dominant, how could Thalassic serve as the impermeable harbor? A question she did not ask; an explanation left unsaid by Leander. But that was not the reason why she rejected the sanctuary proposed by the soldiers. One can go so far as to put restraints upon others in order to safe-keep them from the evils of the world. They believed that they knew what was best. However, it is in that belief that they would take away all free-will. The shelter soon becomes a cage. No longer is the free truly so, but now a prisoner. Though the fault is the prisoner's own, having gone willingly in the shelter. And she would not accept this.

"I leave it in your hands, Nyx," Leander said.

Her head arched in wonder, hearing her name on another's lips for the first time. It was bittersweet. An attraction, a craving, a curiosity filled her interest towards Leander. With his offer the captain may have insinuated that it was her choice, but she wondered if it truly was. She believed he instead led her to believe the choice was hers in order to make her into a willing captive. She would not be incarcerated by such delusion. And even though the soldiers seemed trustworthy, it was not enough for intuition told her that in their company she would be reduced to a detainee whether intentional or not.

"I am sorry, I do not trust you," she said. She did not trust it was indeed her choice to go with them. And so she turned and left, running bullheaded through the grass.

Hector, took aim by instinct at the fleeing survivor, but Leander placed his hand up. The weapon lowered at the unspoken order to stand down. Though she did not see it, a silent understanding passed between them. Nyx was the only thread offering clues to this disease, whether being able to lead them to other potential groups or somehow even being the cure they sought, being a survivor when there should be none. They would not allow her to escape; they would follow to see where she would lead them.

Chapter Four: Leander

Three and a half years previous: On the Marshlands

Through the swamps, through the marshes, through the forests, through the snow, two soldiers hiked. Leander waded in the marsh. It was up to his waist in a frosted sludge and he held his pack high over his head. Dio struggled to his side, the weight of the larger man clearly making it more difficult. They were dropped in unknown Maine territories, and needed to use their skills to survive the cold wetlands and find their way to the check point in a four day period. But as he looked toward Dio uncertainty rose if his partner would prevail. He could leave Dio and complete his training, graduating with high honors. Or carry the weight for two, and not meet the deadline. However, it was not even a choice to Leander. They were comrades and he would not abandon him.

Dio stumbled with fatigue, falling deeper into the water. But before the murky depths consumed him entirely, Leander reached out and grabbed him. Just in time, for the packs hovered dangerously close to the water. With their supplies wet their chances would dwindle to nothing, for they needed a way to warm up after finding a drier area. They had also tied their winter wear to the packs while passing the swamps, and those would provide a barrier against hypothermia soon, as long as the clothes stayed dry. Pulling Dio up, Leander grabbed his pack and put it over his own. The weight pressed against him as he used the rest of his strength to steady Dio and allow him to rest.

"You should leave you know. Leave me behind. If you're late for the check-point you can't go on."

"Leave and miss the fun? Never, man," Leander answered.

"I don't know why they put us through this anyway," Dio said. "Not like we will ever use it."

Was it even the survival and war skills that the training taught, or rather was it the bond created between the soldiers? The training stripped the men of all that they were, and it left them with only each other.

Dio reached in his pocket, shivering, he pulled out a photo now stained with water. Trying to smooth what he could, he then showed the worn memento to Leander.

"My family. My little girl, Cassie. A couple years serving aboard the Thalassic will more than fulfill the requirements of the director position at the local Aquarium. Then I'll be home with them. Man, though, if I knew I would be waist deep in ..." Dio said, breaking into a hearty laugh before he finished. Joking to the end, in spite of the hunger and overwhelming exhaustion. "Never told anyone, but damn, I hate deep sea diving. And here I am applying for service in the Thalassic. In a goddamn undersea colony."

A look at the picture opened a piece of Dio that Leander had never seen before. The cheerful bloke sat with his wife flanked to his side. And squished in-between was a young girl. Missing one tooth in the smile, curly hair that seemed to bounce even in the still photograph.

"Wish I had something like this," he said as Dio placed the photo back inside his pocket.

All his life, Leander had worked toward studying the oceans and serving his country. He had never placed himself first, but rather his work. From the coast of Maine, as a child he would sit and look out toward the dark grey expanse, daydreaming of the time when explorers would venture down below. And now he had his chance. Unlike Dio, he trained not simply to secure another job; rather this was his life. All he wanted was to be below the sea, and soon alongside Dio, he would be. But still something was missing. The thing that he saw in Dio's photograph.

Leander looked out, seeing only overcast marshes in their path. That ... and a lone orchid, a fusion of pink and purple fighting against the gloom. A smile caught his lips as his sight settled on the willful flower, growing despite the odds. It gave him peace. He did not search for such a sight, yet he found it. As with love; you do not search for it. It blooms when it is ready to, as the orchid does.

"Come on, one more day. Don't want to be late. Even if I have to carry you over my back, we are going to complete this together," Leander said. Dio started wholeheartedly laughing again in response, and his laughter became infectious.

One year previous: In the sea below

Leander folded his arms over his decorated uniform. He did not cherish the insignia though, for he did not feel it was deserved. His status came from oceanic research and not from actual combat, though being stationed on the Thalassic offered no opportunity to serve in the front lines. However, some may find that lucky, considering the current enemy was one without a known weakness. The disease or whatever the hell it was that assaulted humankind left even the strongest artillery to shame.

To his left, his friend and comrade Dio looked at the monitor displaying his wife, child, and mother. Dio's family was in the submersible, heading down below the ocean to the Thalassic to escape the havoc of the coming Armageddon. However, Admiral Telphousian had come into the room and interrupted, placing the transmission on mute.

"I cannot allow this, Diomedes," Telphousian said. Acting head of the undersea colony, she overtook command of the Thalassic naming herself Admiral while the true commander was stuck surface side. And with the quarantine in effect, who knew how long that would be. "No one in or out. It is the only way I can keep Thalassic safe from the disease."

Dio did not say anything. He could not. Instead, Leander stepped between the two and pulled Telphousian to the side. "This is his family. They need to board; they cannot go back to the surface. We can place them in quarantine, contain them until it is certain that they are not a threat. And we can learn more from his mother. We can study what we are up against, for here we are in the dark. You cannot sentence them to death."

"Stand down," she said, the words dripping cruelly off her lips. She tugged her arm loose from Leander's hold with one forceful backward movement as she turned her attention to Dio. "I will not allow them to board. Have them go back surface side, and I will ignore the fact that you abused the use of the submersible for your own means, Diomedes."

"I cannot. They will not last," Dio said. He looked from Telphousian to the screen displaying his family. Behind his wife and daughter was his mother. Placed in a container, tubes shoved in her nose, she laid tranquilized.

"My wife said she could not leave her; she had hoped the Thalassic could place her in hibernation until a cure is found," Dio continued. "The tranquilizer they gave her will not last to make the trek back to the surface; they don't have much time."

Dio's mother would awaken, a Chaot. She would kill his family if they remained in the submersible.

"Even more reason to deny your request, though even without her I would say the same," Telphousian said, her voice cracked from the stern dictator to reveal tenderness beneath her fiery locks despite her words.

She turned and left, leaving Dio alone with Leander, and alone with his impending hardship.

Before his friend succumbed to heartache, Leander stepped to Dio's side and turned off the mute to open communication again. He spoke to Dio's wife, his voice one in control, though he himself was well aware of the consequences. "Listen to me. Bring the sub to the east side of the Thalassic. The moon pool will be closed and secure, but I can get you in another way. Just wait for me."

Dio's hand came to his shoulder, though no thanks were spoken. Instead, so much more than that passed between them.

Leander left to prepare. Wetsuit. Breathing masks: his and three extra. Oxygen tanks. Fins. And a medic pack, complete with more tranquilizer. Dio could not come, he would be more a liability than help. Maybe Hector, Leander thought, but he quickly dismissed the new addition to the Thalassic. Hector was only supposed to be onboard to debrief the undersea colony about the situation on land. Though with the quarantine in place, Hector had to stay. His anger toward the Admiral upon hearing that he could not return to fight made Leander believe that Hector would help. However, even though Hector was the only one with experience facing the Chaots, he was not trained in diving. Leander had to do this by himself.

Dio soon came out from talking to his wife over the radio, a smile covering heavy eyes and a heavy soul.

"I should have known that I would be going out in the deep blue sooner or later," he said, trying to ease the situation in his jest.

"I know how you feel about diving," Leander responded, "and I need you with me like I need a hole in the head."

That was only part of it though. Sure, Dio would slow him down for Leander was a faster and more experienced diver, but it was not that simple. What worried Leander was what would happen after they arrived at the submersible. He needed someone who could keep their head on straight in a tough situation, and when family was involved it added a whole new dimension to staying in control.

"Keep the communications and monitor off, or else the commander will put an end to our rescue."

"Just bring back my family. And maybe I will give you a medal that actually bears importance," Dio said in response, though Leander frowned as he remembered his thoughts and how naive they had been. Now he understood the price of meaningful medals, and the weight they truly carried. And the weight of the fate of Dio's family that he now carried, praying he would succeed.

Dio reached over to the emergency hatch. He spun it open before reaching out for Leander's arm to help lower him down. Leander reached back, having his hand rest on his shoulder for a moment longer than necessary, in reassurance that he would succeed in getting his family to safety. Dio closed the hatch behind him, sealing it shut.

Leander climbed down adjusting the pressure, allowing for the tube to be filled with water. As the water crawled up his legs, he adjusted the mask over his face, bracing himself for full submersion.

The water inched up to his chest; finally it submerged his head, and he positioned himself down, hands ready to twist the hatch. The water filled to the top of the tube, the green light flashed signaling the matched pressure of the outer limits. He rotated the handle of the secondary hatch. Soon he would be back in the sea he loved, however it was no longer love that he felt as the sea became more and more an obstacle in his rescue of Dio's family.

He had to succeed. He did not know how he could return otherwise.

And through hell

The submersible came into view. It drifted, meandering in the tug and pull of the underwater current. It was off course, far from the east point of the Thalassic. Leander spent ten minutes longer than he had expected, not giving up on them in hopes of finding the sub.

Finally the sub's headlights had come into sight, a beacon in the dark abyss. But now that he looked at the metal shell, he knew that he was too late. His heart sank, though he still pushed ahead through the sea. He had to continue for Dio. He could not give up for him.

He steadied himself, swimming along the enclosure, and looked in through the oval window. The wife sat. Face chewed off.

Pulling back, Leander turned to the blackness of the sea, closing his eyes, trying to steady his breath. Heart pounded as he turned back to the window. Dio's mother bent over the chair where the wife sat, a metal rod stood erect through her torso. Both dead. Red streaked the dress, red soaked down to the floor. He tried to look beyond the sight, beyond the carnage. He needed to find Dio's daughter, Cassie, needed to find her alive and bring her back to her father.

He saw something move. A shadow. That was all he needed to confirm that someone aboard survived. He climbed over the sub's hull towards the hatch. The water lashed against him, the pressure of an entire ocean weighed him down. Leander emptied his mind of doubts, especially of the image that continually flashed in his head: Dio's wife, Dio's mother, forever in tragedy. What he did try to hold on to was hope; it was all he could do.

The outer control panel was positioned near the side hatch. He swam to it and input the code to commence the pressure adjustment: the entry room into the sub would fill with water to match the pressure outside the hull. Then, and only then, could he open the hatch to get inside and help Cassie. He knew that every second the girl was inside alone—watching her mother's blood fall to the floor—was a second filled with terror. He would have to be fast when the pressure aligns, granting him access to the entry tube that then connected with the main hull. Now he could only wait as it filled with water.

Swimming back toward the oval window, he looked in. Dio's wife now hung, half off the seat.

It had to be the motion of the drifting submersible that had made her fall from her place.

Hair hanging down, the locks resting on Dio's mother, she was so removed from the picture he had seen of her years ago. The picture of her smiling, full of life, deteriorated from his mind as if a fire had been set to the photograph. The flames scorched her image, replacing it with a faceless void. He forced his gaze away from her, looking for Cassie.

The little girl sat in the corner. She sat still even with the turbulence surrounding her. Leander placed his hand on the window, wishing he was there to console her and let her know this would soon be over. He thought of her as his family, though he had never met her. She was connected to him through his ties with Dio. He knew it would be a gamble going inside the sub, the chance of contamination high; but if he could save Cassie, nothing else mattered. She was worth the risk. He would give anything to save her, anything to bring her back to Dio's arms.

The hand turned into a fist as Leander pounded once against the hull as if he could break through the steel. One last look to the girl, he damned himself for what he could not help. He swam back to the hatch, counting down the moments before he could break the release seal and go in.

Minutes passed before the beacon finally signaled ready. He opened the hatch and swam in, sealing it behind him. One last step: pressurize the tube to match the sub's main compartment. Seconds stretched out, time forming a barrier to him. The water lowered, his feet pressed firmly on the ground, and finally the last beacon blinked, confirming safe entry.

He opened the interior hatch. Water sloshed out from around him, as he stumbled through and lifted the breathing mask from his face. He saw the girl hunched over in the corner, probably petrified in shock over what had occurred. Relief came to Leander—he would be able to get her back, he would be able to at least give Dio one shred of peace amidst the deaths of his wife and mother. He walked to the girl, hand out in a gesture of affinity.

"Don't worry, Cassie. Your father sent me. He is waiting for you ... you will be away from here soon. You are safe now, with me."

He took a step. She did not move. She hunched over herself, hunched over an object, but Leander could not make it out. It seemed she trembled in terror, understandably. But something was out of place —not right—though Leander chose to ignore it and focus on his rescue.

The light flickered above. On and off, the light switched. The power of the sub had been depleted.

The light went blank. Nothing. Blackness. Darkness.

The sea for the first time felt cold to Leander. Always had it been so, but for the first time as he looked to Cassie did he actually feel the cold, like a wrath tearing apart all warmth from his soul.

The emergency light flickered on. Before him sat Dio's daughter, she held a piece of her mother's hand, partially eaten. Skin covering muscle. Always would the vile be unearthed.

The little girl looked up. Blood stained her lips.

She stared at Leander. Her pupils were clouded. Skin ashen against the trail of red that fell from her mouth.

The future played before him of what could never be as he took another step toward Cassie. The future of things that would never occur in the face of the plague. It was too late to save the girl. Yet he could not give up, even when the situation confronting him offered only hopelessness.

"It's okay, I'll get you back. It will be okay."

His words could only comfort himself, for she no longer understood.

The girl hissed in an unearthly reverberation. She threw the chewed hand down and ran toward him—hands out, looking to tear him limb from limb, despite his size and strength over her.

He caught her in mid-stride, turned her away from him and held her, making sure the biting teeth did not dig into his wetsuit.

"Don't worry. I'll bring you to Dio; I'll bring you to your dad," Leander comforted the child, not knowing what else to do. He could not kill her. A child. His friend's child. He looked down at the curls, tossing and turning as the girl squirmed in his hands. Lost innocence, his first look at what had come to the world above. The first time he was face to face with what the ocean had shielded him—and all Thalassic—from.

I could tranquilize her, he thought, bring her to Thalassic and hope for an antidote to be found. But as he reached for the med pack, she rammed her head backwards into his, her resilience amplified from the adrenaline that pumped through her. He fell, his body knocking against the controls and activating emergency protocol for escape.

The sub lurched at the activation; Cassie fell back and away from her prey. The underwater grave began to fill with water to match the pressure and open the emergency hatch. Water poured on top of the girl as she struggled forward: her sights solely on her attack and not on the threat of being buried alive by the pounding water.

Leander opened the medic supplies, grabbing the tranquilizer shot. He needed to administer it on Cassie, get the breathing mask on her and get her back to Thalassic. His mind could not focus on the facts: she was a Chaot, she was already lost to them. There would be no antidote. No cure. But all he could focus on was getting her back to her father. He staggered toward her, trying to steady himself as the water came in.

Syringe pointed forward as the girl came to attack, he pushed it in her. The needle pierced her skin, but before he could press down and release the fluid to her system, she knocked it away. The syringe fell into the rushing water, lost to him, the tranquilizer disappearing in the current.

The water continued in. The waves of sea filled the sub, lifting the bodies, Leander and the girl in its girth. She was there, kicking, struggling against the incoming force of water, still trying to attack even as the air diminished. Leander placed his mask on knowing that it combined with the deep sea wet suit would provide the barrier needed against any contagions in the water. He then swam over, wanting to place the extra mask on the girl's face. Avoiding her strikes to attack him, he grabbed her as the water rose to touch the ceiling.

She did not take a last breath of air, her intentions not of survival.

He moved quick, brought the mask over her face, securing it in order to empty the water from it. But the emergency hatch opened automatically as the pressure equalized to the outside, sending in a strong current that tore his grip from Cassie. Free from his hold, she tore the mask from her face. Despite the odds, despite the futility, he grabbed the mask again and swam toward the girl.

He could still get the mask over her mouth and bring her in. She kicked, she scratched in the water, eyes spread wide in a feral stare. He kept trying, even as the current swirled viciously around him as if alive. Cassie gasped; her mouth opening as water pushed itself into her lungs.

Her movements lessened, enabling him to secure her mask. But as he purged the mask to allow air in, he saw her face. Death filled her open eyes.

He could still take her. Bring her lifeless body to Dio. Try to breathe life into her, and even if that succeeded, it would not be Dio's little girl that came back but a Chaot. His action, however heartfelt, could lead to the death of those aboard the Thalassic.

Leander left without Cassie. He swam from the sub, hope sinking as the submersible plunged to the far depths behind him.

He would tell Dio he could not find the submersible. That way his comrade, his friend, could imagine his family had time to go back to the surface. He could imagine his family still lived.

Leander would carry the weight of what truly happened himself. The image of the girl, teeth sunk into her mother's hand, ever-present.

Chapter Five

Solitude had come for Nyx as she ran through the town. She knew the soldiers would be not far behind and so she did not cease running. Faster still, she fled not just the physical but the mental. Subconscious questions filled her head with uncertainty. Much had happened, much that she could not make sense of. The death that entrapped the city, the creatures spurned from hell dubbed Chaots, the soldiers rescuing her only to dart and bind her: all this dominated her thoughts. So she ran and as the scene grew distant, her spirit roused again.

The town's organization hallmarked the usual northeast waterfront communities. Downtown, interspersed with residential areas, hugged the sloping hillsides. This tradition of living within walking distance to the downtown shops allowed city centers to once thrive. Quaint stores did not become replaced by strip malls, as walking rather than driving would still be the main transportation. The ocean appeared just over the tree tops; the constant breeze that once cooled the townsfolk found no rest even upon the eve of humanity's end.

The charm of an old town, not eternal, but evanescent.

She ran along the streets that were empty with the exception of a few cars. On the eve of disaster, she imagined, the citizens must have driven away from their town in hopes to escape. But to where does one go to escape the inevitable? She pictured the cars that probably littered the highways outside of the seaside towns. Many cars may have been stopped along the way as their drivers became overwhelmed with the disease, causing traffic to come to a standstill. She thought about what had likely occurred: the uninfected rolling up their car windows, locking their doors. Frustrated attempts to stop the Chaots from coming inside, almost as if they could stop them in the same way that they could shun the rain from entering. Yet the Chaots would crash through the glass window-shields. Screams. The harbinger of death triumphs. She could only wonder where she had been to escape this fate.

She ran, ignoring the pain from her bare feet pounding along the cement. Ignoring the rancid scent that rose from the corpses in the summer's heat. Not permitting herself to be lost in the black eyes of the dead, she avoided the corpses' stares, lest they try to pull her under to Hades. Her gaze remained fixed on the trees in the distance. The massacre of long ago that played in her mind was only imagined tales of distant times. Fear should not inhibit her, and soon the trepidation passed.

Concern did not come over where she would stay the night nor if she would ever talk to another again. Conversation in itself held binds, for expression was confined to words. Limited. The extent that one could express oneself in such finite structure was oppressive. No desire summoned within her to be with the soldiers, that is until she turned the corner. Then, and only then, did her feelings rapidly change.

This time, not one Chaot blocked her course, but many. She now faced the fire that sprung from the dragon's mouth, for hell stood in front of her.

Twelve Chaots convened together on the street. Tranquility did not exist in the small gathering, for even amongst each other they sought war and feast. Several of them bent over a meal like hyenas. The meal, another Chaot, was still alive under the scavenging. Moans and shrieks mounted from its lips as the prey tried to escape the frenzy. A larger, more muscular one was trying to tear the weaker's leg off—a monstrous portrayal of survival of the fittest. The motivation of this carnal act seemed twofold: to gain nourishment, but the prevalent reason was for enjoyment. To watch its own kind shrivel in torment.

The other two chewed directly from their banquet. One was over the abdomen, intestines strewn between its teeth as its meal convulsed. The second crouched over the head. Its tongue flicked as a snake's over the eyeball, savoring the soft organ, oblivious of all else.

Six of the other Chaots fought, not with weapons but with tooth and nail. Perhaps they quarreled to take down a second for additional cuisine or they simply enjoyed the brutal mayhem. Fighting for the sake of the fight. Either way, she could not discern the target individual or if any fought in cooperation.

One Chaot stood to the side. It busied itself in scratching and nibbling its left arm; its gaze stared off into nothingness. It must have been abrading its flesh for a long time, for the Chaot's fingernails were worn down from the mindless act. On the ring finger the nail hung loose, connected only by a cord of flesh that kept it from falling completely off. The skin where it scratched was ragged and raw. Blood dried in the crevices, gangrenous spores dotted the dermis. In some areas the bone was visible due to the obsessive-compulsive chafing. The disease was not directly responsible for this rot; rather the Chaots' wasted minds could not comprehend the need to properly care for their bodies. Nor did they understand the basics of hygiene, for that required action with no immediate satisfaction. They lived for the moment, more so than herself, to indulge the needs of the id.

The last wore only a loose-fitting hospital gown, no longer sterile white but now brown in filth and age. Tattered cloths flitted around the beasts; it looked as if none had changed nor washed their garments since infected by the disease. The gowned Chaot was fixated on a more lecherous pleasure than the others. It masturbated in the street's corner with a neurosis matched only by the obsessive skin scratcher. The diseased organ was limp in its hands, desensitized by the chronic act.

So secluded were these lepers, so depraved and uninhibited in their actions. So horrid in their form and mind.

The Chaots burlesqued an obscene gathering akin of the maenads of Dionysus, the Greek god of wine. The maenads were his female followers who were indulgent in all of the mind's deep-rooted pleasures and impulses. Mankind now festered with animalistic desires and hungers as the maenads had, with no conscience nor reason to restrain them. The gatekeeper of the mind destroyed, what makes us human no longer intact. Though at first glance, only chaos seemed to reign in their actions, there was order. Order from Chaos. Nyx could not piece it together, for she could not fully comprehend the scene. It was as elusive as trying to capture the winds in a butterfly net. Nonetheless, they could be caught, just like the tornado that gathers the winds for their demolition. And the order was there to be seen by some and used by others. By her, perhaps. But not yet.

The number twelve symbolizes the ideal paragon. Twelve in their idyllic world of debauchery. Add one more to numerological perfection and it can only become marred in corruption and rebellion. Nyx was the thirteenth, coming before the group of twelve Chaots. Even the ones with rotted eyes, perhaps from smell or some undeciphered sense, looked toward her. Hunger swelled in them from her presence—not in the malnourished sense, but in all the ravenousness denotations of the word. And that surge led them to her, leaving prior acts forgotten in order to satisfy this new indulgence.

Exhausted because of running from the intangible, she now had to run from the corporeal as they took chase upon her. Instinct broke within the Chaots when she ran, and they began to take chase, mouths salivating as hunting yelps echoed through the air. They ran like a pack of hyenas towards her—scattered and in it for their own satisfaction. Even the one who was the meal attempted to stand in its slaughtered ruin to go after her. Though as it propped itself up, its intestines tore completely from their cage and the creature fell in death.

Running several blocks, she then cut a corner into an alleyway in hopes to lose them. She ran in silent caution in attempt to hide her location from the Chaots as she navigated the alley's maze. Each step held a possibility to return her to her tormentors, but each step also promised that she would be clear of them. However, there is never any true escape from your nightmares. They are a part of you, as you are a part of them, and despite the silence she knew it would not last.

The alley ended in an overflow of brilliance as the daylight came to view. The buildings curbed along the sidewalks before her; the Chaots no longer in her sight. She did not know whether they still roamed the alleyways anticipating an encounter with her, or whether they gave up their search. But she thought it would be best to hide, and so ran across the street, looking for somewhere safe.

She came to a row of Victorian townhouses, once probably the venerated pleasure of the beach front community now in disrepair. The colors faded with dirt and ash, the structures collapsed on top of each other by what must have been a past fire. Not even a clear entrance was viable in one of the houses; only a misshaped crevice marked the entry into the decrepit innards. Hopefully it would be sufficient, she thought. She shifted between the rubble and squeezed in. Once inside she took some excess debris and placed it into the hole she had entered through. The windows had already been boarded up. Nothing would come in.

At least she could hope.

Her gaze swept the room. Scattering rays of sun lit the lair through the wall's cracks; otherwise, her sight would have been met with darkness.

Long ago the room was a child's space. A crib sat to one side, the wood had pale yellow paint reminiscent of a blooming daffodil. It had begun to chip, yet she could almost imagine the stifled cries that had come from behind its bars. On the floorboards, a petite slipper rested, shimmering in bronze. So tiny were the feet of the creature that once lived here; miniatures of a human in body, but in mind they seemed to amplify the emotions as if giants. The love babies had, the passions of joy, anger and sorrow. Unconfined, restricted only by their infantile inabilities.

The tiny boots fascinated her, preserved forever unlike the host they once contained. The turmoil of the outside was distanced in the rapture of childhood fantasy, and after a while she moved to touch the booties. Though before her fingers wrapped around them, her gaze caught a white object she did not notice before. The world no longer had white outside of the cascading waves, but rather dingy undertones of grey. The purity of white, both metaphorical and material, evaded society's reach. Yet a streak of it remained, a treasure for her alone. It was beneath the crib and she reached out. It was part of a book, the cover was mostly deteriorated by the fire but had preserved the white pages inside.

She opened the book as if unlocking a treasure containing untold secrets—as if it was about to erupt with demons as a volcano spews lava when the cover folds over. Each picture she looked over with unabated curiosity, amazed by the tale the child's book wove. One by one she turned the pages, hungry for knowledge. She read of a young boy's punishment. His journey over the sea. Meeting the wild things. They had wanted to tear into him, but instead they found him to be the most wild thing of all, and dubbed him the king of the wild things.

Tame them. Look into their wild eyes, without blinking once.

Thud.

The noise halted her rapture with the book. Her moment's peace broken as the fanciful stories of nevermore shrank back into the pages. No longer white but tattered, burnt pages were in her hands. The pictures were faded and the words illegible, even though to her they had existed only moments before. She threw the book away from her. Hallucinations. No, memories, a voice whispered. From a time forgotten. She closed her eyes to forgo this memory of childhood's end, though even more desperately she wished to transcend the outside's reality.

Thud. Thud.

The pounding whispered out to her. Each thud was bone chilling, not because of the sound itself, but rather what lay beyond those walls. Chaots. They had found her. And now their incessant thuds continued, the only end in sight being when the wall would collapse.

Maybe it was her smell that led them to her hiding place. Or the smell of fear that made them grovel at the walls, tormenting her to let them in.

But she refused to give in, to allow terror to overcome.

She scanned the room of the Victorian home, hoping to find a weapon. Wishing the Fisherman's knife was with her still.

Thud. Thud.

Still it continued. The repetition. Again and again as if to constantly remind her of what resided outside.

How long would these dilapidated walls hold?

Soon she would know, for the thuds found err to their resonance.

Thud. Crash.

The barricade of the window crumbled and broke. An arm jetted inward in hopes to grab its prey and pull it from the crevice. The hand, torn by the shattered glass, splattered red on the yellow crib as it crashed through. Another thud turned into a crash bringing one more hole to her shelter.

Her pulse escalated; breath quickened, she knew she could wait no longer. Running up the stairs, she headed to the attic and outside to the widow's walk. The rooftop balcony received its namesake from the mariners' wives who would look out over the sea in search of their husbands, hoping they had not succumb to the sea. But now, not even the wives escaped misfortune, as Nyx looked out and saw the swarm of Chaots—both male and female, husbands and wives—below.

She climbed over the balcony, to the roof of the adjacent townhouse and to the edge. The next row of townhouses would offer an escape, it she could jump across the divide and on to the other roof. If, she whispered to herself, holding her breath and jumping before she could form any doubts. Air rushed past her, as did her life, though that is not much to say considering her amnesia. The jump ended, not with her feet securely planted on the roof as she hoped, but with a bang as she collided into the roof's edge. Nyx struggled to grab onto the gutter to stop her fall, her nails digging into the composted leaves that filled it.

Her plan of a quiet escape was also slipping from her grip, for one Chaot heard the commotion and began heading for the second row of townhouses where she now hung.

The gutter groaned as she tried pulling herself up. It shuttered, she grabbed tighter. One last pull up, and she would be on the roof, away from ...

"No!" she gasped but tried not to scream. The gutter bent, her with it, half way down the side of the house. It stopped with a violent jerk, though she did not as she fell the rest of the way. At least she fell directly on an overeager Chaot; he broke her fall, and she most likely broke his spine in the process.

His tongue flickered to the sound of an exaggerated wheeze as if all the air were squished out from him; his eyes rolled back, his legs and arms seemed unresponsive as she pushed herself from the beastly cushion. She could not help the look of apologetic exhilaration as she moved off the Chaot, aching from the fall, but adrenaline making her pause only for a second. The others may have heard, and would soon be here.

She took to the streets in flight. She sprinted over the pavement and into the forests that flanked the town's edge. The creatures turned their efforts away from tearing down the walls of the Victorian townhouse to the wheezing, partially squished Chaot and fleeing woman. Though the sudden escape gave Nyx a sufficient head start, they still pursued. But soon she was a waning silhouette darting into the cover of the forest. Then she was lost to them.

For now.

Leaves replaced the harsh cement under her feet, cushioning her footfalls ever quick. The buildings metamorphosed to trees. Running until no longer the angles of civilization past haunted her, she became surrounded by nature.

She hid in a patch of ferns and laid back exhausted and sore. Her stare pivoted upward to the blue skies. Clouds made their cycle, visible as they slid to and fro over the canopy. She found the rapture of serenity if only for a few fading moments, for though the scene implored tranquility, it still could not drown out the ever sounding thuds echoing in the distance. Were they imagined remnants from the thuds inside the townhouse, or did the Chaots persist in their search? The steps rang out, not of normalcy but rather of strange, erratic strides. The sounds came vibrantly from what should have been dead, what should have perished along with civilization, but did not.

The Chaots now rambled closer, unseen but not unheard. She edged herself from her hideout in the ferns and crawled near a tree that was covered by vines and leaves. She pushed against the bark, letting the foliage wrap around her in an effort to camouflage herself.

Grasping the low-lying branches and using them as leverage, she climbed up and away from the ground, praying the Chaots could not climb. From the elevated position, she looked along the forest's floor to catch view of two Chaots walking, animated in their deadly stroll. They were the same ones from town, having followed her with unrivaled determination. Veins throbbing in the chase, bursting in a paradise lost, these destroyed shells of humanity searched.

She looked up, not wanting to witness the terrors below. However, it was not the skies that graced her sight; it was a dead human in the branches above. It was not alone. Feasting upon the carcass was a Chaot, a different one than before. The soulless being once upon a time had called himself the civilized.

Now he was savage, resembling a jaguar hiding its prey from scavengers. The Chaot moved with an animalistic grace in the tree. He could have trained in jujitsu in another life; nimble movements from branch to branch gave him an elegance, a gentle grace, that enchanted her. For the first time she did not abhor the infected beings, but saw another side. For the first time she saw the Chaot as 'he' rather than 'it'. She saw her own desire reflected in him. The sun streamed between the leaves, igniting his copper skin in luminescence; each movement intentional and wildly beautiful as he stalked his new prey.

Her.

His eyes lacked the spark of social intelligence, yet they whispered knowledge of a secret known by the Chaots alone. To be truly free. His tanned features were stained in blood—old and new, prey and self. Gaped teeth smiled at her, as if in laughter over the fallacies of what humans were. In Nyx he found a new hunt and new desires. Waiting no longer, the human beast quickened his descent down the tree and pounced toward her direction.

Part of her wanted him to take her as his own, to bring the secrets of the Chaots to her in sadistic whispers. Every moment the Chaots lived in the id. A freedom from societal construct that could only be released in the Chaots' embrace. But she prepared to fight him, knowing this freedom was false.

However, before they could collide, a gun sounded. Shots whizzed by her, two bursting in the sound of war. The bullets directly hit the oncoming predator, ending his hunt. The explosion of flesh tore on impact, causing the Chaot to lose his grip on the bark. Tumbling downward, the once graceful body rammed into Nyx on the branches. Both forms fell, colliding in midair. She hit the ground again, though this time it was she who broke the fall, the Chaot on top; the earth as their bed. Close to death, the Chaot moved with futile instinct, through sheer tenacity. He tried to grant his dying wish: for his teeth to sink into her, for his hands to tear her body apart.

She had wanted to finally understand the Chaot. Curiosity had replaced revulsion when she saw the tree dweller, yet faced with death she had no choice but to fight.

She reached up around his throat as she used all her strength to keep the snapping jaws away. Her hands sank into the wound near his clavicle where one bullet had hit; the second bullet had embedded itself in his abdomen. She did not have time to think of who had shot as she attempted to pry him off of her.

She channeled everything to evade the infectious bites. Her will, her desire to remain uninfected, fueled her counterattack. For though he had obtained a type of deliverance from society, the Chaot was a mere marionette to the disease. He epitomized freedom, but look deeper and find only an illusion she realized. Underneath, only darkness and death resides. And she did not want that.

Unearthly groans spilled from his mouth as he sought one last testament of satisfaction. He brought his head down again and again in reflex, teeth gleaming in the light that escaped the folds of the canopy. She grabbed a branch that had fallen in the fiasco. Clenching it, she brought it to the head of the creature. It hit the Chaot's forehead with finality, ceasing his movements. With one last push, she removed the now dead form from on top of her.

Falling backwards, the Chaot faced a long eluded end. She stood. Her rage became palpable as she hit him again; the stick tore away flesh and bone of the departed in the repeated striking. For moments, she had wanted the Chaot to descend upon her in order to understand his secrets. But he did not; he could not. She was thankful in his death and her salvation. It was lies that the wild eyes had offered, the beautiful copper Chaot was only a pawn.

The thrashing with the branch continued, but before she could bring down the branch one more time a grip came around her arm. Hector held her firm, not wanting her to continue in such unequivocal rage. The hold surprised her considering the Chaot's blood on her and the risk of infection she presented. A hazmat glove concealed Hector's skin, but still she did not want him to take a risk for her. Her clobbering of the Chaot displayed a part of her soul—an anger uncontrollable, a wrath unconfined. In his hold though, Hector stopped her downward spiral, and for that she looked gratefully towards the one who held her at bay.

Hector looked back. His face contained relief in finding Nyx but also a distance that separated him from the potential infected: her. With the striations of blood marking her, he did not know whether he would be forced to put her down. One thing seemed certain to him—he would soon find out. But even if he had to put a bullet through her head, the least he could do was calm her. To bring an end to her beating of the lifeless evil, for that had made his blood run cold, more so than any appalling acts by the infected themselves.

From the darkness of the forest, two figures appeared behind Hector. The two Chaots from the town moved to the scene with a hungry delirium. She pointed behind Hector at the approaching Chaots, to warn him that she was the least of their problems for the moment.

Hector let go of her, turning toward the two Chaots. His gun blazed with an indignation to destroy, yet with a composed self-control in his attack. Watching the demolition that he now wrought, Nyx was still. She let her arm drop to her side and with it the branch, that was covered with the innards of the beast. The weapon fell from her hand to the ground. She backed away from the war-torn zones and toward the solace of forests. She could escape this blight, and simply leave.

To ignore, to not face what may happen. That Hector's subsequent target may be her. She had to go against the possibility that her fate would be the same of the devolved human that now withered behind her.

Devolution. Her memories called from the haze, hearing voices filled with scientific authority surrounding her. There is no such thing as devolving. Only evolving, only moving forth. Nature adapts, metamorphosing into the most successful course of evolution, into what is the fittest. Even if we do not see it as advancement—it is.

And so, she did not wait for the outcome of Hector's battle with the two Chaots, not wanting to see if she would be Hector's next target. She ran from him toward obscurity, looking behind her toward the shots and then above, wondering if another tree-bearing Chaot would jump down upon her. Looking everywhere as she ran through the forest—except right in front of her.

And because of that, she ran straight head long into another.

A muffled groan came as she collided against Leander and fell down. At first thought she assumed it was a monster and she backed away from the outstretched gloved hand. Idle wishes came and left that she had not abandoned her only weapon, the tree branch. However, as her gaze reached Leander's, relief came, but inevitably her instinct prevailed: to get away. To run. Not just for her own safety, but for his.

"No," Leander said. "Stop."

His voice digressed from its duty-driven timbre; passion melting the formidable. The sight of Nyx, seeing the blood on her skin. Did he believe he had lost her to the disease? No. Hope flickered visibly in Leander's face, or so she believed, and he would not give up on her yet. It was possible that the Chaot's blood had not entered her system. She stopped. She did not flee. The hope in his eyes was like the gem hidden inside Pandora's box. She did not want to lose it, and she knew she would if she ran.

Hector joined Leander and Nyx, having finished off the two Chaots. He readied himself as if awaiting the orders to neutralize the situation if it should escalate. Heavy inhalation, the breath escaping from his mouth in rasps behind his mask. Controlled, but telling of the battle he had just finished.

She knew if the disease had invaded her, the soldiers would kill her now to avoid the threat she could become. Regret and remorse: both were abandoned in times of the post-apocalyptical war. The only option was death to the contaminated—her end for their continuation. For their survival.

Backing away from the two, she knew the likelihood that Hector would shoot her. Yet she remained, hesitant to make the first move.

Trees scattered, shaking in the distance. The wind ... or something else?

Hector spoke first breaking the silence between the three, breaking her impression of him. A formidable voice, but not as crude as she had expected. Not animalistic nor of a brute without mind, but strewn with intelligence. Not as a scientist aged in book knowledge, but instead with dignity, understanding, and a wisdom that could never be taught.

"You have my word: I will not chain you again. I will not kill you," Hector said.

And with those words, she let go of her fear and stepped forward. Her decision irrevocable, to walk alongside these warriors.

Chapter Six

"Since you would not follow us, we followed you," Leander said, his voice muffled through his hazmat mask. Outfitted in protective gear, he removed all trace of the Chaot blood from Nyx. He made sure she was not wounded for the blood to intermingle with her own. After a period of waiting to see if the imminent threat of being turned passed, Hector had left to stand guard. Dio and Megaira were determining the location to proceed in their mission, leaving Leander to take care of Nyx. Take care of—whether that meant simply to cleanse or to kill her if her behavior spiraled down, only time would tell.

Washing her skin with antiseptic cloths, Leander cleansed the blood from her. Along her cheek and across her forehead, he wiped away the contagion.

She wondered if he feared she would change into a Chaot, yet no trepidation showed on his face. Perhaps he learned it in the army: never allow the predicament to be known to the wounded. That way it allowed the victim, as well as himself, hope. Hope was something they could not lose—what she had seen in Leander's eyes and heard in Hector's voice. Or perhaps she read him wrong. Was the lack of concern tied to being distant, for when faced with a potential enemy it was always best to remove all emotion.

"Giving you the choice to stay or leave was the only option I could think of at the time. It would have been impossible under the current circumstance to force you to come against your will. Yet, alone in this wilderness, you would not last. And you are important to us. We could not let you go, we had to find out how you survived for so long. But it was my fault. I thought we could better track you, keep you out of harms way while seeing where you led us."

Leander said, speaking to her while he continued removing the remaining fluids. He shone an ultraviolet light over her skin, wiping away the particles invisible to the naked eye. "We lost you for awhile in the town. Finally, we found you in the tree with the Chaot, and that was when we intervened. I wish I made a different decision. I cannot change what happened, but will do my best to protect you if you will let me. Will you stay with us now, Nyx?"

She did not respond at first. Why did she stay, she asked herself. The Chaots for one. They would impose their will on her even more than the soldiers. She chose the lesser of the two evils, if it even was a choice. Leander has stated that they could not let her leave, so the question he asked was merely extraneous. But what enticed her to stay was her growing interest towards Leander and the soldiers. Curiosity called, she had to abide.

"I need ..." You. To understand you. But she could not admit to this need. "... to understand what happened."

That was not it at all, and he seemed to read through her partial truth. However, he did not push her. The wind picked up as if in sequence to bring her hair astray.

"When you understand, will you still stay?" he questioned, albeit reluctantly. It was a question he did not need to ask; he knew the answer. If she no longer desired to walk with these soldiers she would simply and unequivocally leave. She was the dissonance within the melody of life; her chords played inharmonious yet flawlessly. Though her footfalls away would seem abrupt and misplaced, to her they would be perfect poetry.

"Will you?" she asked back, as a smile took her lips, so ebullient in posture even after the terrors she had beheld. It seemed as if he was about to answer, but instead he took out a pair of scissors from the med kit.

"Sorry, but I'm going to have to remove your shirt," he said, beginning to cut it away after her nod of permission. She flinched as he removed it, for it was the only remnant from her time with the Fisherman, proof that he was not simply of her invention. She could not lose his wisdom. Leander gave her several white cloths to cover up before removing the residual fluid that had soaked through the shirt to her skin. With the Chaot's blood removed, he could see that her skin was not broken. Given that and the duration of time that had passed without side-effect, she was well beyond the threshold of risk. If the tree-dweller's blood did contaminate her, the symptoms would have already deemed her life carnal. And though she did not see fear before, she saw a subtle relief now come over him.

"I would like to take a sample of your blood," he said. She knew why without explanation, for if the disease was as destructive as it seemed, any survivor could be seen as a potential subject to research in hopes to find a cure. Perhaps having almost lost her had brought reason to Leander—for it was not just her he would have lost. And though she hated to be seen as purely a subject, she held out her arm so he could take her blood. This would cut any ties he had to her as research, she hoped, and what would be left was solely their bonds as individuals.

He took an vial of her blood and concluded with a clear disinfectant over her body to complete the sterilization. It was cool, almost reminiscent of the ocean's chill. She shivered underneath his touch. As she did so, he paused, not wanting to overstep his bounds. He knew war time allowed no place for relationships. For love. But love was the most dangerous of combatants, for nothing could bar its merciless torrent from the gates.

"I wish we had a Hazmat field uniform for you that would fit, but what we have is too large and hence ineffective. This will fit large as well, but should not pose too much of a nuisance," he said as he gave her a shirt, boots, and combat pants.

He turned and walked back toward Hector, leaving her alone with the clothing to provide her with some privacy. She put on the clothes, though was not accustomed to the feel of so much fabric constricting her.

Clothing. Conversation. Comrades around her.

Confining. Controlling. Capturing her.

Nyx walked next to Leander, only catching an occasional glimpse of the others far ahead. Megaira led with Hector securing the path; Dio carried up the rear to make sure none followed them. The two soldiers had returned from scouting with relative success. They had met up soon after Leander had finished decontaminating her; Nyx had only been able to make out whispers of the previous exchange. What she heard had been a puzzle, but who better to decipher the paradox than the one who walked besides her.

"Why do you need me now, you have my blood," she questioned Leander, unexpectedly interrupting the silence.

She caught him off guard, for most of their conversations had been one-sided. He embraced the turn of events with gratefulness, though aware that she might slip again into her shell.

"If there is a chance you are immune we would want to do more tests. But the chance of immunity is ... well, from the reports that had come in to us before we lost contact, there was none. The disease is prion based, such as mad cow disease. One hundred percent of those exposed face the inevitable. So though I have your blood that is most likely a dead end. But you survived, out here somewhere. And I hope some answers may come from knowing how."

"And a type of duty," he continued. "The integrity of our humanity is all we have left that sets us a part from extinction. It is important to realize what we stand for, rather than sink to the level of the Chaots. The infected. It is important to help those in need."

"Tell me more about the infection," she asked. He had spoken the word in a way that inferred an intentional infection. She had believed it to be a disease before, but now it seemed like more. "What happened?"

A pause at her question. He found it strange she did not know. How could one not know?

"I only am aware of some of the details. I expected you, a land survivor, would know more than I do."

"Land?"

"Yes, land," he answered, realizing she did not know what the Thalassic was. "We are from below the sea, a part of an underwater colony, the Thalassic. It is an establishment for scientific government research based off of Maine's coastline. It is how we survived, while most of the rest of humans ..."

The sentence was left unsaid, for they did not need to be reminded of those that now ran in human body but without human soul. Rather, he proceeded to explain exactly what had happened to create such beings of uninhibited strife.

"The War began. We always knew that when it came, the fate of the world would be decided in its battlefront. In hopes to destroy the enemies and not the land, germ warfare commenced as the primary strategy. It specifically targeted the humans while leaving our amenities and resources untouched. The Thalassic is unaware of the specifics, for we lost contact shortly after the outbreak begun. Being underwater granted us safe refuge for it separated us from the outside, unbreachable in our security and completely independent. However, we were left in the dark when the communications surface side failed."

"From what we gathered from intelligence," Leander continued, "the infection is caused by a type of military-designed prion that served as a bioweapon, let loose by our side in the air and waterways. It was supposed to render the enemy dead by targeting the brain and ending life immediately. I believe the creators responsible did not predict the outcomes of releasing such an atrocity to the world. They tried to wield a beast which could not be tamed, for the prion had a mind of its own."

Our side. She studied his face, seeing the weight of sorrow as he spoke. Soldiers do not give such orders, they are pawns set upon boards, the only choice given to them is which side is the lesser of two evils. Often that choice is even removed, and who they fight for is determined by where they were born. She could see that he did not agree with the use of such weapons, but also probably did not even know of their use until too late. But rather than make excuses, or lie to her, he told her the facts.

"Death did not come to the targets. They were not immune though; the contagion still affected and destroyed specific regions of the brain. It created what had chased you. What we call the Chaots, since chaos rules them."

"If the contagion had killed upon contact then the targeted areas would have been easily contained and quarantined as what was planned. But those who survived as half-human—as Chaots—spread the infection before any quarantine could be established. The bio-agent was used against us as well, in a desperate dying attempt from our enemy, not to 'win' the war, but to make sure we also suffered the consequences. The disease propagated because of these unforeseen consequences. It carried like wildfire worldwide, being unbiased with whom it destroyed and made into another vector," Leander finished, looking toward Nyx, his gaze showing confusion as to how she could have survived the Armageddon without knowing it had ever occurred. Part of him probably wished to blame it on post traumatic stress, that she had forgotten due to the nature of the horror, or a possible head trauma. Another part must have known it must be something more.

His story did not sadden her nor make her wish the war had been prevented, since it was from a time before. A time that did not matter to her, for it was beyond what she could remember. Not that she lacked empathy, it was as if it was a story of battles in past history. If you wished the past to change, in turn you also wished that you did not exist. No matter how small the point of impact, the ripples reached out indefinitely in time and would change the face of the world.

And the creation myth Leander wove was just that—a myth to her. The Chaots and the end of humanity simply was the world she now lived in and all else represented fairy tales told of legends of old to explain why. The infected in her mind made into wild beasts, a beauty in their own right, even if twisted. And she believed one should not pity the beasts nor seek to destroy the prides which hunted among the gazelles. Though beware the predator's fouled bite and strike to live if need be.

But these Thalassicians were not like her; they sought return to the past, to a civilization that never was civilized to begin with.

"We waited for almost a year aboard Thalassic wondering what was happening on the surface after communication was lost. First we waited to ascertain that the air was clear from contagion. Luckily Chaots themselves can only transmit the disease through direct bodily fluid contact—the bio weapon remained airborne only in the human-initiated attacks. Yet even after establishing the air's safety, the Thalassicians continued to wait. They hid behind excuses of why not to venture upward—from seeing if the threat would somehow extinguish itself, even to the idea we should abandon the hope of ever living surface side again. However, one cannot sit around forever in safety but naiveté."

A grimace conjured along his mouth as he spoke, causing her to wonder if indeed all of Thalassic was behind his squadron's movement upward. Surely if they were self-sufficient some would wish to stay underwater beings and not risk their own contamination. She could only guess how many would support Leander in the effort to come from the seas to the land.

"It was why you were not initially greeted with open arms, Nyx," he explained. "No one survived up here that we knew of. They all either became a Chaot or died at the hands of one. So now I ask again, how did you survive? If you are somehow immune, however unlikely, we need more than a vial. If you are part of a community of survivors, we can help each other. Either way, you could be what we are looking for."

For a moment she thought of telling him that she was not the sole survivor of the land. The Fisherman ... but was he just of her fancy? No knife, no shirt, nothing left from him except perhaps a delusion she conjured for companionship? And so she spoke of the only thing she knew for certain.

"And as I say again," she said, wishing she had more to give him, "I do not know. I do not remember. I am here with you now and that is all I can tell you."

Nodding, he desired more but knew that it was the most he could ask for. All he could truly ask for was for this wild one to simply walk by his side. And never one should remiss the small treasures that the world now granted, for they were truly far and few in-between. And Nyx was a gift to him. In her freedom. In her careless unbound spirit. So similar to the creatures that mankind had become in their lack of inhibitions, but yet so unlike them. She was the breath of fresh air that had been restrained for so long.

Even if an unsung Trojan Horse awaited deep within.

"Where do we go now if not to Thalassic?" she asked.

"We were deployed to come to land and to see how far the disease had polluted this world, if the Chaots had replaced humankind in its entirety or destroyed themselves. And to understand if there will again be a day where we can walk this surface without threat. We would like to find a cure, or at least come across a clue as to how to reverse the effects. The last Intel tells of an effort here, secluded on this island of Acadia to counteract the disease. Optimistically the research compound contains answers for the future of humanity and where we now go."

A pause. He took a sidelong glance at her. Long hair brushed her sides in such carelessness; she seemed more desperate to feel the breezes that meandered the trees than to understand his story. He noticed that her boots were off; her feet reveling in the moss and forest grasses. Leander could not help but smile at her spirit. However, another part of him wondered if indeed she did escape the prion in the days of Armageddon considering her unconventional ways. That thought dissipated as abruptly as it had come; no one could survive even partially the contaminates.

"I have skepticism after seeing what had become of man. How does one repair what is now in such disarray? A cure in a vial is what is hoped, but in reality seems impossible judging the damage done to the brain. We hope the Chaots' behavior is not caused by an irreparable ruin of the tissue, but instead it is a blockage or pressure that can be relieved ... gods only know. We could not study the disease first hand, and only have the intel initially sent to us."

His talk of immunity was just a pipe dream, he knew this truth, knowing the epidemiology of the disease. No one was immune for prions took what was present in every human, PrP which is a healthy cellular prion protein, and taught these proteins themselves to misfold. Prion diseases are incurable and not treatable. No one escaped its wrath.

A branch clawed at him as he shoved it back. The forest was an encumbrance to him, yet one welcomed. Living in the confines of an underwater base and remaining sane seemed a conundrum. How long can one go untouched by the wind and sun and still want to live? It was why the risk to venture the land was necessary in his mind. The Thalassic could only last so long below the waters before giving way to its own mayhem.

Nyx remained silent at his story, waiting for him to continue. For moments only footsteps were heard as they hiked forward in search of the research facility which may, or may not, hold the salvation to a civilization lost.

"Many of the Thalassic were adamant that we remain below. I see that as giving up. I cannot do that."

"I understand. To sit and wait for death to come is already death," she said.

"Yes. I was therefore issued several soldiers in hopes to find a way for humanity to reclaim our land."

"Issued?" A voice hearty within cheer called from the background, one obviously eavesdropping. It was Dio, coming up from behind. "No one issues me. I believed that I joined this suicide quest of yours with open arms, boy."

"Ha, that you did Dio," Leander said, welcoming the interruption. To talk about their troubles, and a quest that had yet to carve a ray of hope in the dreary skies, presented a forlorn mission. Yet Dio always offered a good laugh to even the most discouraging of journeys.

Increasing his pace, Dio joined Leander and Nyx. He reminded her of the Greek god Dionysus; his demeanor akin to one who would rather fulfill his desires of merriment than war. If only he could do as the god could and control the maenadic feasts of chaos.

"Don't listen to this one's duty driven mumbo jumbo. Truth is we aren't supposed to be surface side," Dio said. Leander narrowed his eyes not wanting their disobedience of commands to be such public knowledge, but did not impede the confessions of his cohort.

"We left the Thalassic undermining the system," Dio continued, ignoring Leander's expression. "Admiral Telphousian lacked any spine to issue such commands herself. She wanted safety for the Thalassic—but nothing more. We could not wait in our safe haven when families were suffering above, people whose fate were unknown to us." A crack in Dio's voice when he mentioned families caused her to wonder if he had many loved ones who had died during the pandemic. Yet his tone returned to a quick witted cannon as he continued spewing forth facts Leander probably did not wish her to hear.

"Of course our heads might be had by the Admiral upon our return; who knows what she will charge us with. Treason? Mutiny? But hell with her if we bring back something grand. Some hope that we can come topside. Better yet, some hope that we can save the infected. Hence, Leander acted despite the politicians and their two-faced schemes, and gleaned himself our cozy squadron here of the righteous, not so law abidingly fit, soldiers." A laugh turned sour as Dio glanced ahead to make sure the fourth soldier was not in audible range. "Megaira though, be careful of her. She is only in it for the action. I don't think she likes you, and that's an understatement."

"No," Leander cut in, "she does not mean any harm. And it's more than action she seeks." He said no more in explanation as he glanced ahead—not seeing, but knowing both Megaira and Hector were at the lead. Even though she had not yet spoken with Megaira, Dio's caution only served to rouse her curiosity. Though what truly piqued her intrigue was the esoteric guise of Hector. He spoke only when called for. His actions unambiguous but unconventional. She had thought Hector would be the first to kill her if she became contagious, duty trumping anything else. Yet he surprised her when he had pledged he would not harm her.

"And Hector ...?"

"Fearless and unwavering," Leander said, "Hector would sacrifice himself without question in the line of duty. Not like us, who are soldiers in the face of this conflict but little more. He is one who has lived and breathed battle during his entire life."

He stopped abruptly—not wishing—or perhaps unable to go on. His features grew disconcerted, making his boyish face look older than he truly was. The rest of Hector's riddle was left uncoded and unsaid. His life seemed it would always be an enigma as puzzling as the Fisherman had been.

"And Dio overstates," Leander continued, changing the subject, "and embellishes our disloyalty of the Thalassic. We are not insurgents looking to revolt. We act for the best interests of humanity as a whole: that is our mission and in that we will not falter."

Chapter Seven

Night fell. It was dangerous to stay idle, yet continuing in the dark presented its own risks. Not only would the soldiers miss any indications of the laboratory, but they would be more vulnerable to the dangers of the forests and the Chaots. The Chaots posed a threat more dangerous than the predators of nature for they were not motivated by the instinct to feed alone. They had moved beyond the natural world of survival into the perverted, beyond genetics into the synthetically risen. This made the Chaots capricious, unconventional killers, hence by far the most threatening.

The Chaots' behavior was also unknown, whether they hunted at night or day, in a group or alone. From what Nyx perceived thus far of the infected, she saw a myriad of variations, and night time offered no safe haven. She suspected that not all the Chaots would rest during the night. And, at least with a camp, they could monitor the circumference and provide security.

Precautions had to be taken. They set up a perimeter of trip wires around the camp. The technology constituted lasers rather than physical cables. Invisible to the eye, if triggered by an interrupted beam it would alert the soldiers to take immediate action. The tents were composed of mosquito nets that rested over the low laying branches. Summer allowed them to go without sleeping bags, though come autumn the chill of the Northeast would have made it unbearable. The warmth was on the soldier's side, for the luggage of genuine tents and sleeping bags posed difficulty in a scenario of attack. In an additional defensive measure, one soldier would stand sentinel over the camp, rotating out every two hours.

Hector watched first. He headed off with vigilance after the camp and security were established. Nyx found comfort in the belief that nothing would get pass the warrior. A fire would be too risky to ignite; it would attract the Chaots like moths to a flame. Therefore, they chewed pre-cooked freeze-dried rations in hungry silence. She abhorred the taste, her last meal being vivid in her mind. If only she could go back to the sea to delight in freshly caught fish—to eat meat immediately after the kill. If only the ocean air replaced the heat, the salty winds caught thick in her hair and not the damp sweat of the humidity now present. But still she threw some of her meal to within the forest in hopes the falcon of the beach would find it and share in her fare, though as she did this the others looked strangely at her ritual.

Food finished, the four sat around in the darkness. They knew that they should rest but the adrenaline running through them would not allow it. Leander sat next to her, only a few inches between them. His inner conscious hoping that proximity would somehow anchor Nyx, but that was not the only motivation. She captivated him; the siren whispered such mystery in her sweet but undecipherable behavior. Shifting on the rock-covered ground, his arm brushed hers. Her skin cool to his warmth. She did not pull away, and he took a small delight in that before chastising himself for behaving as a schoolboy. It was wartime; he should not be so heedless in his emotions. But when her eyes caught his, he could not help but be lost in them.

Dio was the first to break the peace, his voice a low hum over the distant winds. Tone deep, for it was a tale he wove for them to listen, and not interrupt.

"My ancestors were native to this area—the Wabanakis—the Dawn Land People. How much I have of our beliefs and blood left is trivial. It has been a long time which I have sought to find comfort in their mythos. But now in the face of the Armageddon, I look back to my own blood to find reason in the world."

"The Dawn Land people," Dio continued, "believed in harmony between animal and mankind, that in turn led to harmony in the universe. In the hunt we did not choose to kill, but the animal chose to give itself to us. There was no good or evil in our life at the heart of it, for evil cannot be tied to actions nor to people. And now there are Chaots. Some would say they are evil, but I instead turn to what is left of my heritage."

"They are evil, Dio," Megaira interrupted, disbelief in hearing him, out of all people, calling the Chaots a non-malignant presence. "Look what they have done."

"Everyone has two sides," Dio said, trying to shed some light of the Wabanaki beliefs to them. "Even the Wabanaki creator Koluskap had a twin brother, Malsom, to counteract his benevolence. And in each of us lays both a Koluskap and Malsom in our conscience—in each of us is a two-headed monster. And the Chaot is Malsom finally showing his face."

The tale fascinated Nyx, Koluskap and Malsom coming together to form a tapestry similar to her own story. It was as if two forces contradicted inside her. One wished the incorruptible feel of nature. One desired a darker need. When she had attacked the tree-climbing Chaot, she felt—pure and simply—good. To feel his skull smash, the blood spray upon her skin, released her. And previously along the shore fishing, this galvanized her need to hunt more, though not just for fish. She needed a challenge to satisfy a craving she could not yet identify. But she could not speak of her dark half to the soldiers. To speak of her own Malsom, would mean their mistrust and possibly her death. They believed her to be harmless; if she should shatter this image, she was not sure what would come. And right now she did not wish to leave the soldiers, for she needed them. Not necessarily for protection, but a more innate pull: she needed the Thalassicians to gain understanding of her own place. The more she was around the humans, the more she understood what set her apart.

"So Malsom is evil then?" Nyx questioned, but in truth she understood. There was more than good and evil, something greater than the two that could be achieved. She also spoke in hope of absolution for her own dark half. If Malsom was not evil to Dio, perhaps neither would she be.

"No, not in our terms," he answered. "Remember evil in the Wabanaki culture cannot be attributed to people. We are balanced in order for harmony to ultimately exist. And that is who the Chaots are to me; not evil, no matter what they have taken away from us."

Shadows played upon his face as he spoke. He looked between each of them, seeing what he could of his comrades through the forested night, before drawing in one breath and speaking again. It was as if he did not tell the tale, but his ancestors rose from their graves in his inhale, and spoke through his exhale. "You see, in the beginning there was only the forest and sea. Animals and people were created to live in consonance. However, humans began to take advantage of their environment, exploiting both the hunt and the animal. And so finally the Chaots were created from the dissonance—not a horror spawned from hell, but as a savior to somehow find the equilibrium again between nature and people."

"That's bull," Megaira said, shaking her head. She leaned back, looking towards the heavens in order to abandon whatever heresy he tried to throw at her—after all she knew he would fight by her side come tomorrow, no matter his outlandish take on the Chaots.

"And is what you believe any closer to your truth?" Dio questioned.

"Most beliefs do share common threads," Leander said, almost acting as a referee between the two. As captain, he could not afford to have too much conflict split the soldiers. "At the basis of all myths are the monsters. If they were not present, heroes could never arise. The Greek heroes developed because of the monsters, not in spite of it. And even though they lack the supernatural form, monsters are present in the Christian religion too: Jesus needed Judas to betray him in order to be crucified; therefore, he could demonstrate immortality by rising from the dead. Judas is the monster needed for the hero to achieve his ultimate destiny."

"Yes, and because of that, monsters cannot truly be seen as evil. Rather, they are liberators in and of themselves, allowing the hero to transcend the common path," Dio said, despite Megaira's breath of annoyance.

"If it were a god," Megaira said, "I believe they brought this disease to us in retribution not in salvation nor liberation. There is nothing good to come from this; we have damned ourselves and will never return to what was."

"Now we again live in the time of myths and legend," Nyx said in accordance, "where satyrs rule the forests."

Megaira looked at her; it was not as before, not with a stare that identified Nyx as the enemy or a hindering object. But human to human, though Nyx would not go as far to say she saw friendship. But possibility for more manifested.

"And where Nymphs roam free," Leander whispered, finding it difficult not to look at Nyx as he spoke. A smile hinted on her lips as she caught his gaze. He smiled back, shyness in his charm, but then immediately looked away as if ashamed he should find happiness when so many were suffering. Clearing his thoughts back into rationale, he spoke, "The Chaots fundamentally are not some god's vengeance poured from the skies down upon us. Remember, it was humanity that had engaged in biological warfare. At the heart of it, we are responsible for our own fate."

"What was the war about," Nyx asked.

"The war was ultimately political in nature," Dio said. "The Bavarian Coalition desired a worldwide government under a single group rule claiming to bring about peace. Not everyone agreed, believing the intentions of the Coalition were not so selfless, and so the Uprising formed. The Coalition attacked the Uprising, hoping biological warfare would end things quietly, but it got out of control to say the least."

"Whatever the cause," Leander said, "the issue now is if we can overcome the monster set before us. If we can transcend our mortality and become the heroes."

The four sat in silence for a time, wondering if the last remnants of humankind could rise above the challenge. Years from now, Nyx wondered, would the Chaots be a myth that is told around the campfire: the Chaots portrayed as fanciful as monsters. The Thalassic soldiers, depicted as the heroes, slaying the Chaot. Though what would happen if it were the Chaots who won—would the soldiers then become the legendary monsters? Gazing upward, she looked toward those heroes that had been painted in the stars, wishing that the legends of old could guide her in her own challenges.

The stars shimmered with an exuberance lost since long ago. It had been eons since the stars encompassed such formidable wonder and fascination in their breadth, for the sky had been polluted previously by man-made light. Now electricity died, alongside those who had harnessed it, causing the rebirth of beauty in the night sky. With the absence of city lights, the stars regained their ancient splendor. For the first time, Nyx and the soldiers could see what their ancestors saw. Details glowed in the galaxies; brushstrokes painted in starlight illustrated the conquests of heroes, gods, and monsters.

Leander pointed out a constellation to her. He had known of these stars solely on star charts for they had been too dim to see in the pre-apocalypse world and impossible in the undersea environment he endured the last several years. He had embodied the H. Hanson quote that 'we are just mollusks, shut up tight at the bottom of a dark, cold ocean trying to make sense of stars we cannot even see'. With clear excitement and pleasure, he now could see those stars, even if the rest of the unseen web remains unseen. He showed her the constellation of the dragon Draco, and then the neighboring five star Lyra.

"Lyra is named after Orpheus's instrument," Leander said to Nyx. "The brightest of the stars is said to be a jewel in his lyre named Vega, the Falling eagle. You seem to enjoy Greek mythology; do you remember that myth?"

"Most. Orpheus is the musician who faced the Underworld to bring his wife back?"

"Yes," he said, and she saw that he was pleased she remembered. Perhaps he thought her memories could come back if she still retained some knowledge of before. But thankfully he did not bring up her amnesia as he continued speaking about Orpheus. "And though he moved Hades with his music and had him agree to release Eurydice, he failed to follow the conditions. He looked back before they were out of the Underworld, and so he lost her forever."

"Is Orpheus himself among the stars?"

"No. After Orpheus lost Eurydice, he died at the hands of the Maenads, the crazed followers of the god of wine," he responded. "They tore him limb by limb and threw his body into the river Lesbos; there was not much left of him to put into the stars. His lyre also was thrown into the river but was found by Apollo, who had originally given the instrument to the musician. He convinced Zeus to place it within the heavens to honor Orpheus."

Death at the hands of the Maenads, she reflected on his words and how they paralleled her view of the Chaots as Maenads. Hopefully the fate of Orpheus would not be theirs.

"Are you glad you decided to stay?" Leander asked. His gaze moved away from the stars to look at her. "If you were alone you ..."

He could not finish his sentence for it would reveal his feelings, something he could not do, stopped by the nature of their circumstance. Accordingly, she spoke so he would not have to. "If I were alone, I would miss such stories and tales of the Wabanaki and the stars."

"Ah, but I am a one story type guy," Dio said, cutting in. He saw the way Leander looked at Nyx, and he was glad that his friend had found someone to take the focus off the horrors that befell humankind. However, one was not thrilled over Leander's attraction.

Megaira sat stone cold, a misguided sense of resentfulness chiseled into her. She opposed taking Nyx into the company to begin with, and now the commander's smitten behavior made her believe it was more than a mistake. No longer could Nyx see the shimmer of fellowship between herself and Megaira that was there moments ago. It had shriveled, disappearing under Megaira's concept of her hindering their ultimate goal. Luckily, Dio saw this anger and started to talk to Megaira again about the differing possibilities of why the war started. He must have been hopeful that he could distract her and afford the two some privacy.

"Promise that you will tell me before you do leave, Nyx. Say goodbye. Do that for me," Leander said.

"Just for you then," she said in agreement to his lighthearted request, trying not to be too unsettled by Megaira's animosity toward her.

He smiled in gratitude, relaxing from his otherwise duty-driven conduct. "What would I do without you?"

"Worry less?" she answered, moving her hand to brush against his. In the bare essence of it all: as he was to her, she was to him.

"Exactly," he said.

"And what would I do without you?"

"Hmm ..." A cringe creviced Leander's forehead as if deep in thought, the indistinct conversation of Dio and Megaira the only noise as he mused over her question. "Worry more?"

"No," A playful tone in her response, given to the playful answer. Leander knew the opposite would be so, for if anything, he was becoming someone she did care for, and would worry for.

"I know then: become a singer and go on to a long and prosperous career?"

Humor posed an peculiar exchange to her; it was foreign. Alien. Yet still desired. She paused finding the words appropriate to continue their banter, "Everyone knows it is as a guitarist and not a singer that I would excel as."

"Have you ever even played a guitar?" A chance to get to know her, a chance to break through her wall to see even a small part of her past.

"No," she admitted, knowing that she had never even heard one played before. Only the orchestra of the skies rang familiar. "But I'll find a teacher somewhere, somehow."

Maybe the Fisherman would return to teach her again, of all the skills humanity had.

"Nyx," Leander said, falling into seriousness. It was a chance he had to take. "I have to know how you survived. It could mean helping other pockets of survivors."

"I told you. I do not remember," she said. She pulled away, as he responded with a darkened expression as she saw the struggle within him. He could not allow his feelings to detract from what could potentially help the remnants left of humankind.

"Leander—" came an interruption. Megaira stood, focusing on her commander as if Nyx did not exist. "—she is lying. Stop treating her as if a comrade or a friend. She is the enemy. The only land survivors are probably the ones who are to blame for the Chaots!"

Leander stood, his height slightly taller than Megaira, but his presence dictating even more of a variance. "It is not your decision, Megaira. We will not go around accusing or convicting survivors without evidence."

"The evidence is that she survived. Why should she, when no one else did!"

"Stand down and leave Nyx alone. Or face me," Leander continued, his voice inflexible, "I am going to replace Hector now so he can get some food and rest. I suggest the rest of you turn in for the night as well."

Silence steamed off of the frigid fair-haired soldier. Nyx was not threatened by her outburst, but rather intrigued. Megaira was the sole one who saw through the naivety. She sensed the threat she could pose, whereas no others could. Neither Nyx nor Megaira knew the truth of the danger or the extent of it. But both understood it was there.

Hector returned; the demeanor of the story-telling ambience dissipated in his presence. Nyx could tell that the other soldiers regarded him with reverence, but the kind that also separated him from them. He would never cheerfully weave the tales of Dio nor feel at rest in banter. A heavy-hearted rogue—if not for war, she could not imagine where his place in society would be.

Dio left for his tent to get rest before his watch, and Megaira sat near Hector cleaning her gun and its cylinders. Nyx was about to retreat for the night, when Hector stood and motioned to her. Megaira's lips twitched in anticipation, hoping that her fellow soldier had finally decided to take Nyx out to the back to either chase her away from their squad or kill her. She preferred the latter.

Nyx followed without pause. If he chose to release her into the wilds, she would welcome it. As one takes a feral animal back to where they belong, she hoped the warrior would revoke her commitment to the soldiers. But he turned to her, and spoke with a camaraderie in his tone.

"Together we live. Alone we shall die. But the Chaots die together, every moment taking from them another piece of their humanity. Nyx, I need to be assured they will not strip that humanity from you."

He held his revolver out before she could answer, though not in hostility that he did so.

"We use assault rifles for combat, but I think its best you start with this. This revolver holds six shots, less than a semi-automatic, however it has a greater reliability."

Hector placed the weapon in her hands, directing her how to load the gun. Then he stood behind her to align her stance and aim. The physical power contained within him clear as he moved her to the proper form. He instructed her on all aspects of the firearm, but they did not discharge any bullets due to the sound, not wishing to give away their location.

"And if I am without a weapon?" she questioned, giving Hector back his gun. She knew the answer even before it left his mouth, and looked forward to learn how to fight—not with the manmade, but with more primal skills.

"You are never without weapons; you must learn how to kill with your hands," Hector replied, accepting his gun back to explain close range combatives. "Since you are not muscular, you may not believe you stand a chance in hand to hand combat. It is not about the mass of your body but your ability to use equilibrium, momentum, and leverage in attacking an opponent. And not only physical balance, but mental. Do not allow fear nor anger to blind you. Seize the unexpected, for if an opponent is ready and expects an attack you will lose the advantage."

He turned her, placing one arm underneath her neck and another on the occipital region of her skull. She felt where his hands touched, and the angles that he used as he gradually twisted her head.

"Break the neck if from behind or even at the side of your opponent, but do so when it is unexpected to gain the advantage. Remember that by using leverage you can defeat a larger and stronger adversary. Use the natural, instinctual movement of your own body to bring them into the unnatural, and hence control their fate."

He demonstrated once more on her, before showing her the proper hand placement, torsion, and movement on himself and techniques to bring him down to her level. "But it is best to not rely on only your hands. Use your surroundings or anything in your possession. Slice their carotid artery if you have a sharp instrument. If you have a blunt item, use it to cave in their skull. Fight dirty, be fearless."

"Feels better than the gun," she said, as she moved to repeat his actions. Nyx practiced kicking him in the leg to bring him to her reach, then her arms drew around his head in an imitation twist. Then she learned the weak points one would focus on to kill. Much better than a gun, as she could feel her pulse quicken, practicing her onslaught. She let him loose, before rehearsing the movements several more times— each from a different angle. No rest, even as sweat pearled on their heads, as he went on to the next lesson.

"In fighting face to face, use the eye gouge, head butt, or collar grab choke," he said, and then subsequently demonstrated the three tactics.

He focused on the choke for it presented less likelihood of fluid contact between the attacker and attacked.

"Remember, timing must be precise. If you move too soon, the enemy will anticipate your attack. If you move too late, the enemy will attack you first," he paused, one hand grasped her shoulder. She anticipated that he would show her another technique, but instead he simply looked at her in solemn decree of the most important lesson. "Strike to kill," he said. "Nothing less."

"I will."

"I have no doubts, Nyx. Your innocence is only so deep. I saw you with the Chaot from the tree. I saw your rage. And I know you will do what you must."

The branches of the forest trembled in movement. Hector fell silent, quickly pivoting his gun's aim toward the intrusion. A Chaot did not emerge, but Megaira. She came through the dark of night, as it threw shadows across her face. Despite the dim outline of her face, Nyx perceived the smile gracing the Megaira's lips fall suddenly when she saw Nyx. She had expected Hector there alone with the outsider taken care of: dead or gone. The illusion shattered, however, as she saw her comrade standing near to the other, speaking in companionship. Resentment and jealousy came as Megaira stared upon the fabricated green-eyed monster of Nyx.

"Hector, I thought ..." Megaira began.

Hector turned to Nyx, removing his hand on her shoulder in parting. "Remember all that I have said."

"Good night Hector. Megaira," Nyx said, knowing that Megaira would not return her farewell. Taking leave and into the mosquito-net tent, Nyx left the two behind. She wished to let sleep come, for it would be the first she could remember. How would dreams feel? But she could not, for the conversation between Megaira and Hector interrupted the quietude of the forest.

"I thought you would get rid of her!" Megaira's voice resonated in a hushed shout.

"She is not the demon you imagine," Hector replied.

"She is not the harmless survivor that you picture either."

"I never stated such. But why is it that you do not want her among us? Even if she is the enemy, she is presenting no imminent danger. If anything we can learn from her. She could be immune, she could give knowledge to what happened on the land."

"We see what happened, death. She is not talking of how she survived, which means she is hiding something or is a trap. And if she is immune, it's too late anyway. Everyone is dead or far gone! We should just kill her and bring her body back to study if you want to research a cure," she said, though Nyx could not tell if the tone was in seriousness or exasperation to kill her. She knew one thing—that Megaira wanted her to hear that threat. "Anyways, I do not trust her. And you know as well as I we do not have any epidemiologists or biologists who specialize in anything other than marine biology! They would not know how to make a cure from her, if even she is immune. Though no one can be immune, you know that."

Hector was silent, and in her anger she started repeating what they had been told many times before. "We cannot be immune to this Prion disease. I don't even see why we search for this fabled antidote; there can be no cures, no immunities, no resistance to them. Vaccines cannot be made for prions due to their high heat resistance. Death, or becoming a Chaot, are the only outcomes. The land is not ours anymore."

"Then why did you come." Hector spoke, but it did not seem like a question and, considering the hateful pause which followed, was definitely not one which Megaira answered honestly.

"The research station is, and should be our only target for this mission, as it was before. Then I hope you will see that our place is in Thalassic. And Leander is compromising the mission because of her. He even mentioned her possible immunity, when he knows that is impossible. If she ever becomes contaminated I will kill her. And I'm beginning to doubt if he will, or if he would rather compromise our safety."

"He would never allow his feelings to interfere, as we do not," Hector said. His voice grew subtle, a hint of tenderness that Nyx did not expect. The affection towards Megaira becoming clear, even if strained by the situation. Nyx turned away in the mosquito net, wishing to afford them their privacy but the proximity deemed otherwise, carrying the soldiers' voices.

"When this battle is done ..." Megaira said, but then paused mid-sentence. The future that she hoped for was left unstated. A dream with Hector by her side, but it would only ever be a dream, asserted as he spoke.

"It will never be over, Megaira."

"We should have just stayed in Thalassic. We could have lived there. Together."

Hector's silence indicated that the barrier he allowed down for moments was already being constructed again. Megaira did not know him if she believed he would be happy while sedentary in the Thalassic. In reaction to his reticence, Megaira tromped away; the underbrush and fallen branches cracking under the weight of her steps. Nyx heard a parting hiss coming from her, damning Hector for being anything but what Megaira desired. Damning him for being anything other than what she needed.

Chapter Eight: Megaira

Twenty years previous: In the time before the war

The little girl in mismatched pigtails looked at the live feed recording in the waiting room with awe. She clutched onto her dolphin stuffed animal, so much so that some of the stuffing popped out from the opening in its stitches.

"Look momma! He's doing the same thing as me!" she said, pointing at the television. Megaira looked over to her mother, hoping her excitement would be shared but her mom just sat there, taking a long, annoyed drag from the cigarette. She knew the researcher had asked her mom to please dispose of it. She didn't know why the researcher did not allow the cigarettes but hoped her mom would have listened. Meg didn't want to leave this place.

When they first got here, she had been brought into the back room to figure out a puzzle box. It was painted black and the researcher demonstrated how to open it up. Knock on the top, turn a knob, pull down a handle, then knock on the side and lift a lever. Then the little door on the front unlocked and a treat popped out! She was so excited to do this herself and get her own treat but that was not even the most exciting part!

The researcher escorted her back to the waiting room and turned on the live feed tv. There sat a black furry creature right where she just was. A chimpanzee, like from the zoos! And it did the same task, repeating the steps the researcher showed it and getting a treat.

"He's just like me!"

Her mom did not respond again, though that couldn't stop her amusement. Her mom often took her to different labs, though typically they were no fun at all. But her mom said she had to contribute and be useful somehow, because otherwise she was pretty useless. And the research studies gave them some money to help out. Not that there was anything special about Meg, they were just studies needing normal children participants. Most parents did not want to bring their kids or even consider it; her friend even said that Meg was going to end up with three ears! She did not think so, but they were normally boring. But this time was so awesome! Seeing the chimpanzee and even getting a treat was the greatest thing that had ever happened to her.

The researcher came in again, a big smile brightening her face. "Did you like seeing Sulango?"

"Oh yes! That was so cool!"

She laughed and reached out to offer her hand to the child. "There is one more box to open and treat to be had, if you are ready?"

Meg took the lady's hand, and was led back to the lab again. Another box was there, though this time it was transparent. You could see everything inside it, all the mechanisms that made it work. The researcher did the steps again, and Meg sat there with a big smile on her face as she repeated the steps and then got her treat. Then she was led back again to the waiting room.

The chimpanzee soon appeared on the television screen, with the transparent box in front of him. The researcher showed him the steps ... but Sulango did not do all of them! He just skipped some, and only turned the knob and lifted the lever, but the treat still popped out for him. She sat there, confused. Did she do something wrong?

Her mom finally spoke up from between her puffs, though her voice nonchalance and annoyed at being there, "That monkey is smarter than you."

The researcher came in, same big smile as she kneeled down to the eye level of Meg. But rather than her excitement of previous, Megaira burst into tears. "I'm dumb! I did it wrong, I'm sorry."

"No! No, you didn't at all," she said soothingly, patting the top of the pigtail mess that sorted the unkempt blonde hair. "You see, this experiment is to just tell us how Chimpanzees are amazing at problem solving. They can see something and figure out how to solve many basic problems better than any human. And their memory is amazing too. One experiment shows that they can remember patterns shown just in short bursts to them, better than even adult humans."

"But I see more than just showing how smart these apes are. I see how special this makes us and how it may have been the reason we evolved the way we did, and have society and culture. You see, you had such strong belief in the ritual, you ignored the fact that some steps were pointless in opening the box. This does not make you dumb! Rather it shows how important this belief is in humans, it is the reason why we were able to form a society and become what we are. So this experiment should not just be about how chimpanzees are great at problem solving, but how the human's propensity to belief is what helped our evolution to what we are today."

Obviously the confused young face that stared up at her caused the researcher to continue in hopes to clarify herself. "Belief helps us build on the thoughts and ideas of others. It allowed us to create space shuttles and be able to have underwater sea exploration. It lets us create art and society. I trust that flicking this switch will turn on the lights. I have no idea how it does, but trusting others allowed me to study other aspects of science and build on them. Belief makes us rely on others, and this is how society is formed."

"So you did not do it wrong. You are showing how special humans are," the researcher continued, and though Meg could hear her mom scoff in the background, it did not matter. Her previous excitement was returning.

"I want to be just like you when I grow up!"

The researcher smiled in return and pushed some of the stuffing back into the brains of the poor dolphin. "You know dolphins are chimpanzees of the sea, they are so smart. And you can be anything you set your mind to."

"Stop telling her lies," her mom rebutted, grabbed the hand of the little one and pulled her away. "We have been here long enough, we have other appointments."

Her mom hurried her away, of course after getting the pay. But Meg did not care, all she could think of was what the researcher had said. Chimpanzees of the sea! She loved the ocean, she wished she could live forever in the sea, like a mermaid! That would be so much better than where she lived now.

Several days previous: In the time after the war

Satin sheets clung to Megaira's skin. Sweat trickled from her, enveloping each curve. Regardless of the cool deep sea that surrounded the Thalassic, her quarters felt as if a sweltering oven. One hand propped her head, the other teased the sheet, beckoning her partner to return to their haven.

"Hector, stay," she murmured, sitting up and pulling the sheets loosely around her as if challenging Hector to come and pull them off.

He did not answer. He dressed and started to head toward the door.

It was a vain attempt to find a heart inside the hollow husk of a soldier. Once, she believed he would have more to give, once upon a time as the fairy tales go. She should have known, though perhaps that was why she was attracted to him, that she did know. She knew it would never be more, and part of her wanted it to be that way. She could not help the occasional pull for significance, but if Hector ever responded positively? She would probably leave him, needing to maintain her independence.

Still, she persuaded him to stay and forgo his duties. Climb the impossible mountain, push the rock too heavy, as Sisyphus in the classical mythos. Sisyphus was a Corinthian king who had betrayed Zeus. In eagle form, Zeus had found love with a nymph and had carried her away. But Sisyphus, who had always been deceitful and murderous if to his own advantage, told the nymph's father where Zeus had taken her. Therefore Sisyphus was punished to be chained in Hell, but instead used trickery to chain Death himself, which caused disorder in the earthly realm. Finally though, he was sentenced in Hell to attempt to push a rock up a mountain, though when he neared the summit the boulder would roll down. He was bound to eternity to repeat this task. The comparison was not a far stretch considering Hector was like an immobile boulder and Thalassic mimicked Tartarus so closely, and she, as the Greek king had been, was punished for an eternity in the underworld.

"Come on stay." She stretched under the sheets, allowing each movement to be visible to the soldier. Each gesture deliberate yet impulsive.

"No," he responded. Hard, cold, the stone of Sisyphus. "Not while there may be others above."

What he meant was not while there was a war to be fought above. He probably cared little of any survivors, he just wanted to fight. She sighed, oh, how she could read him. However, he completely misunderstood her.

"I did not mean that. I just meant for a hour, away from your duties toward the Thalassic and Leander."

Despite herself, she was hoping again that there was more to him than his steel exterior; the question was: was he worth it to her?

"I am going to meet with Leander," he responded. "We leave come dusk. I have to go."

The sultry climate stood opposed to the frost growing between them. But he took a step back to her, and suddenly the impermeable mountain seemed to collapse in an avalanche. Care and concern carved his features as he looked to her.

"You stay aboard Thalassic, promise me. I want you safe," Hector said, bringing one hand to sweep her blonde locks over her shoulder.

He would never understand. She wanted to be with him—not protected by him. Hell if she could not protect herself. Slipping her hand down the side of the bed, she searched underneath it. First her hand hit a very familiar object, which once was fluffy and comforting but now made her hand retreat in embarrassment upon feeling its worn fur. Definitely do not want to bring out my old dolphin, she thought as her cheeks blushed, and she continued her search. Finally, she found what she wanted and pulled out the assault rifle stowed securely underneath. Weapons were not allowed in the private cabins, for the discharge of them would only compromise the underwater compound. But she was not one to abide by any rule that separated her from it.

"I don't need you concerned for my safety," Megaira said in a gesture of stubbornness. Not that it was a misguided stubbornness; she was an ace in assault tactics.

"And that is what I like about you," Hector said, taking the gesture in play. He smiled as he threw a pillow on her. "Though promise me. Stay here in Thalassic."

Promise ignored, Megaira walked the tunnels composing the Thalassic to find Leander. She would not have Hector dictate her prerogatives. And to hell with him if he decided what was best for her. Or perhaps that was what caused her dissension: he did not care for her. Somehow his order for her to stay behind showed her that he did not want her by his side. And this expedition to the surface was truly just a way to throw her off his back.

Walking through the circular halls, she felt each step weighted as she considered the true reasoning behind Hector's demand. Finally, she found Leander in the weapons area. Preparing for his unauthorized mission, he looked up suddenly upon her interruption.

"What are you doing here?" she asked. She knew, but decided to use it to her advantage. "Nothing behind Admiral Telphousian's back, right?"

He shook his head, knowing damn well what she was trying to do. Blackmail, to keep her quiet and the mission secret. "What do you want, Megaira?"

"To go with you."

"Hector doesn't want you to go," Leander said. "You know he really does care for you in his own way. And it is too dangerous up there. Plus, we are going against direct orders. If found out, we will lose our rank, maybe worse. I don't want to place you in that situation."

She sighed; Leander was worst than a protective brother. Of course, as an only child, she supposed part of her enjoyed his brotherly demeanor.

"Why don't you just leverage how the Admiral feels about you. Give her what she wants—maybe she will then give you what you want. This mission, proper troops," she said.

"You know how I feel about Tilphê. I cannot lie and put forward false feelings even for the endorsement of this mission. I won't play with her heart like that."

"Then if you don't allow me to come, I will tell her. Both of you will be behind bars, and she would probably enjoy putting you there—then she could finally make you hers."

Leander frowned, his face embittered at her threat. "You would put yourself before the good of society, Megaira?"

"Would you put Hector's wishes above it?"

She had him, she knew it. He would do anything, from going against orders to dismissing Hector's wish, if it was for the 'good of society'. But she knew better, society was damned and all she could afford to care about right now was the good of herself. It may sound selfish, but she learned even before the outbreak that all you really have is yourself. That was the one and only lesson her mother had taught her, albeit indirectly.

"Fine. You can come."

A smile broke her face, as she joined by his side. She wrapped her hand around the largest assault rifle and pulled it from the rack. "You won't regret your decision."

"I will as soon as Hector finds out."

And that was sooner than later. Hector walked into the weapons locker. Face emotionless, he looked at Megaira and then Leander, nothing behind the hard expression. He pulled a revolver and rifle from the rack, still wordless.

"I can handle it, Hector," Megaira said, answering Hector's unstated yet clear discontent. "You know I can help you guys up there."

"I am not worried about whether you can handle yourself," Hector said.

Leander backed away from the beginnings of the quarrel, placing his weapons of choice in his utility belt and pack. "I'm going to get Dio, obtain some medical supplies, and we will meet at the moon pool at nineteen hundred."

He left without a goodbye; Megaira did not blame him as the tension rose between herself and Hector.

"Then what is it?" she asked, hushed, as she touched Hector's arm. He tensed. "You just want to leave me behind? I don't understand why you do not want me there."

His tension eased as he placed his arms around her. To finally feel his warmth rather than the coldness, but to know he would soon close up again was torture. He was a warrior; he needed war to be himself. Otherwise his spirit was tortured; otherwise, he was as the ghosts of lions that lay idle in the zoo. He needs the hunt, the fight ... not love. And she knew this. Yet still his warmth enticed, his presence lured her to him.

"Before Thalassic ..." he began. He paused, and she loosened her grip to look at him. He never mentioned the time before he was stationed on Thalassic outside of the formal debriefings, but now he spoke. "I fought the Chaots. But they were not just Chaots to me. They were my squadron who had turned. I fought against those I stood besides, I fought my own comrades. This disease, it takes your soul."

He pressed his lips against her cheek as he murmured in her ear: "I worry I will have to stand against you."

"I understand," she said, relieved, realizing he did not doubt her skills or ability to stand strong. "And do what you must Hector. And I will do as I must."

He kissed her. Their lips met for mere seconds, but the passion shared would live on in her mind.

And through hell

The submersible broke the surface. Testing the air, assuring themselves that the bio-agent was indeed gone from the atmosphere, Leander then pushed the hatch open and the four looked out, the first time in over a year they saw the moonlight.

Salt air filled the cabin. Fresh air.

Megaira breathed deep, finally grasping the point for heading upward, becoming aware of the life she had missed. The unprocessed air, the wind that whipped through the sub and around the

Thalassicians, the sounds of waves and seagull caws, all of this she did not even realize was lacking in her life, did not realize she even missed it, until now.

But what waited away from the open sea? What waited on land?

They would soon find out.

The moonlight bounced along the rocks scattering the shore. Each shone as if a moon to itself, granting a beautiful vision of land to the sea bound soldiers. Megaira smiled, and for the first time it was not a journey to be besides Hector, or to test her training, but to simply escape the underwater shell that kept her for over a year. She leaned over, putting her hand between the rocks to touch the muddy soil of the earth.

The King Sisyphus has cheated death once. Now she felt the same, escaping from the underworld to again be alive.

"We're here," she called out, as if now they could stay here. It seemed peaceful, removed from any threat of the doomsday long past. Maybe the Chaots had killed themselves, she thought, and all those months were spent below for nothing.

A dog bark responded to her proclamation. She laughed, as if the bark corroborated her hope that the end of war had come. Now was only nature, only peace.

If only it could be so simple.

The dog bark came again, not in happiness though. Not in welcome of people returning to pet and groom him, nor as a carnivore on the hunt. It made her arms freeze, not the best thing when what they should have been doing was readying her gun. The dog roared; the sound crossing the line to into the fanatical. Over the rocks, the dog ran, and as he came to sight she saw his mouth foaming.

Gun ... gun ... she thought to herself, but was still caught off guard in her euphoria moments ago.

Hector stepped in front of her, turning to the charging animal, took aim, and fired.

The dog fell, its blood splashing unto the moonlit rocks. Megaira said nothing, felt nothing. The joyous homecoming broke away from her exterior, leaving her with nothing left except the mission.

"Did the disease cross the lines from humans to animals?" she asked, her voice shaky. Her confidence of animals faltered as if the chimpanzee whom she adored from her childhood had escaped from behind the television screen and came to chase her down, taking the identity of the dog to do so.

Dio looked over the dog. Megaira wondered if he still respected the culture of his ancestors as he looked with reverence upon the animal. Leander came to his side to visually examine the dog.

"Looks like rabies," Leander said. "Without humans to try to control the virus, the outbreak is probably escalating in animals around here. Nothing to do with the disease itself."

"Let us hope we only run into crazed dogs, and not crazed humans," Megaira replied. She stepped out from behind Hector's protection, placing a hand on his arm. "And I can take care of myself from dogs, cats ... even the occasional person."

She joked, yet her voice was far off. Cold crept within her soul as she tried to return to the elation of being surface side, but failed.

"No offense, but it did not seem that way to me," Dio said. She always believed Dio had it out for her, and his critical glare only proved it to her.

"No, everything would have been fine. I just did not want to go around killing dogs, and so waited a moment to be sure."

"That moment could mean your death next time," Hector said.

Great, it felt like everyone was ganging up on her.

"Next time, keep your gun in your holster, Hector," she retorted, "and you will see I won't hesitate."

She said that more to herself than anyone, as she looked at the dog. Perhaps there was still a chance the plague was self-eradicating. But seeing that dead dog, the saliva dripping down the open mouth as if the virus still lived, she knew hope could not be afforded. If it were, she would be ill-equipped to handle what hides, pass the rock shores, behind the line of green.

My gun will be in my hands, ready to kill, next time. She swore that to herself.

Chapter Nine

Victor of the dawn, the sun rose as a flaming chariot. Awakening those under his path, Helios took the reins to bring light to the new day. The god played secondary to the pantheon in ancient times, only on the island of Rhodes did his worship manifest beyond the trivial. Though now as he came to the Acadia island in the western hemisphere, his adoration again became forefront. Scaring away demons that haunted the night, lighting the way for the those who most needed him, Helios found the veneration of a true deity. The soldiers watched the vibrance of dawn fight away the night, and aspired that they too could battle the personified darkness—the Chaots—and win as Helios had.

Allowing the light to lead them, the five broke camp and began again to hike toward the uncharted destination. This time Leander and Dio took the lead, Hector the rear, and Megaira hiked with Nyx in the middle. The men were out of eyeshot, but she did not mind. They were becoming a restrictive presence, an anchor cast within the roving seas. How one could stand such an accumulation of people was beyond her. Especially Leander...his presence confused her. He was the haze before sunrise, where nothing was clear, where nothing made sense. She waited for the sun to rise to see straight, to follow her wayward path. But with Leander she was trapped in that foggy interval between wake and sleep, night and day. She desired to be away and on her own, but the pull to stay—the pull toward Leander—overwhelmed even that.

But destiny had its own ideas. Megaira took her arm and shoved her to the side, her gun trained on her.

"Don't get any brave ideas. I'm not going to shoot you, unless you force me into it. You don't belong with us. You endanger us ... you don't want to endanger Leander, do you?"

She could shout out for Leander, but knew the moment she took a breath to do so, a bullet would be in her. She did not blame Megaira, she only did what she believed best for the soldiers. And considering Nyx's own confusion toward Leander, perhaps this was best for her as well. Never, not even in her forgotten life, had she ever felt such connection with another. It scared her this unknown, it should not have, she thought, but it did. Megaira was right. She did not want to harm Leander. She did not belong.

"This is where you part," Megaira said, her gun motioning for Nyx to go into the forest away from the soldiers' path. "Do not come back."

Nyx hesitated. No matter the fear of her feelings, she did not want to leave, but right now the choice was not hers to make. She could not refuse nor fight against Megaira and turned wordlessly and left. She could do nothing to prevent her forced departure, not yet anyway, and within her heart she felt again the beckoning of the wild, of the solitude, of what was known and familiar to her.

Shadows rose from between the maple and spruce trees; the dark gaps encompassed a lure as seductive as sirens. Black holes, they were, that threatened to swallow one from existence if they came too close. And as a black hole, the shadows relentless pull acted as gravity to Nyx, pulling her further from the soldiers into their event horizon.

Birds called their chorus down to her as the distance grew between herself and the Thalassicians. Cardinals in their scarlet crowns, their song a beautiful array of whistles. In their melody was the charm of the forest and of nature. But a distinct vocal offset their song, a scratchy overture from above. It was almost as if the disease began to rise, interrupting life in the skies as it did below. Yet it was only a blue jay. The sapphire plumage just as stunning as the cardinals', even if its vocalizations did not ring as beautiful. As they sang, she wondered what had happened to the animals in the wake of society's demise. Prosper? Or find the new predator, the Chaots, to be worse than the humans. Though it seemed the birds flourished as did the fish seaside, untouched by the monstrosity that had befell the law of the land.

Flourished, maybe. But still hunted nonetheless.

There was one feathered presence that did not sing in the cheerful croons of the others. It stalked the songbirds. The peregrine falcon—she mused it was the one she had seen from the beach and she wondered if it had found the meal she left for it the night before. In the sunlight she could see the chocolate colored back and streaked feathers, hiding a small amount of down, marking it as juvenile. She caught the view of the silent presence every so often, either sitting in the branches or flying above. Or now, where it hunted the brightly colored targets. High in the sky, the falcon tracked the flying blue jay. With sudden, incomprehensible speed, the falcon dove as a guided missile cutting through the air towards its mark, offering no hope of escape. At first with closed talons it rammed into the bird, before circling back and taking the jay. The prey lashed out—pitifully so—it had no chance against the bird-eating raptor. A bird eating a bird: was this cannibalism? No said the voice of facts, the voice of reason and scientific understanding. Cannibals feed on the flesh of the same species. And the falcon was far removed from the songbirds. A predator, not weak as its prey.

Were the Chaots cannibals then when they preyed upon the humans?

The voice remained silent.

She roamed deeper into the forests; her footsteps took her further and faster away from the group as she tried to track the falcon. Soon she was lost within the maze of backwater trees. Calls from behind her escalated as Leander must have realized she no longer walked behind him. The soldiers shouted her name, even risking their own location as they did so, in hopes that she would return. She wished to go back to them, but what would she return to if not Megaira's bullet. If not immediately, then surely come night.

"Nyx!"

Her name again called by the soldiers. A tremble came across her, a shiver in the summer's heat. Her spirit tore. Part of her wished to return. Megaira was a problem, yet not one that she feared, for she feared more Megaira's prophecy of putting them in harm's way. But then she heard something in the distance, drowning out all else. A mismatched sound, not of the forest nor soldiers' calls, indicating more than trees. And part of her became determined to stay her path, to investigate the idiosyncrasy she heard.

The noise grew clear. Low, but audible, a guttural chorus whispered between the maple trees. The words were not words; the meaning was meaningless. But together it strung a harmony that had deeper implications than surface value. Closer she came to the source. Staying low, she moved some branches to peer out and into the abyss—and now she stood facing the event horizon.

The falcon's hunt still vivid in her mind, but replacing its image was the predator of the lands: the Chaots.

A gathering of at least thirty appeared to her sight. And how many more were hidden in the trees, she thought. The Chaots she could see stood in a crescent clearing of the forest. Unlike the twelve she had seen in the city, these did not engage in any salacious acts, at least not now. Instead they stood. Humming. The whimsical chanting grew powerful, the tide of time present in their voices.

Physically they emulated the town's Chaots. In ailment they withered, covered with festering sickness. Almost akin to lepers did they live; as legs, fingers, eyes were lost and incomplete in each human form —victims to raging viruses of rot or self-fulfilling bouts of cannibalism.

But internally they appeared different. She saw more. They hummed in an unified group, focused on an act that brought no ultimate reward. She could even see disparity amongst those of the forest gathering. A distinction in awareness presented itself as some were inspirited in their incantation while others lagged and struggled at the chore. But what was clear was that some remnants of the scope of human intelligence must have remained to invoke such a gathering.

The added dimension of Chaot behavior confused her, for before she believed these beings were without an advanced awareness. A complete slave to the disease. But now? Did the pathogen affect its victims each differently in its prognosis? The town's twelve Chaots acted in the ways of the singularly insane. Separate in mind, unaware of the wants and needs of the other, and deviant in their group individualism. Conversely, this hive that she stumbled upon revealed another layer. The Chaots acted as a cohesive whole. There was always a chance that their conformities were indeed not unique but instead the Chaots were progressing beyond the initial pandemonium.

The Chaots faced the same way, to the west. Away from Mecca, away from Olympus, away from the rising sun. Their blank eyes stared out at the horizon, but for the life of her she could not see what the Chaots saw.

But she also knew what she did not see. No beds, no hearth, no altar, no shelter. She could not tell if this place was their permanent habitation, or some kind of ritualistic place of worship. It seemed to be just another part of the forest to an outsider's eye; the trees, the plants— all stood the same. Nor could she guess if this was a kindred clan of

Chaots, or if once the humming ceased, they would disperse as seeds to the wind. Something told her this was more than simply a sporadic meeting though, that coincidence could not bring so many Chaots to the same place at the same time. There were more than appearances to this symphonic conclave.

Look beneath, and you will see.

She remembered the justification Leander gave for not killing her when she was chained in the abandoned playground. She spoke. It was what set her apart from the Chaots, the control of communication, being able to voice her desires rather than simply act on them. The Chaots chanting composed of various sounds proved otherwise; these creatures did have forms of communication. But what did they chant to? Why did they chant?

It could be the birth of a religion, the ancestral makings of a prayer to the unseen immortals. Soon the nonsensical hums would become words, giving birth to language, and then to form tales of gods and myths distinct to the Chaots. The humans soon would fall to extinction and would live on only as a legend to the Chaots. Perhaps it was beyond religion, beyond atheism, and into another realm. Or it was a ritual done without knowledge of why—even to them—but rather just a vestige of humankind. An echo of whom they once were, awaiting to disappear like all the other mannerisms of the civil.

Lines of good and evil, right and wrong, were ever blurred inside her mind. She did not know how to interpret this scene for she was led to believe the Chaots were absent of sanity. But as she looked out from hiding to observe the gathering of the wild creatures, she could not help but see a society at its roots. In the aftermath of war, a group—not civilized by any means—nonetheless spawned a new civilization. A manifestation of conformity amongst the crowd. A new species stood before her, rather than 'sickness', it now became a dawn to a new age. Not something warped and perverted as the soldiers would see. Not something to cure, for they did not start the final battle between humans. The Chaots did not cause the end of the human's rule upon the Earth, but we did. It was not their apocalypse but our own.

She understood why the soldiers fought: self preservation. But it was more than that, they also desired the Chaots death because of fear. Fear of the unknown and known. The Chaots were too close a reflection of what they knew, reminding them of the end of *Homo sapiens*. The soldiers struggled to prevail against the odds, but they did not realize the victor had already been chosen. The new reign of *Homo ferus* begins, with her a witness to it.

The wild replaces the wise. Nature triumphs the logical.

But will it end in one generation? Genetics were not at work in this evolution; Mendel's laws of inheritance could not prevail. Look to Lamarck, the voice of scientific reason echoed, inheritance of acquired phenotypes not by way of genetics. Once absurd. But not with prions, prions are the exception. They are heritable. They will act in conjunction with evolution.

It would not end. Even now, she could see an infant held in one female's grip, a living testament that nature endures. Its teeth dug with vigor into its mother's arm. Not human, never was. Born Chaot.

Nyx saw the beginnings of a new species in the infant. But like so many other ape species, there needed to be more. Though she was not sure what she looked for until she saw it.

In the midst of the group, one Chaot stood out, one Chaot above the rest. His hair a dusky brown. His skin tanned and coated with dirt like the others. But unlike those that stood around him, his arms and face were spared the full extent of corrosion. Only ample scars were visible, marking the battles he had fought—and apparently won. He stood as if he had a direction, a path to follow, where the others just ran sporadically without goal. But with him, came a cohesive direction. They surrounded him as if he was the central force, venerated and in control: the deep seeded order behind all chaos.

He was the leader. The alpha of the Chaots.

The Pathfinder.

Pathfinder, she mused for the name felt like it was meant for him. A memory, she wondered. But his goal and purpose seemed to be to reign. Emerging from the aftermath of one era, he would lead into the next.

Turning as if in answer to her unspoken question, the Pathfinder looked past his followers to find her. She could see his bronze eyes as he stared into her soul, and she pulled back behind the tree—more in fear of fantasy than what was real. His stare was pervasive as if forged in the fires of Hephaestus. To be caught in it, one surely would be thrown in the same flaming hearth.

He had taken the reins and stood before the Chaots. And now that he had sighted her, he could pull those reins to guide the Chaots to her. Destroying her, ending the journey. But the Pathfinder made no move.

She began to question whether he had even seen her, or if it was her imagination alone that believed such.

She risked looking out from her hiding place once more. Though the Pathfinder no longer stood amidst his followers. Where had he gone?

Just a figment, as the Fisherman had been. A mirage. The order the Pathfinder imposed in this chaos was as likely as an oasis in the desert. Believe the mirage, drink the sand, and die.

"Nyx!" Leander called out through the forest.

The chanting noises stopped; heads turned from the west toward the soldier's voice. She ducked underneath several low-lying leaves for cover, cursing Leander. He put himself at risk for her. She had to get back to the soldiers and warn them, despite Megaira's threat.

But her decision came too late.

A hand reached out, stopping her by tightening around her shoulder. Intrigue piqued, she wondered if the Pathfinder had come to her side, not as a mirage but as reality. She turned to face him, but met disappointment. It was not the leader, but another Chaot. Blonde hair and fair skin shone beneath the dirt of the monster, almost akin to a porcelain doll. Eyes as sheer as the ocean's waves would have been luminous, but unsettling red lines etched across the white sclera. He contrasted greatly in looks to the tree-dwelling Chaot near the city but shared one common thread in her mind: the overwhelming feeling that she was now in the presence of the gods. They had been created not as some error of warfare, but through the divine.

Despite this conception, she would not be restrained against her will. She took a step away to free herself; but his grasp grew tighter, preventing any escape. His fingers pressed into her skin. His nails were like claws in their yellow lengthy appearance.

The Chaot did not move at first, other than to keep her at bay. He made no efforts to bring her to the others, or to hide her away as his own. It was almost as if he was accepting her as one of them, welcoming the long lost one home. The strange thing was, she wanted to see where he led her, embracing her allure to these strange creatures, no matter the darkness that shadowed them.

Leander called again from the distance. The believed moment of kinship between them ended. And this time, the soldier's call caused a grumble of alert from the gathering below. Starting as a quiet alarm, it snowballed into a duet, a quartet, and finally a loud rise from all their mouths. It did not signal her interruption; the group alarm was directed to the soldiers, the outsiders.

The one besides her joined in with the chorus. His call was so powerful in its reiteration that as he vocalized a loose tooth bursted from his putrid gums. It fell with a thud, hitting the dirt of the forest floor. What would have surprised her if not for the circumstances was the disregard he had to his dismantled jaw. It was as if he had grown accustomed to pieces falling from him that the Chaot no longer took notice.

The rousing warning of this infected male petrified her; she did not know what would come next. What stopped the Chaot from satisfying his needs now, tearing away at her skin as a barbie on a pit, she wondered even though she could guess the answer. The id contained more than hungers for the feast, and the flesh could be used to serve other appetites. He could control his urge to kill and eat, at least for moments, in order to engage in other limbic desires.

His alarm stopped in cohesion with the others, replaced by grunting breaths. His tongue flickered in delicious excitement along his lips in anticipation of her. The organ, cancerous and shriveled, moved out from his mouth, along her cheek to taste her salty freshness. The wet trail lined her face. She could only hold still, hoping not to incite him further.

He grabbed her with both arms, dragging her away. Away from the other Chaots and from the threat of the intruders, away from any interruption. She damned herself for hesitating from fighting back, for ignoring Hector's lessons of attacking before too late. Fear, his other lesson, had now hindered her. Though it was more than that. Curiosity. And curiosity now caused her to pause in action. The Chaot may bring her to the Pathfinder, or even reveal the mysteries of her soul, bringing a fate that had long evaded her. She could not fight back, for then all the answers would slip away to obscurity. But she knew she had to fight back for the soldier's sake.

The trees shadowed their figures, hiding the duo from display. The Chaot stopped about thirty feet away from the group and pushed her down and into a hole. She fell several feet, but her descent abruptly stopped upon impact with the ground. Dust and dirt dispersed around her, making it difficult to see. She touched the edge; deposits of the rock rubbed along her finger. It was limestone. Then her hand came to a wooden board, placed there to probably secure this cave. The walls integrated a fusion between the uniform structure set by the cave's creators and a natural expanse of hollow earth. Parts seemed wet to the touch, a sign of its slow erosion—nature taking its claim on the manmade structure.

The fall did no damage, she thought, nothing substantial enough for concern. What would happen next was. She immediately tried to run after standing, but the Chaot jumped on her and grabbed her. He stood still, waiting with her in his grip. Her sight adjusted to the lair and she looked around, hoping she could gain some information of her surroundings to help in her escape. It was an underground cave system beneath the forest, one that still reeked from the usage of past times. She wondered if it had been built in a last hope effort to shelter survivors from the plague of Armageddon. The Chaots of this gathering may have been the ones who built this cavern before they had become infected. Or perhaps they were the ones who penetrated the grounds, bringing chaos to the shelter and eating what hid inside. Or a mix of both, and only through the disease it joined two enemies together, fighting no more as they became one.

Fear shimmered within her sweat in this sweltering complex. The Chaot turned her toward him, his gaze catching hers through the cave's dark. Wrapping one arm around her trembling form as he grew close, the second hand came over her mouth to prevent any screams. He was face to face with her as he imprisoned her in his arms, awaiting the threat from above to vanish. Waiting to quench his desires.

He transformed into a minion of Hades before her.

Echoes of the alarm grew distant inside the harbor of the cave. Only her own inhalation rang in her ears. Her breath became more erratic through his fingers as she stared upward. A few shards of light illuminated the cave. The light retreated from the world above, however the quietude of above did not last long, as sudden explosions replaced the chorus of the Chaots. The soldiers had come. Only their heroic inspiration to free her led them. And though they were brave, this place was the territory of the infected. The Chaots had the advantage in the dark, dank corridors of the forest.

The fair-haired Chaot pulled his catch closer to him, as if she were the doll at his whims. He had no intention of releasing her or bringing her to the Pathfinder. She had to fight. Without her hands free, she did what Hector taught and rammed her head into the Chaot's. Another tooth shattered and broke away from his jaw as if he were actually made of porcelain. His hold loosened for seconds, and she was able to free one hand and go for his collar. But he rammed forward himself, grabbing her around her head as if to decapitate or smother her. Tighter he pushed his arm around her face, she could not breath. She struggled against him, but soon that struggle just became an uncoordinated fight wanting air again. All she could think to do was bite him; she clenched her teeth down on the Chaot's arm in hopes to free herself from the death grip.

Iron bitterness poured within her mouth as her teeth cut through his flesh, but no screams answered her act of insurgence. Instead laughter escaped from her captor as he shoved her aside. The laughter seemed to continue though he had stopped, for she then realized the full repercussion of her act. Of what would happen. She was exposed to the disease. The prion was now in her system.

She knew she did not have long. Mere minutes until the sickness ravaged her body. The soldiers had drilled her with the epidemiology of the prion and she knew it would overcome her sanity without remorse in moments.

What does one do when they know they only have minutes to live? Cherish memories of long ago, reliving childhood delights and dreams? Yet she had none. Treasure moments of passion, a first kiss … a first touch upon another's flesh? But she had never experienced love nor lust. There was no 'other' who she had shared life with. Even to look to the sky and bask within its splendor for the last time, she could not do. She only saw black, the bleakness of the underground. A beauty though overlooked by too many. The aberrant was what captured the grandeur of life itself. What would come from the cookie cutter scenes, the seemingly attractive all but the same? In consonance we find stagnation. In dissonance we find true beauty. And so she braced for the prion's takeover, ready to become a Chaot. Ready for the discordance that would come.

Outside she heard the horde of Chaots surrounding the soldiers. The Thalassic warriors continued to assault the gathering with no regard of their outnumbered situation. In her mind's eye she saw their faces pinched in sick delirium; they moved to destroy those who threatened their existence, threatening the Chaots' in turn. She could do nothing, only hope that the soldiers survived this ordeal. Only to pray to the ancient gods that Leander, Hector, Dio and Megaira would endure. But to what end? She still awaited the infection's repercussion. Then she would be a Chaot, and if the soldiers survived this ordeal, Hector would be forced to break his one promise to her. He would be forced to kill her.

The Chaot was on her again, this time pulling her through the maze, leading deeper and deeper into the caves. Twisting throughout the channels—rights followed by sharp lefts—finally he slowed. He pulled her around to face him. His motive ever present in his limbique stare. In one abrupt movement, his hand came up to wipe away the bloodied slime that streaked her mouth from her act of rebellion. A thumb moved downward on her chin in a brutish caress. He looked toward her with an animalistic sensuality in his claim; did he even wonder if his disease would work into her, warping the girl into his Bride of Frankenstein. One finger, almost rotten to the bone, came up to his mouth. His lips puckered and blew signaling her to remain quiet. Not that she would obey if she had a choice, but even if she did yell out no one would hear in the turmoil above. But his act: it separated him from the mindless descriptions that the soldiers had told her of the Chaots. What were they truly?

She nodded in understanding, knowing in a few minutes it may not even matter what he would do to her. The contagion hovered over her, like a dark cloud threatening to burst. It was irrefutably in her bloodstream due to her bite. Why it did not take her yet, she did not know. She could only wait and see if the fate would come or if only uncertainty would follow.

Her gaze came to the Chaot. Her attention captured by his unnatural eyes, haunting her with questions. With answers.

He pushed her down to the floor with sudden force. Edging near the corners, she searched for a weapon but found nothing. Her will and determination pivoted greatly between one moment and the next.

Courage loomed within her, waiting for release. She should not curl in fear, hidden behind shadows. She had to escape. For moments though, she allowed dread to overpower her mind, unable to plan an attack.

Who then was the more despicable: the Chaot who stared with gaping repulsiveness from without or the girl whose soul broke within, unable to take control of her own fate.

It was a wanderer she was ... but a wanderer lost.

"Why?"

Voice shaken, lips smeared within the rancid blood of the infected, she grasped for an understanding as why her fate should be tainted by cruelties and anomalous defects. But before the answer could be posed on the monster's tongue, she turned her head away, disgusted not with the face before her but with herself. She never wished to question 'why', or to query what was before her. Yet her own voice had just now betrayed her spirit. Why she had asked, rather than simply accept what was before her and act.

She did not look off into the blackened solace for long, for the Chaot crept forward and pried her filth-covered face toward his. He made her stare at him, made her see the fate of what she would become. Or was it something else that persuaded his actions? Stare. Stare into the beast, stare into the eyes of the maker. Stare a wild beast in the eyes, and become it or die. And she would not surrender. Only inches lay between them, and she forced her eyes to meet his soulless gaze.

A voice came outward from him, not human in its tone, but an unnatural stunted hiss of decay which seemed to say '*You mine*'.

Teeth bared under the festering lips as they pulled upward. Hunger for flesh written upon the face of the Chaot. Breath hinged as terror began to chill her from the inside out. She could hardly focus or move or even steady her increasingly panicked exhales as the teeth came closer still. She would not plea though; she would not crumble to the ground in defeat. Not yet and not now. Somehow she had to prevail against the odds. Hopes of overcoming the mighty drove her to search the dirt-covered ground again. Her touch came to a splintered outbreak of wood that kept the cave walls from folding in. She grasped it, allowing the dark to cover her actions, and waited for the optimal moment. This time she would act not too soon nor too late.

The Chaot's hand trembled in unconfined anticipation as he reached out and tore at her pants, ripping through her clothes. With a section of skin exposed, he touched her thigh. Fingers came up along her body; grotesque worms as they slithered upon her flesh. Dirt mingled with blood smeared across her as he pressed his hand to between her legs. His actions were driven by urges beyond his control; the Chaot sought to bring impurity to the perceived innocence laying before him. A shred of desire hid behind the mound of hatred and fear, though she could not understand her fascination in these creatures. Disgust that should have shown, as the soldiers had toward the Chaots, did not materialize. Rather, she felt an unbalanced revulsion and yet feeling that this was where she belonged.

The disease did not bring these thoughts, she told herself with complete certainty. Though it should have happened, it had not yet come. She had her will, her wits, her mind, and was not ready to submit to the infection nor this Chaot. She would never be ready.

She smiled through clenched teeth. Deranged as her captor, her smile glimmered white against her dirt-covered face. The Chaot could no longer withhold as he pulled her to him in an attempt to meet his unsatisfied desires. She felt the weight of his body press close to hers. Holding the wood slice, she shifted as he pushed toward her. Hector's wisdom returned to her, reminding her to use her opponent's momentum to her advantage. To not let fear dictate but rather instinct. And the Chaot did not see her as a threat, wherein she found her edge. She would not become a marionette to his liking. She tore the shard up into his oncoming torso, sinking the piece deep inside him.

He screeched. The sound was unearthly, almost as Frankenstein's monster's cries cross the Arctic snow. He did not die yet though. The pain manifested as increased lechery, even if her attack did serve to weaken his overall strength.

The Chaot grabbed the stick, pulling it from his wound. A sucking sound emanated as the weapon came out; the engorged blood poured down from his injury onto her body that lay below. He hit the wood shard hard against her cheek, striking her for her disobedience. No screams came, only a silent urgency. Trying to get away from him, she struggled underneath his form. His hand clenched her neck. He pulled her to him as if she was a toy to tinker with, dragging her mouth to his. His lips were not puckered to elope hers in a tender first kiss, instead teeth raged open with one intent—to bite her face off. Then he would have her.

A sudden bang interjected, bringing silence. The quiet interlude gave her hope, for the alternative was her own screams if the Chaot succeeded in his feast. But the gunshot caused the monster to stop from his calamitous path. Though unlike before in the forest, the shot missed. Delivered in darkness, it was doomed to fail. It did succeed, however, in causing a distraction and in that she found her opening.

With no weapon except her own fortitude, she took advantage of the wound she had caused from the first assault. Striking hard and quick for the moment of redemption was fleeting, she rammed her hand inside the gaping hole of his abdomen. The hot juices of innards surrounded her fingers as she entwined them in his organs. The fair-haired porcelain pawn of Chaos turned to her—in pain, in surprise, in angered wrath. But too late, as she tore his insides out, pulling her hand away and bringing his intestines with it.

He fell on her, desolate in his embrace. Eyes still open as if looking at her, in an everlasting accusation of what she had done.

She rolled his weight off of her. The infected fell with a thud to the ground. She did not stay to welcome the one who caused the gun shot diversion. She could not trust herself for she had tasted the sweet apple seeds of the underworld, the blood of the Chaots. Now she believed herself doomed; no one could save her. She did not want to risk hurting the soldiers if her mind should suddenly go. Fueled by not wanting to harm them, she found steadiness within her feet and began to run deep into the underground.

She did not get far. The bronze-eyed Pathfinder stood in the shadows, stopping her way.

He stood alone, looking from Nyx to the crumpled Chaot behind her. He had witnessed everything. The outcroppings of light found his face as he stepped toward her, lighting up his features so she could see. He was arrestingly divine, even if clearly a son of Chaos. It was not retaliation of his fallen comrade he sought in his coming, rather the act contained an expression that she had not yet seen in a Chaot. The desire to understand, and perhaps to be understood.

He reached his hand out to her, in an unarticulated gesture to join him.

She was not ready.

She ran from him. Doom stepped its course alongside her. The prion contaminated her. The direct contact between the contagious blood and her own was unquestionable, leaving doubt in her knowledge of the disease. Maybe the time between exposure and symptoms were longer than the soldiers had warned. The prion therefore could still come to take her now, or minutes from now. Was her fate to become a Chaot? Even the Pathfinder seemed to know that she was a part of them.

"No," she said.

An answer to her silent questions. Spoken aloud to represent her conviction that she would not become a monster, if ever the Chaots truly were monsters. Whether monsters or gods, both took a form similar to each other. Beauty and abhorrence under one guise. Even mortals could not see Zeus in his true form, for only death would arise from the sight. This left the question if his beauty caused such death, or was it a monstrosity of the gods that roused the end to the spectators.

Within the distance, she heard several grunts from other Chaots. They appeared as a constant cloud ahead through the darkness of the cave, but she realized their movements had a goal: to surround her. To finish what her now-dead captor had started. To ambush her and show her the only alternative in her rejection of the Pathfinder's offer would be death.

One noise bore a familiarity; it was from the one who had saved her upon the sun-drenched streets of above. Hector. Though this would give others cause to approach, it only caused panic in her for he presented no exit to escape.

You have my word I will not kill you. His previous words of valiance endured throughout her thoughts. She could only guess if they were still valid now that she had contagion upon her lips and scratched body. She knew what he would see—a threat. No longer a person, but a shell containing infection. And he would kill her. Or she would him if the chaos took her.

So she ran through the darkened corridors, through the catacombs of the cave.

Away from the Chaots. From the soldiers.

From herself.

Chapter Ten

Nyx ran further into the tunnels. She ran from Hector for his protection, the threat of infection ever present. The only way to escape, the only way to see the light of day once more, was alone. But the deeper she went, the darker it grew. The further she ran, the possibility dwindled of finding an exit. It felt as if she would be lost forever in the complexity of the cave and her mind. But what the sight of Hector could not do, the sound of gunfire did. She stopped.

The shots were not directed at her, but towards the Chaots filtering into the cave. Hector must be surrounded, she believed, at the mercy of their inclinations. She should be by his side and realized that what truly trapped her was not the threat of infection. What trapped her also defined her: her fear. The phobia of being captured under another's will had become a self-imposed harness. She had to unleash the binds of her fear and not be hindered.

Do not run away from the reaper, for that allows death to dictate life even before your time, and that was what she was doing. But the disease did not transform her, it should have already if ever it would. It would not serve to protect herself or Hector if she continued the spiral downward into the cave, concerned about a fate that may never be realized. And so, she turned from the oblivion to follow Hector's gunshots. To help him as he had her.

Through the darkness and uneven rock formations, she retraced her steps and came upon Hector. He did not see her, his back was turned and he was facing the Chaots. In moments she assessed the situation, realizing a dire outcome. The soldier took arms in an impressive display, though he focused on what was in front of him. She could see a hidden figure to his side; coming up from his left edged a vile creature. It crept through the shadows, presenting the true threat to Hector. Nyx's angle allowed her to discern the attacker. Shades of grey and black made it impossible to speak of colors, but the Chaot's silhouette painted a picture of long hair tresses and curves unmistakably female.

Nyx ran her hand along the cave wall in search of a weapon. A rock loosened, and she took it though kept her attention on the Chaot. The predator of Hector became the prey as she stalked the stalker. When she drew close enough, she brought the rock down in one swift hit. The stone's edge pounded against bone in a devastating shrill, implanting itself in the Chaot's skull. An excruciating screech melded of surprise, pain, and death sounded as the skeletal pieces shattered. Though that screech ended abruptly and the infected she-beast fell in a heap, spasms animating her body as death came.

Hector turned; he looked from the Chaot at his feet to Nyx standing near with the rock in her hand. It was Hector who now expressed a silent gratitude to her. He put his gloved hand on her shoulder. The soldier's touch was coarse through the glove yet warmed her spirit. Did he realize that she had been exposed? He did not see the blood on her through the dark, she thought, wishing to tell him, but she could not yet.

Through the interlaced tunnels, the two ran from this hell. He cleared the way through the demons' hole to freedom. Gun blasting, she heard nothing save for the deafening thunder of his weapon. She just saw. Carnage, death. The gunshots tore through the Chaots with ruthlessness, killing many to pave the way. The grim applause of death's sirens finally sings to those who should have traveled across the River Styx long ago as the Chaots died.

Daylight came in splotches as they almost escaped the underworld in order to stand once more in the forests of the living. But before they exited the caves, Hector paused. Turning to her, he could only murmur her name. "Nyx ..."

No longer did his voice reflect the hardened tenor of a warrior. Something else haunted his tone as his gaze came across her body coated in blood. Her lips caressed by red rivers. Did he mourn her passing already? Or feel sorrow in the weapon he would pull, the bullet he would fire to save her from a fate of the beasts?

Wiping the blood away from her own mouth, Nyx looked to him. She wondered if she strayed from normalcy, would Hector still be by her side.

"I am not infected," she said. A lie. Though was it deception if the reality held true. She did not turn into a Chaot; the prion did not torment her as it did with the others. The contagion was inside her, but the symptoms had yet to ensue. "But ..."

She was going to tell him everything, how she was exposed. He stopped her though, shaking his head to stop her confessions as if to show her he understood. Or maybe it was a show of obstinacy, he did not want to understand, he wanted the lie. At least the result of her words rendered what she wished. The uncertainty disappeared from his features; it became replaced by the belief that together they would survive this mayhem. Though behind that dream flickered a reality. He knew what she was about to say to him. But now he needed the fantasy rather than face the truth. If his decision would be fated to haunt him, so be it. He will embrace the consequences.

"Clean off. Now."

She understood the urgency and implied reason behind his order. If the other soldiers were to see her like this, they may not be willing to believe her story. Especially Megaira. Immunity is not possible with prion diseases, despite whether this showed evidence to the contrary or not. This scientific certainty could cause Dio and Leander to also falter. And though her friendships between those two were beginning to cement, they may not see her. As soldiers they may see the blood and a comrade that had already fallen. They may shoot her, to save her from the fate of the Chaots. But Hector had given his word to her, and to him that was all that mattered.

As Hector stood guard, she swabbed the blood from her face and body with the disinfectant cloths that he had pulled from his equipment as he stood guard. Pale skin showed dimly in the cave's light after each stroke removed the blood. The scratches that abraded her legs stung as the cleanser swept over. Face and then neck, her lips tasting the potent antiseptic as it passed over them. Tearing off her shirt, she used the replacement given to her by Hector from his pack. She then rubbed her torn pants, trying to get the traces of red off. She put dirt on the stains that refused to relent; the dark navy color of the slacks helped hide the red. Hector kept close eye on her, perhaps counting the time that passed, and with each moment he seemed to believe more and more that she was indeed uninfected. Tossing the soiled shirt, leaving any apprehension behind, they began their final trek out.

The sunlight struck, drenching the two emerging forms from the cave. Hector came first, an escape from the underground—from Hades. Should he look back, and as Orpheus have his Eurydice lost to him forever? But unlike the poet of ancient lore, he repressed the urge to turn and make sure she was behind him. And thereby he avoided the fate of the tragic Greek hero, as Nyx emerged and stepped to his side.

Her hand enwrapped into his own. Her flesh was dirt-ridden, though her intentions were as pure as the silks spun by the black widow. It was neither passion nor electricity that ran between the two, but an indescribable union. Brother and sister, not in blood ancestry but of a common clan. A loose alliance between nomads, for she saw him.

He was not like the others, no matter how he tried to hide beneath the soldier's uniform. He fought not for values of government and justice, but for the intrinsic calling of the hunt and honor. An animal hid under the guise of warrior. A hero emulated only in situation. It was his honor alone that allowed him to walk among men. He clung to it, for otherwise he would be no different than those he destroyed.

Chapter Eleven: Hector

Over one year previous: In the rocks above

Hector stood atop a rock pillar towering over the city of Kalambaka in Greece. He looked out over the mountains; the city nestled between the pillars granted a beauty that he had never seen before. Kicking a few pebbles off the side of the cliff, he watched their descent and, as the seconds passed, their disappearance from his gaze. In spite of its beauty, this land was also deadly. One wrong step would end in a crash three hundred meters below, following the pebbles' path. He glanced upward, the sun warm on his face. The sky was clear and tranquil, such a stark contrast to how it will soon look, with flames and black smoke blotting out the sun. But for the moment, Hector felt at peace here, in this sacred place, despite his mission.

Behind him was the Meteora monastery, whose foundation clung to the pillar's summit. He understood why the monastery had been built here, and why it was still inhabited. Being amongst the clouds, surrounded by an unearthly, almost divine, splendor was only part of it. The isolated and impenetrable fortress also served the purpose of protection, for his mission to acquire the monastery's weakness proved almost fruitless.

Almost.

The towering location physically safeguarded the priests; however, its Achilles' heel was the priests themselves. And so Hector successfully established a rapport with them, and even though he tried to prevent it, they grew on him as well. Strange, that they would be so welcoming of him, a representative of the very government they opposed. But as a sergeant he would put aside any concern, any hesitation. And in his next visit, being welcomed with open arms, he alongside his squadron would carry out their orders.

The Bavarian Coalition considered the monastery a threat to the one world government, and it was his duty to eliminate this threat. A threat, maybe, but not in any militaristic nature. Its people had no governing body, no weapons. Its threat stemmed from its independence. It did not need to depend upon a paternalistic government to direct them, to tell them what to do or how to live, or tax them in order to do it. Anarchy some would say, others would say true individualism and self sufficiency. The results to Hector however, were of beauty and serenity. In the town itself, the people. And at its apex, in the monasteries atop the pillars. But it did not matter what he believed, for the threat of this town was these ideas, their teachings of independence from the ever encompassing world government. Their opposition to be under its rule. This is what damned them.

And damned himself. Killing priests ... what else could the Bavarian Coalition ask of him? But he was a soldier, he had to follow orders. Conscience and second thoughts were a risk on the battlefield. Not only on, but off, for orders needed to be followed. The Coalition punished insubordination worse than any injury of battle. And so he complied, not for his own skin, but for his squadron.

The wind swelled against him, as if waves were crashing in succession upon his form. It threatened to pull him from the cliff, and bring him to his death as if his thoughts were known. A guardian of the monastery, the wind roared in hate of his presence. Yet the priest showed none of its abhorrence. Rather, he came in greeting. Older than Hector, cloaked in robes beneath robes. A sedate smile on his face as if he alone had wisdom, and certainty of his discernment. Did he know I was ordered to neutralize them, Hector thought. Probably.

The priest ushered him inside and away from the wind chill. Hector knew it could be a trap, but it was too good an opportunity for recon for him to pass up.

"I am Athanasios," the priest said, offering Hector bread and tea as he sat opposite of him. "I am told you traveled a far way, I hope I can give you what you seek."

"Priest, you cannot be that naive."

A knowing smile crossed Athanasios's lips as he sipped the tea and listened to Hector continue.

"You started something that you cannot control," Hector said, "and if you let me I can help you and your people. Speak to the Uprising, renounce your ideas and give support to the World Government. This is the only way to prevent bloodshed."

Or was it? He knew the Bavarian Coalition would silence this monastery, and that this was not a meeting for truce but one to do reconnaissance. Yet Hector had to try to talk sense into the priests.

"Our ideas? Though we would be honored to be the origin of such ideas of freedom, they have been always been present within the human spirit. And we did not start the Uprising."

The priest refilled Hector's cup, and then sat back with his hands relaxed around his own. He spoke in broken English, as he smiled with generosity towards one who should be his enemy. "Whatever the origins, it has brought a chasm between those who want freedom and those whose purpose is to rule. Though you should ask yourself if I were to denounce the Uprising ideology as you say, would it truly stop bloodshed? The Bavarian Coalition is only the start of a totalitarian new world order where people are subservient and peace is anything but synonymous with their goals."

Athanasios accompanied Hector to the cliff's edge to wish the soldier farewell. If only one soldier could impact what would happen, but he felt at a lost to do so.

"I understand why you are here," the priest said. Hector tensed and grew silent. Was the welcoming a façade to make him too comfortable and then kill him? The priest must have saw these thoughts, for his smile grew at Hector's misunderstanding.

"No, no. I meant why you are here. I know why you climb these cliffs."

"I have no time to philosophize. Neither should you. You do not understand," Hector responded. He knew it was against orders, but he wanted to warn them. He knew he would be back in arms, yet caution slipped from his lips. He stopped mid-sentence, unable to compromise the mission.

"I understand," Athanasios responded, "But you do not. No one saves us but ourselves. No one can and no one may. We ourselves must walk the path."

Hector stayed silent, torn between two worlds. One of duty, and one that did not want to be a part of manslaughter. "You do not need to walk it alone, priest," he finally murmured, hoping the quizzical rhetoric would inspire Athanasios to act. "You should take refuge before you are stampeded upon."

"We must walk the path ourselves," Athanasios repeated, "And you will need to embrace it fully, no matter the price. It is a price that we priests are willing to pay. We will not run."

The priest turned from Hector and looked out unto the town resting below the sheer vertical cliffs of the pillars. His smile never left, perhaps knowing that one day Hector would grasp his counsel, and the world would again be right.

But for now the cryptic words slipped past Hector, taken by the wind. He looked back one last time after he prepared the rock-climbing equipment for the repel down. Amongst the clouds, secluded and sacred, the monastery served for refuge from various enemies throughout its existence. He almost hoped that Athanasios would see past his lies and push him off the pillar and to Hades below. Instead the priest offered nonsensical advice, and Hector could offer nothing in return except the silent promise of a bloody return. A soldier, he repeated to himself, knowing that he would follow orders, go down and ready his squadron, and return to attack.

"Have you ever read Plato's Allegory of the Cave, Hector?"

"Enlighten me, old man," Hector said, hoping that the longer he delayed in his repel down that the more sense he could make of what the priest said.

When Athanasios spoke, his whole manner changed into one who delights in storytelling. His voice grew deeper as if Plato himself rose from the grave to tell this age old story through the priest. "Imagine a group of humans inside a cave. They were bound tightly, unable to move and facing the stone walls their entire life. They could not look away. All they could see were the shadows on the cave walls that were cast by the fire behind them. This was their reality, this was what they knew. Imagine if one became free, how he would see the true world. There would not even be words or thoughts to explain it."

"This is how we are. We are in that cave still. Even science is restricted, for it is limited by humans themselves. Our senses. Our perception of time. Our ideas of reality itself. But what is really outside our own metaphorical cave walls?"

"Are we but brains in a vat or in a simulation? Are we insignificant beings or rather, in stark contrast, does our consciousness create reality? The only thing we are certain of is that one's own consciousness exists. This is the singularity. Outside of that we are akin to Plato's cave dwellers."

Hector listened. He understood some of what the priest said. He knew that though the priest spoke of brains in a vat, neither a physical brain or vat was needed. It was just a spark of consciousness that emerged. Not even the universe or time was a necessity, only that one thought was needed for reality to come to be. Was this more likely than the normalized perception of the universe? Could we ever know for certain?

What would come when the thought ended, he wondered. Or was it not the 'end' that would come but rather the consciousness continued eternally in a constant loop. Had he walked this path before; will he again, fated for eternity to look out at this sky and ask these questions again and again. Life began to feel as if a book read many times, the words never changing and the characters locked into their path. Yet each time it was read, though the words remained the same, the journey was anew.

"Plato had also wrote of the Allegory of the Sun. To truly see our reality, we do not only need a sense, such as sight, and an object for the sense, such as the city below to see. We also need a third element. In the case of sight, we also need the sun. If not for the light all would just be black. Perhaps when you find your own sun, you will see truth."

With that, Hector looked toward the actual sun. A glimmer caught his eyes from behind the clouds. The sight he saw signaled to him that the fight no longer remained in his hands. A jet roared above the pillars of sandstone and the positioning told him one thing. The Bavarian Coalition must have deemed his squadron useless against the remote monasteries, opting for the air force's more direct and absolute attack. And considering the natural beauty of the rock pillars, skillfully carved over millions of years, Hector knew they would choose biological warfare over nuclear or conventional weapons. He turned to Athanasios, finally being able to return advice as he shouted above the wind's screams: "Get indoors, seal off the monastery!"

His orders were to kill them, but in his perspective those orders derailed with the presence of air artillery. Hatred roused from the sight of the planes, for it meant that the Bavarian Coalition had deemed him —and his squadron—expendable. If he helped the priests survive, so be it; all he could hope was that this trivial act of decency be repaid with the safety of his squadron in the city below.

With Athanasios running inside the monastery, Hector secured his climbing equipment, ready to repel. He looked over the vertical drop. It truly was a sight worthy of the gods. The rock pillars rose in an unearthly splendor, as if Titans breaking away from the earth and reaching to the skies to pull Zeus from his throne and back to Tartaros. To Hector though, the pillars transformed from the majestic to a hindrance, serving only as a barrier between himself and his squadron.

It was a barrier, however, that he overcame. He jumped. Secured with rope, Hector repelled down the cliffs with the speed of a falcon hunting. Trying to make the most of each second, he risked everything. Falling seven meters, followed by tethering to a lower anchor and another fall, he repelled his way down the sheer drop. The sandstone crumbled with each downfall, threatening to spit out the climbing anchor and drop the soldier to his death.

He did not falter, he could not. His squad was at risk; he had to be there for them.

The aircraft swiveled in mid-air, realizing Hector's assumption by dropping several bombs over the city. He used one hand to secure himself to the sandstone cliffs and one to go through his backpack, finding and subsequently fitting a supplied-air bio-filter respirator over his face. He began to sweat, making it difficult to seal the rubber mask; sweat from repelling down, he told himself, not from fear.

Flames did not come. Smog did. An expansive cloud of white flooded over the buildings of Kalambaka. It settled over the valley like a milky ocean with the rock pillars as islands above the sea, though soon even those islands would face the flood. He did not retreat back up the cliffs; he continued down. Loyalty to his squadron now served as his only authority.

In the fog below

Fog drifted in and out, causing moments of total blindness. Hector held his rifle ready, looking through the sight, using its thermal vision to track the surroundings. Below the rock pillar, he ventured forth into the biological mist and to the edge of the city where his unit's base camp was established.

He saw no one. No bodies. No survivors. Hector continued to his squad's encampment, counting on the chance that somehow they were prepared and had also seen the aircraft. Hector knew the reality of that happening was slim, despite his far-fetched hope. The jets used by the Bavarian Coalition were lined from the bottom with high-intensity light panels and low acoustic signatures proving them to be all but invisible from the ground.

The soldier's camp showed no sign of life. It offered no hope that his squadron survived; yet, it also offered hope that they may not be dead yet. Hector rammed his fist into the tent's pole; the metal bending at the force. Uselessness was not an emotion he was privy to; as a soldier he needed to fight, and in this smog he could do nothing.

He turned on the encampment's radio to contact the Bavarian Coalition in order to find out if his soldiers were given the order to withdraw from the area. Hopefully, for again he knew the protocols of war better than what was stated on the operandi. If the command center gave fair warning, they could not attest for the success of their covert operation. A leak might occur.

"Come in, Soldier 70-98-7 here," he said. "Secured frequency, code omega peregrine. Why were weapons deployed at this locale—our squadron was still on assignment."

An answer did not come, at least not one to his question. A metallic voice responded through the speaker: "Report situation, 70-98-7."

"I have my gas mask in use," Hector answered. "I was not present during the initial assault. All seems abandoned—both by the civilians and my squad. No dead are accounted for."

A pause of static followed, before the voice came again.

"DM Prion Bio-agent was dropped. Fatality rate should be immediate at one hundred percent. Make sure bio-filter is secure and do not take off your mask. Repeat: do not remove mask."

If the fatality rate was as said, corpses should be lining the streets. Yet Hector was not about to remove his mask to test his assumption.

"Why was it discharged, the threat was null. The civilians were unarmed—my squad was present." Anger broke in his voice, though he knew that he would receive an insufficient answer. Orders by way of orders; the radio controller would not have privilege to that information.

"You must withdraw immediately from the area. I will arrange a transport at coordinate alpha five at thirteen hundred."

"I have to search for my squadron first."

"Thirteen hundred is all I can do. Under any circumstance, do not remove your respirator," the radio controlled said, pausing for a moment before offering one last piece of guidance. "Do not be late."

"I need more time. There may be other survivors."

Static answered.

And through hell

Unknown noises flared in the distance. They guided Hector through the city, as if sirens urging him into the depths of the germ sea. And here he traveled, in the bottomless fog, searching for his comrades and hoping that it would not be bodies he found. Could it be that in the face of this attack, the people of Kalambaka took arms against his squadron and now held them captive? At that thought, Hector removed his rifle's safety. If the tides had turned, he knew he must fight against the local civilians. He must free his fellow soldiers.

Moving in opposition to the breezes, Hector forced the bio-agent fog to part in his wake. It did not matter who the true enemy or true victim was. He was a soldier, one who thrived off war. Athanasios may have believed otherwise, though there was one truth: Hector hunted. He needed this, for without it he was merely a shadow. And a hunter is what overrode whatever insights of pity he had, and instinct replaced it.

The thermal vision module mounted on his firearm picked up a harlequin haze against the monotone backdrop as Hector looked behind himself. He was being followed.

Whatever situation arose, one could adapt and fight—or die. And so he chose the former, limiting his movements and hence what was projected of him through the fog. His respirator caused considerable noise and disrupted the fog due to the fan forcing air through the filter. It would give away his position, and so he turned it off but kept the sealed mask on, gauging that he could hold his breath for three minutes. He took the chance he had enough to neutralize the pursuer.

Hector acted in stealth, using the mist rather than being encumbered by it. Keeping himself low, he retraced his steps back and behind his pursuer. Something was amiss, but Hector could not place it. He concentrated on subduing whoever followed him. Not killing, for they could simply be one of his own or even a civilian, but he had to act. Delaying even for a moment could place the upper hand in the potential adversary's and he could not risk that. Standing behind him, he took the blunt end of his weapon and struck it into the skull base. The form fell.

Quiet, quick.

Something else moved. Hector heard it and turned. The fog folded in on itself. White. But he saw grey splattered in the bleached fog, revealing many shadows. Every shift in the gathering rippled the clouds as if water disturbed by a skipping stone. Breezes, breathing, any movement caused a skip in the fog. One shadow in the mass of many took a step. Circles moved outward. Another step, another ripple materialized further along in the distance. Hector looked through the thermal vision module; a portrait of hues wept together in a multicolor rainbow. The threat revealed itself in the throbbing mass of heat, a threat of many, of at least twenty humans in front of him.

But he saw more than that. These people were not civilians confused by the bio-agent that entrenched their city. He saw the multicolored human forms swarm upon a smaller figure. Spine chilling screams of pain and rage coalescing into one unnatural, eternal cry from the mob as Hector watched it being torn apart; though whether it was a dog or a child, he could not tell.

In an immersion of stealth and urgency, he took to the ground and toward a back alley. He needed oxygen; his lungs burned as each second passed. But even more-so, he needed an escape from the hell he witnessed. He entered the alleyway and activated the gas mask's fan again. Breathing deeply, Hector stood ready. The alley was narrow between the buildings, offering the perfect stand against the shadows he saw. As used in Thermopylae, the war tactic still offered hope in a battle of the few against the many. Taper the enemy by way of the environment. Narrow the pathway thus assuring that the entire bulk of the attack would be gradual and only from the front.

Noise erupted behind contradicting his tactic. Pivoting his weapon to fire, Hector turned to face a man. His clothes were old and his hair dirty; several empty whiskey bottles littered the ground near where he sat. Most likely homeless, Hector surmised, posing a negligible threat.

"Get inside," he instructed the vagrant, the mask making his voice seem artificial. "Seal off the entranceways. Remain inside."

The man said nothing in response. Probably drunk. Hector's attention shifted back to the entrance of the alleyway and the perceived danger. Behind him, the man stood. He took one step toward the soldier, causing Hector to shift his firearm once more to behind. The man became clearer. The vagrant's eyes gushed with blood; his nose and ears did the same.

"Stand down. Get inside."

Hector repeated his commands. A warning in the undertone, for if the vagrant continued Hector would have no choice. And no choice was given—the man advanced. Hector fired into his leg.

Screams came forth, but even through the pain, the homeless man continued his approach. Hector took aim again, firing into his heart. To go from instructing safety to killing a civilian was an inescapable drop, and one he handled with composed control. With the vagrant neutralized, Hector immediately turned his attention to the entry, knowing that the gunfire would lead the enemy to his position.

And it had. Except it was not a foreign rival that he saw. It was one of his comrades.

Relief came. Followed by alarm.

A ribbon of scarlet dripped from his comrade's nose. An unfamiliar depth laid behind his eyes of one driven beyond madness. Even though the soldier's movements were unprecedented for humankind, Hector could read them anywhere: they were of attack, not kinship. Its aim was to kill him.

To rip him apart.

He fired. Through the heart this time, skipping the futile step of warnings. His comrade fell. Sorrow tried to break his emotions, but Hector pushed it away. These were his fellow soldiers, but as they attacked, he was left no choice. And if remorse overcame him, he would fail. All he could do was build a wall, one which was impenetrable. A wall of fortitude to block his emotions, in order to kill those who once fought by his side. Another came, this time Hector shot him through the head with the same effect.

His comrades struck the ground, dead. His friends. His brothers in arm.

Hector could stay here. Die himself in this chaos. Or he could make it to the coordinates and escape the fate that befell his brethren. It was not a choice though. Survival being the sole option, to live to fight another day.

Leaving the alley and back to the cover of the toxic clouds, Hector ran forth to the street. Killing those who moved to attack him, he made his way through the city in order to get to the pick-up coordinates in time. Hands came at him from the fog, trying to grab him, bring him back and consume him. He mentally separated himself from the slaughter he sowed, and from the carnage he now reaped. Die or kill, there was no other way.

No longer could he consider them brothers—or even human. Humanity did not animate their forms; no rhyme or reason arose, or rationale. Chaos had taken them; Chaos was all that existed now. All that moved, all that they were, were Chaots.

Chapter Twelve

Hector and Nyx emerged from the cave. Above ground stood the other three soldiers scattered in the forest's plateau. They secured the perimeter, having dispersed the band of Chaots. Some Chaots had not made it; their corpses slept in silence before her. The foliage no longer scattered the sun's rays to the forest floor; smoke and ash replaced it. The massacre weighted Dio; his jolly spirit dwindled. Only a glint of his former self persevered as he saw Nyx safely emerge. In stark opposition walked Megaira. Gun alert, its aim shifted momentarily on her just waiting for a sign to continue the carnage. Eagerness spewed from her tightly wound body.

Then there was Leander. He rushed to her side.

A tempestuous call, stronger even than the waves of the ocean, lured her to his embrace. He was now the siren to her own desires.

Hector let his hand slide from hers as Leander took her in his arms. Hector went ahead to be on the lookout, motioning Megaira to follow. Megaira did not look happy about seeing Nyx alive and again with them, but heeded Hector's unspoken command and walked off with him. Nyx buried her head within Leander's shoulders as his arms offered her warmth from the chill of the barren caves, glad to feel him but also glad his gear provided a barrier between their touch, still worried of the possibilities that loomed.

"I thought you ran from us again. I thought I had lost you," he murmured within her ear.

"I did not want ... I would not leave you," she said, though did not tell him what happened, how Megaira had banished her. She would not, for she knew Megaira was right in her intentions and did not want to make more of a rift between them. Instead, she offered Leander a faltered smile and a more emotive embrace, clinging to him to forget all that had happened. To forget the insatiable affinity she had seen in the monster's eyes. To forget her exposure, a continued cloud above her. In Leander's arms she could abandon everything and return to the threads of normalcy. And even though her heart stirred to be with him, the wind of her soul resting to a breeze, she needed answers about the Chaots. Her query could not wait, for who knew how long she had—if the symptoms would come, albeit late. Curiosity lingered in urgency, causing her to question rather than find repose in her escape.

"The contagion. How did it come to be? You spoke of a prion?" she spoke, hoping to understand the disease more, and understand if she could still turn and still be a threat.

Leander loosened his arms from around her, startled by her pursuance of what caused the disease. But he spoke, first tentatively as if trying to draw back his emotions. "Prions are infectious agents, but different from viruses and bacteria. They are composed of proteins and do not depend on self-replication. Instead they affect the proteins already present in the host's brain, causing them to mis-fold and affect the infected's behavior."

He hesitated, still confounded by her sudden inquiry, for she had previously seemed indifferent. He was not unwilling to grant information; his reluctance was based on the distinct feeling that she was not telling him everything. He continued, hoping his doubts were ill found. "Examples are Kuru among the Fore tribe of Papua New Guinea and mad cow disease which caused Creutzfeldt-Jakob Disease in humans, though thus far, prion diseases have been limited due to their long incubation periods. Due to this reason, they have never been used in warfare situations. Supposedly the pandemic was caused by a new, previously undiscovered type of prion, one whose infectivity decreased the time between exposure and onset of symptoms to null, creating a devastating weapon."

"I thought you were a soldier, not a scientist?" she questioned, somewhat surprised that he had a more biological grasp than she expected.

"I am both ... to a certain extent. I entered the forces of the Bavarian Coalition as an officer, already having earned my degree in oceanography in the Naval Academy and was subsequently stationed aboard Thalassic after training. Though my major focus was not pathology, I did take courses in all facets of biology and is why I understand the basic structure of prions," a somewhat embarrassed smile broke out along his features, as he continued in explanation. "I am not a soldier as Hector is, I never saw war until now."

She knew he wanted to stop talking about the disease, wanted to simply be glad she was back. As did she, but she had to know, hoping that some shred of knowledge may help her understand why she had not yet become a Chaot. "And what does the research station you are looking for have? What do they know about the disease?"

"We are uncertain on the specifics," he said, not wishing to convey that unsubstantiated hope was the only thing that led them. "The Thalassic lost contact with the mainland and Bavarian Coalition soon after the pandemic struck. From what we can conclude they were searching for the origin and design of the contagion."

"But I thought the Bavarian Coalition were the ones responsible for using the prion?" she asked. "Shouldn't they already know about the prion if they were the ones to create it?"

"Yes, they used the prion. But the group commissioned to engineer the bioweapon, as well as all their research, disappeared after the initial attack. Without them, the Bavarian Coalition had nothing to go on. So they recruited other scientists to study the prion's construction in hopes to understand how to eradicate it."

"Why?" she asked. She understood technically why: their survival versus the Chaots, always would your own survival be chosen. But why not try to find ways for the survival of both, humans and Chaots, for were not the latter once friends, family, comrades? Her question was met by the expected though: his expression buckled in wonder why one almost mutilated by the Chaots would question their destruction.

"Humans were not meant to live in the fringes of life," he answered, "not meant to revert to cannibalistic animals without reason, without society. We need to eliminate the disease for with the end of the prion, comes our ability to rise from the ashes and to begin our civilization anew. They are a threat, you should know that Nyx. They almost killed you."

She could not hide her frustration; her thoughts being anything but identical to Leander's. Would he believe her as human if her life was ruled not by reason but by whim; would he seek to eradicate her? Lawless, winged and unconfined. She epitomized the poetry written long before her time. Unwilling to cave under the pressures of an unknown civilization, unwilling to conform, she could not accept his view.

She could not accept that if she should turn, he would want her dead.

"Eradicate it," Dio said, the interruption breaking his more good-natured humor. The usual smile and laugh did not cross his face; rather, the atrocities of the past, the darkness that lay behind his outer happiness, came forth. "The Chaots are not evil; they are people such as ourselves. But I cannot say the same for the disease. That is why we have to destroy it. It took everything ..."

His voice cracked. Everything, he had said, and it was clear he thought of everyone who had been taken from him.

"Dio," Leander said, as if he witnessed a dam that stood strong in spite of the torrential downfalls, suddenly shatter. And he was tentative as to whether he should help repair that dam, or allow Dio to let what he had been harboring loose. "Your family. I need to ..."

"No, Leander," Dio replied. "I know. I always knew what happened."

Grief alongside memories overcame Leander's features. He stood silent, unable to answer to his friend.

"I saw it. Through the video feed on the Thalassic, I saw everything," Dio said. "I know you did everything you could to save my daughter. I know you even tried despite her already being infected. Not telling me the truth, believing it was for the best."

Hatred was clear in his voice. The hatred of losing his family. And more so in himself for hiding away in Leander's lie, in wanting to believe his family may still be alive despite seeing their watery grave. For not being strong enough to accept the truth. Yet the hatred found its reprieve in absolution as he spoke of forgiveness. "Do not bear that weight alone; let us fight the disease together."

No words could reveal Leander's feelings; nothing could atone for him not being able to save Diomedes's family. But the weight lessened, as Leander brought his hand to Dio's shoulder and a re-found brotherhood passed between them.

"We need to destroy it, Nyx," Dio said. The words hard; the words unyielding in their resonance. "Not the ones who are infected by it, they do not need to be destroyed. The disease itself is evil, that and those who created it. And those who turned their backs away from the infected, leaving them to die rather than help."

At the last words, Dio looked at Leander. She saw something pass between them, an understanding of exactly who he referred to. She wondered who it was that turned their back away, who could make Dio falter in his stance that none are truly evil.

"Don't forget that, Nyx," Dio continued, bringing his gaze back to her, giving her a wink to assure her he was back to his old self. "But I'll let you two talk, I am sure Hector needs my help with the nav system. God's mercy be with us if I left him to lead us himself. Probably will try to make us climb a cliff to cut off a few minutes of our hiking time."

He left the two, this time giving a wink to Leander, as if he could blatantly see the captain's feeling towards her.

She smiled at first in goodbye to Dio, but unspoken questions raced through her mind. They saturated her consciousness until it felt as if she would drown. She had felt absolution through Dio around the camp, but now guilt. What was her life before? What was she long ago?

What was she now? A creature of the wild and not the wise, she understood more her connection with Chaots than with humans. It became clear in Leander's wish of an ideal society and her need for none. He could not see that she was not one of them, and never could be confined to his civilization. And it became clear in Dio's justified reason to destroy the disease, when she desired only understanding and not its elimination.

"Hey, Nyx ..." Leander said.

He caressed her arm sensing her discontent. His desire clear to take her in his arms again but she did not turn to face him. He led her to the side, away from the ears of the other soldiers who busied themselves with the global positioning system. They plotted directions to the research compound, paying no heed to the two. Around them the wind quieted to a hush, sweeping between the trees in a never relenting lattice of a maze. The hive of Chaots lay in dispersed purgatory, but it was as if they still watched. Watching under the shrouded shadows of the forests depths, a waiting maelstrom in a restful ocean. The Pathfinder was near, she knew it.

"I know I will never understand you. I know that what separates us is a chasm equal to the land and the air. But ..." Whispers said by Leander with such tenderness, but what did he expect from her? What could she promise that was not impossible to uphold?

She wanted to understand Leander. With her gaze on his, he stepped closer, wanting to show her how he cared, but not knowing how to except with words of truth.

"Let me protect you from harm. Each time you leave it is if I lay exposed and the thought of losing you crushes me."

Shaking her head in negation, her hair fell back from her shoulders. Her heart caved, for she wanted him. But he could not save Dio's daughter, and Nyx knew he could not save her. Therefore, she had to push him away, for she feared that if he failed another under his protection, the loss would destroy him. "You cannot keep me safe, you cannot shelter me from the outside. For that is when life ends, when fear overrides and hope is no longer possible."

"You cannot keep me safe," she repeated, chiding herself for the words but unable to stop their flow. She had to separate herself from him for he blurred things even more than fear could. If she was to turn, if she was to be a Chaot, she could not allow him to be close to her. She did not want to hurt him. She had to push him away. She had to protect him. "I am not yours to save."

Leander nodded somberly in acceptance. He was a soldier, and his deepest instinct was to safeguard what was important to him. Normally it had been to preserve what the world government deemed primary, but for the first time he found something of his own will that he desired to protect, for the first time since losing Dio's daughter. Nyx's bitter denial of his affections roused rejection in his heart. Only the truth came; she had no use in lying whether in viciousness or in a well-intentioned equivocation. She did not want him, he believed. And so Leander started toward where Hector headed off, no longer able to converse without showing his true emotions, his hurt. He motioned for her to follow in silent gesture. Dio stayed in the rear. Megaira moved ahead to share the location-based positions, eyeing Nyx on her way.

"Come night," Megaira said under her breathe as she walked past. Though truly Nyx did not care about nor fear her threats.

They continued for hours. Sweat dripped down their faces, washing away the dust and dirt of the cave. And in the passing of every minute with no symptoms, Nyx knew she must be in the clear. She began to wonder if she should have said those things to Leander, wishing to protect him from her. The tension thickened between the two and an unrequited desire brewed to a boil in her. Finally after miles of silence, steps were heard from behind. Leander stopped, aiming his weapon towards the oncoming movement with one arm and putting his other in front of her. The inherent tendency to protect surfaced in him, even after their prior interchange. But instead of the grotesque glimpse of the infected, Dio came into view.

"Hey, how come you guys have all the fun when I'm back here covering your asses?" A jolly voice bolstered out. Leander holstered his gun, saying nothing in reply. Looking to Nyx then Leander, Dio could guess at the heartbreak stirring in his commander. He could also probably guess what Leander, and even Nyx herself, could not: she cared for him, despite her words.

Another tremor whispered in the trees, this time in front of them. Again, Leander removed his gun, only again to have a false alarm as Hector came to view this time.

"A waterfall is ahead," Hector said, looking to the three. His somber gaze was heavy upon her, almost as if no emotion brewed in him. She had believed something had stirred between herself and Hector at the cave: comradeship, fellowship, kinship. The wall dividing the warrior from Nyx crumpled as a friendship budded. She hoped it was not already lost. She searched his face, remembering the feel of her hand taking his as they fled from the underground. Remembering how he said her name after the horror that confronted them. If only she could see the common threads that interlaced them. But Hector stood solid, emotion could not be allowed on the battlefront, as he continued. "It will be a good place to set up camp for night is coming."

In the darkness they shall hunt, when light no longer can prevail.

Silence. Now it was three that Dio looked between, trying to think of a way to lighten the mood. Finally, he spoke, humor being one human trait that often outlasted the strongest adversary to atrocity. "Sounds good. It will be nice to take a swim as well. Not that the dirt takes away any of your allure, sweet nymph," Dio said in jest as he half bowed to her but then immediately turned his gesture to Hector. "And especially none of yours."

Nyx smiled in return understanding that wit served to say what never could be. The remorse will always be there, underneath the layers of humor; however, Dio would always be there for her as well, even with the gap between their beliefs. Standing to the side of Hector, she interloped her hand through his uncompromising arm. She felt him tense underneath her touch; not fueled by desire like she had felt from Leander, but rather uncertainty in the face of friendship. Or maybe he was still uncertain of her prognosis.

"My guardian from the likes of the satyr," she said, smiling to Dio. "Hector, you will protect me from this drunken goatman, will you not?"

"Of course, milady."

Dio laughed at the seriousness of Hector's reply amidst the humor of the conversation. Tightening her clasp on him, she moved with the warrior away from the others. Leander's expression remained hard regardless of the humor, his heart still unsettled. She saw this too, and knew she had to give him space. Therefore, she followed Hector to the fountain he had discovered. First the thundering song of the waterfall came to their ears, followed soon after by the visage. The brilliance of Hector's discovery laid hidden in tangles of green, only for the worthy to find.

"You surely can find diamonds in coal, my savior," she said to Hector mesmerized by the beauty before them. But his attention was not on the water, it was on the one at his side.

"Nyx, you need no warrior nor savior. From what I have witnessed you endure fearlessly all that you come across. You run alone. And I thank the gods that the blood on you truly was your own and not Chaot, for I had thought—and feared—otherwise."

He had believed the blood was hers. She wanted to tell him otherwise, but was worried what that would incite, and if it would lead to her becoming a lab rat.

"Yet, you still helped me escape from the cave?"

"I would have helped you escape even from the depths of the Underworld."

Silence unleashed itself upon her, for his response was something that she had not expected. She thought he still stood behind an unbreakable barrier, but he did not. So many of those she had met had wished her to be confined in some way, even if they believed it was for her own good. But Hector was different, he saw not a fawn whose girth could not withstand life, but rather he saw her, as she had seen him. Camaraderie cemented between them.

Except one thing he erred in: If she was fearless, why did she hold onto the lie that it was her blood. She hated to hide the truth, but she could not tell him when she did not even know the whole truth herself. If no one could be immune, what was she? And if she was truly fearless, why then did she fear her feelings toward Leander?

Chapter Thirteen

Jagged stones surrounded a transparent, glistening pool of water and river. An adjacent waterfall thundered and smoothed the rocks beneath its path. Vines suffocated the girth of the waterfall while birch trees dipped in precarious angels around its shore. Nyx peeled off filth encrusted clothes without thought of proper etiquette. Seeing what she was doing, Hector turned to give her privacy and watch for the others as she undressed. When a splash was heard signaling her departure into the waters, he turned again but did not join her. Rather like a frozen gargoyle, he kept a protective watch.

"I'll be fine," she called out. She hated to be watched, though even more so she hated to watch Hector forgo the joys life can give. He nodded in leave, and headed back towards the others.

Alone, she ducked her head underwater, going deeper beneath the crystal waves. She let the current seize and toss her about, wishing it to wash away the bygone of the conflicts. Lips opened, allowing water to enter and rinse her mouth from the rancid vestige of the infected blood and letting the current take it away.

The prion imposed no prison to her soul. Perhaps the pathogen was no longer contagious or able to jump from host to host. The potency of the prion may have diminished over time. Soon it would die away as the last Chaot fell. Its fate to be the same as its victims—damned.

A chance remained that immunity protected her. However, Megaira had said that no one could be resistant. Either death or transformation followed the initial exposure she had said. The chance that Nyx alone was impervious to the disease seemed unlikely. Yet she still indulged the thought as her body sank deeper into the water's permeable cold. Maybe she was too different from the other humans, therefore, the prion could not infect her. She lived without barriers preventing her actions, and so the disease could not manifest itself, for she was already wild.

Or maybe her past sealed away the answers. She had never even asked herself why she could not remember it.

The water overtook her, pulling her further into its girth. What the tide did to her body, an epiphany did to her mind. A hypothesis formed: maybe it was possible that she had been a Chaot. That was why she had no memories before the beach. It was why she often acted solely off impulse—a remnant of what she had been. But then she was somehow cured.

It would complete the puzzle, solving why the Chaot's blood did not affect her. Though the piece fit perfectly, explaining so much, it did not make sense to her.

Memories resurfaced of when she explored the room in the Victorian house. When she had found the child's book, she had imposed her own memories to the faded pages. Memories of when she had once read Where the Wild Things Are. But it was not simply the visual recollection, she also unearthed a feeling. She had always been uninhibited, finding affinity with the small boy when he initially set off to explore the realm of the wild. Even as a child, she was uncontrolled and unintimidated by the ways and wariness of society. And those memories were from before the outbreaks had occurred, making her hypothesis questionable. Spirit and independence were not equivalent to the Chaot personality.

The water rippled as her head emerged, breaking through water and thoughts. Deeply she breathed in the air and looked out to see Leander dive into the pool fully clothed. He swam to her across the water in a graceful yet powerful stroke. As he closed the distance, she could see the wavering panic in his face.

"Gods, you gave me a heart attack; I thought you were drowning! You were under way too long."

She swam near, wishing she could take away everything around, every barrier both real and emotional, to be with him. "Leander, I am sorry for before."

"Don't worry, Nyx. I'm just glad you are alright. You give me no rest," he said and laughed in attempts to ease any of her guilt over what had happened between them.

"No rest for the wicked," she said between breaths to replenish the air before diving under once more, making sure her kicks to submerge splashed Leander. No sooner had she gone under did she feel his hand grasp along her leg. His movements were playful, but she could not help but feel stirred by his caress. His grip turned firm as he tried to pull her up to him, but she managed to escape down in the netherworld of the deep, aided by the waters' pervasiveness.

Ignoring the currents that separated them, she planned to dive deeper but the awareness of his body overpowered her. Needing air and hoping for clearness above, she kicked toward the surface. The water yielded to her emerging form; she breathed, yearning for lucidly but finding none. The pull toward Leander was stronger than any riptide, but she fought it. She faced away from him, to instead see the distant silhouettes of Hector and Megaira that were partially hidden by the trees. They were preoccupied with each other, pleasantly so. Hector had brushed the blonde hair of Megaira aside, letting his hand linger by her chin. She returned the gesture, warmth melting her cold persona. She could not find Dio, but he most likely rested amongst the forest's splendor.

She heard the faint sounds of the captain swimming behind her, a soft discontinuance from the waterfall. Ripples broke around her from his movement. She could not understand her own intentions, whether to follow her primal attraction or be wary. In love one loses their freedom and freedom could never be lost, for it would mean death.

She swam away.

Getting to the shore, she climbed from the falls and dressed, seeing that Hector had left new clothes for her. Rather than go to the camp, she began to walk between the trees and away from Leander, to disappear into the forests—to again feel the winds—her solace of chaos.

Only for moments did she find respite from passion, as the ferns parted and Leander hurried to her side, having had first changed into fresh clothes himself. Relief came to his face as he saw her, but only for seconds it remained. Wind brushed along her form, giving her the beauty of the wild, punishing him with what never could be his.

"Nyx, who are you?"

He asked again as he had on the playground, though this time it was not to understand her shrouded origins. This time he asked to find what made her within. Why did she run untamed when all others clutched burdens to their souls? Why she was unlike them?

"I am me," she said with a neutral expression; no emotion, trying to distance herself. To explain her capricious will in the same rhetoric as an explanation of the course of nature would have been insane. This was the fact, as she understood it. I am me. Why question, why turn away from it?

"Yes, but tell me more," responded Leander.

"I'm the same as you."

"I know," he said, smiling at her sincerity as he lessened the distance between them, "that you are not. You survived surface side when no one else did. You look upon the Chaots like no other. You desire freedom more than anything else, yet you restrict yourself in order to protect it."

"Let me in," he continued. "Let me understand you."

At first her expression painted confusion at his request. If he had felt how she had and sensed what she felt, there would be no need for her to explain herself to him. One cannot define indescribable emotions to someone else. It was almost impossible for her to comprehend his inner workings, and sometimes she looked at him wondering if he was truly real. If she could not understand him, how could she ever have him understand her.

Her touch came to him and trailed down his arm. Her repression failing, her urges demanding they be fulfilled. She cupped his hand before leading him to the gradually darkening, foreboding forest that captured her joy.

"You wish to know me. My impulses, my ideas, my joy. I cannot explain it, but I can show you... perhaps."

Looking at his face for moments, she wondered exactly how one follows impulses. Her path had always been impromptu, on instinct and not planned. The exception was with Leander. She restrained her emotions toward him, unnerved by what would come. She was unbridled, he was the bridle, together they posed ambiguity. Perhaps if she could show him her own type of freedom, he would run by her side —wild—rather than impose the threat of the tame.

"Follow your impulses. Sometimes it is best not to ask why."

Surely he would argue that in life one must ask why in order to understand the motives and outcome. Strong but vague impulses could not rule life for one must curb the id to live safely and under order. Uncontrollable chaos leads only to death and anarchy. However, flip the coin over and life becomes another way. Life is the moment rather than the sum of all of life's possible tangents, it is when all those tangents of the future and past coalign into one. The present, the moment you live in, chaos itself.

He did not argue. He did not pull her back for fear of what lay ahead in the unprotected forests, whether it be Chaots or something else. He silenced himself to listen and allowed himself to simply experience her in an attempt to understand the unpredictable.

"Just live. Live for moments, here, with me."

She walked further still, Leander followed.

The forest quivered with each step they took, some maple trees hardy, some on the verge of collapse. Echoes surrounded them. Sounding off tree to tree in an ever-changing symphony of tone. Soon the words lost all meaning, as the resonance, blended with the forest's sounds, endured. Eerie, but beautiful. Was it Echo who chased them as she had once did to her Narcissus? Wishing to warn them of dangers, but in the end failing.

Trees, personified as guardians, kept watch over those that invaded the territory of nature. In such unrefined glory they stood. They leaned in upon the two travelers. They hovered over them as a canvas's border; walls without the imposed decor of the city homes. The trees reflected the King of the Wild Things' room, as the walls fell away, climbing with vines. These forest's walls did not segregate as the man-made ones, but opened many more doors than they closed.

Barely audible murmurs filtered through the forests. It could have been simply the wind against the branches. Or even Chaots in their distant screams of what remained of humanity. Despite the admonition, they continued.

"I hope it is living I do with you in this moment."

Though he smiled, clearly enjoying their time together, his hand coddled his gun in case trouble did come along.

"If you never search for trouble, life would be repetitive."

"Maybe, but life is more preferable than death," he answered, "to me at least. I want to grow old and grey."

"If I grow old as you wish, laden with cobwebs and the tedious, please dust me off," she said, as the eclipse of trees grew darker now that the sun dropped below the tree line. "For you should never run in fear of the reaper, for you then allow death to dictate your life even before your time."

The black shadows of night consumed her form as she walked ahead, hoping to lose Leander for moments. Turning, she circled back around the captain. She stalked as a huntress. Each step absorbed her weight evenly, not intruding upon the environment.

"Nyx, are you okay?"

No response to his words. He readied himself, looking through the trees, hoping he had not lost her to unknown forces once more. Waiting minutes that felt like hours, she crept behind Leander and without warning jumped on top of him in jest.

Laughter escaped her lips, hoping that she gave him a good scare, hoping he found a break from the mundane however small.

"I could have shot you," he chided through a stifled laughter and accusation, knowing quite well that the joke could have taken a turn for the worst. In the middle of the Apocalypse, creatures swarming from Hades in the midst, her prediction that he would not mistake her as a

Chaot and strike was foolish. But here she laughed, not understanding the other possible outcome of her action, or more likely not caring.

"I do my best."

The smile of fulfillment coloring her face disappeared as a sudden noise stole her accomplishment. It came from ahead, closer than the previous sounds. Straying to Leander's back, she stayed behind him as if the sound could not penetrate through the soldier.

"Wait here. I think something is out there," he whispered. He looked back at her, put one hand up as if to warn her of the hidden threat and reason with her to stay. Then he turned away. And as he moved forward, she stayed behind.

Her hand lifted tentatively, to touch Leander as if to pull him back to her. Her gesture came too late as he moved out of her reach into the growing twilight. She could not lose him to chaos, for her own immunity did not necessarily mean his. All fell quiet in the minutes proceeding. Mouth parted slightly, ready to express her wish for him to come back, to stay with her. To break her isolation. But words did not come, as she felt a coiled grip lace around her body and mouth, silencing her.

The call of the wolf lingered in her mind. Already she teased Leander with her 'disappearance'; this time when danger did arise he would assume she was playing once more. She almost bit down upon the living cage with intent to damn her captor, to smite him with her wrath as she did before. Yet she did not have a chance to bite, as she was spun to face her perpetrator.

"Got you!"

For a moment she almost screamed. The fear had mounted; her heart beat as if on its last pulse. But reality prevailed and she shoved Leander with playful intent, acting as if she was not guilty of the same only moments ago.

"You will never have me." But despite herself, three other words lingered in her sentiment, never making it to be heard out loud: *yet you do*. They were lost to her as her focus grew away from the rhetorical and more within the emotional.

Leander standing close.

Again she became breathless, but for reasons much different than before.

"I know that. Though you have me."

He infringed upon her wish to be unbound by another. He had followed her in the city, despite his promise to allow her to leave. He had come to her rescue, though she never desired to be saved. Despite her sentiments spoken when she exited the cave, he still pursued her. And now he had her. Stealing the one thing she had—being without attachment.

One could never be free if they had an anchor tied to them. And he was becoming the weight that moored her from the open seas. Before she wandered, without rhyme or reason, without anyone for her to turn back to.

Only forward, only present, and care for only herself.

But now?

Now her gaze lay restless on Leander. Stepping backwards, she moved away from her realization and away from him. Another step, yet she tripped on an exposed root, and fell back. The mossy ground pillowed her uncouth landing, stopping her gait, but not her tongue. "Then live under falsehoods."

The attempt at good humor as if teasing him failed, and the hurt at her comment was genuinely spread upon his face. Her words displayed the splinter of truth that she was terrified at what he could become to her. What else could she do but make him think that she did not want him. Such untruths left her lips dry, for she was a being fueled by passion and not such restraint. But even if she spoke truth, she could not use such restrictive verbal consonance to hold the meaning of her emotions.

"At least I live. And I live more than you," he spoke, direct in his sentiment. Direct in his affection. "Because I do not fear how I feel for you."

A pause, as silence was her lone reply to what he confessed. He did what she could not: even confined by human vocabulary, he conveyed his passion. And exposing so much of one's self was something he had never done before. As a soldier he guarded himself both physically and emotionally. Going against his training, he revealed his emotions, baring his soul for her to strike him down and wound him more than any weapon could. Though she was not the enemy.

He offered Nyx a hand to pull her up; she hesitated for a moment before accepting. Rather than stand, she tugged him down to join her. Off balance, he fell to the dirt. A short laugh followed but was cut short as his gaze found hers again. He cared for her, in his words, in his gaze, it was clear. Yet, she struggled to give him what he wished.

Her hand went up to cover his eyes as she shut her own, whispering to him as she obstructed his vision. "You need not see me."

Already he knew what she looked like. The dark brought with it a mask of clarity. No longer chained in the sense of sight, for the visible does not always convey the truth. Eyes closed, and blinded to false images, all could be felt. Leander. His breath. His heartbeat. And it was what she desired now, allowing her hunger for his flesh to consume her mind.

He brought up his hand to touch her face. She almost retreated from it, as emotions surged throughout her. She longed to sense him completely, and his caress on her cheek made her emotions uncontainable. Feelings pivoted, for without the confused blur of sight, came the chaos from within.

She moved toward him, close and yet not touching, her own hand benevolently grazed his features, as the blind would do. To be able to see what could not be seen.

The feel of his breath seduced her. She leaned forward to sense it against her skin, to feel each breath against her lips, which were so near to his. It brought such warmth that she moved closer still. As if to taste the forbidden.

Rather than give in to a fate of inhibition, she pulled back. Her movement made no sense even to her—to restrain herself in order to not live in restraint. But somehow the nonsensical contained a reality, for he already burrowed in her heart. Her fear was that he would completely engulf it and bore throughout it. To move so close to another was to lose yourself. A cage would fall upon her if indeed their lips met, sealing their fate forever. Sealing both destinies.

"I cannot."

She said in a failed attempt to break her desire. Her hand left his eyes and she opened her own, to bring her from the sensual to the concrete. What she saw was a reality where she could never have what she desired and feared at once. The weight of desire unrequited remained thick, though she thrived to be immune to its effects.

"I don't ask anything of you, Nyx."

"I know. But I cannot, I need to live," she whispered, completely within a downfall spiral of her fervor. All she desired was to taste his lips and flesh. But yet she denied it all to herself.

She was so fervent within desire, but unknowing in devotion. Love was an anchor, trying to tame the untamable. Never could he truly understand. He asked for nothing, but it would be everything.

"Then live."

A quiet persuasion escaped his lips, holding an undertone of passion. She moved close again, lacing her body near his own. Tremors ran cross her fingers as she caressed his face and trailed her touch along his features, this time with open eyes.

One truth stood alone, despite her conflicts of intimacy. She desired the moment, as only she could, but the concept of love seemed unattainable. He had stolen a piece of her, with him her spirit mused no longer in isolation. The warmth that radiated from him called silently to her, her breath a shivered pause of bemused appetite to want what she should not have.

Why limit the limitless? How could she place boundaries on her actions? Her heart pounded as his breath intermingled with her own. Even the air had difficulty in stirring between the two as their mouths moved closer. All uncertainty was set to the wayward; she could not restrain herself. She needed to feel his touch, to be consumed by it. But as their lips were about to become one, as they were about to kiss for the first time, a scream intruded. Through the jungle it resounded, loud and foreboding. Its call originated back toward the camp, causing both Nyx and Leander to jump to their feet, the moment between them gone. The kiss never transpiring, now lost in the folds of time that never was.

"Stay behind me," was all she heard from the Thalassic captain as he started running back through the forests, gun held at a ready in response to the haunting cries.

Chapter Fourteen

The end of the unfulfilled passion was left with her, but was replaced by concern. The cries they had heard, could still hear, felt as if they would never leave her mind.

Flooded emotions swept within Nyx as a river dammed for eternity to never reach the sea. As Leander left her sight, the dam collapsed and the water rushed through. For if she found love, the story would end. If happiness came then so did stagnation, desiring to forever be in its eternal bliss. But to her that was death. Love was the executioner and she was not ready to head blindly to the gallows. But now, even as lust dampened its hold on her, she knew it would rage again. Now though, she was given a chance to ignore that desire, and pretend heads would not roll.

Allowing the carnal urges to subside, she began to run behind the captain to the camp. Screams of peril filled the air, as beacons through the forest. Scenes played out in her mind of bloodied massacres as she followed. Though even her imagination could not brush upon the brutal realism as they approached the camp.

Hector's right side was covered in blood. Not his own, but of a Chaot whose insides now stained his hazmat clothes as well as his military knife. His expression held rage as he threw the knife. Sailing through the trees, it struck its target, implanting itself in another of the infected. Megaira blindly fired her gun toward the vines, shouting random obscenities to her unseen victims.

Nyx searched the scene, tracing the onslaught of the Chaots and soldiers to try to find the last of the Thalassicians: Diomedes. The nighttime dark impeded her vision, but the starlight mingled with the intermittent light of gunfire helped her search. Yet she could not see him anywhere.

Dead? Off chasing the enemy to amplify his kill-count? Or maybe he was taken as she had been, a captive for later pleasure; at least that scenario allowed for the chance he could be saved.

"Dio," she said, knowing that her voice through the raging sounds of gunfire would go unheard. By her side Leander had already begun joining in the chorus of bullets now blanketing the raid of mindless warriors.

Did Dio simply disappear from reality as the Fisherman once had?

No, unfortunately not. She saw Dio hidden by the tall grasses. He lay covered with blood. No wonder the aggression which poured from the others—seeing one of their brothers now succumb to death. Death, or something else, which now crept upon the once lively man.

She ran across the shallow stream past Hector in order to be by Dio's side. But as swiftly as she sprinted to get to the fallen, Hector brought his left arm out to halt her. The pain rose from her chest as her body collided with his outstretched arm. Was it Hector who stopped her now or had he been enslaved by the contagion? Was it solely the Chaot's blood on him, or alas his own blood that mingled with the prion.

His voice stopped her dubious questions, as speech unaltered by the disease rang within her ears. Hector was not contaminated. Though no relief filled her heart in the meaning of the broad tone.

"He is lost to us."

"No—I see him—let me go to him!" Her voice filled with denial, for it was impossible for her to believe that one so amiable could succumb to a dismal shell.

"No, Nyx. His blood is now infected."

With a soldier's intent, Hector withdrew his holstered gun. He targeted it at Dio. The sounds of war exploded around them as Leander and Megaira continued the slaughter of the raiders, but Hector ignored all. His attention shifted from Nyx to Dio, his gaze portrayed a silent acceptance of what he had to do. "He would have wanted me to end it before it begun."

Said out loud, but Nyx knew it was said for his own ears as Hector aimed the weapon to his downed comrade.

"I will not let you!" Her arm reached for the gun, trying to tear it away from the warrior. She knew that if the Chaot's blood did not affect her then Dio still had a chance that he would not turn. Fervent were her efforts to stop Hector, however there remained no question that his strength dwarfed her own.

Again he brought his arm to her, almost as if to push her away so he could clearly see his target. He needed to bring peace to his brother.

"It did not turn me! It may not turn him!" she said, wishing to save Dio even if it meant admitting she had not told him everything. He looked to her, she saw the reprieve he had shatter, the belief it was her blood from before. If he now believed her to be infected, would he kill her as he set out to do for Diomedes?

Before Hector's decision came, Leander ran over to Dio.

"Stand down, I can neutralize him, we will find a cure out here," Leander said. Confident words from one who had yet to even find the research station, let alone know exactly what clues it would hold. But he stood strong; his figure dominant from the heat of battle. His leadership blatant. The raiding Chaots had been dealt with. If only he was not off wandering with Nyx, but with his own soldiers, she wondered if he thought this and if he now regretted what was between them. She saw the responsibility of a potential death cemented along his features. And he had heard her, her lie about being exposed to the contagion weighed on him. Though he assumed authority and concentrated fully on righting what had happened.

"Dio will be healed. I will get him back to Thalassic," Leander continued as he took a syringe from his supplies and injected two doses into Dio's forearm. It was the tranquilizer once used on her, used now to bring sleep and quiet to the hell that stalked merrily on the eve of nightfall. "Even if he already turned it may be possible to reverse the effects with what we find at the lab. I will not give up on one of my men."

Gun reluctantly holstered, Hector knew the likelihood of what Leander hoped was near impossible. The warrior would not want the fate that the captain now wished upon Dio. But he would fulfill his duty and do as ordered. He could only appeal to his ancestors that Leander's optimism would prove true.

"Put a bullet in me if it ever came to this," Hector's statement lamented a melancholic chord as he turned from the sight, washing his hands of what was. He scanned the horizon in order to assure himself that the camp was indeed cleared from the monsters.

Nyx did not answer. If it ever came to fulfilling her oath she was unsure if she would be able to. Killing another seemed to be easy, as the death of the fish required for her hunger or the Chaot that was stoned by her hand. Yet, the murder of one close to her held an unique difference. The soldiers were becoming too near to her heart and the consequences of such bonds frightened her.

Her gaze turned from Hector to Dio. Leander set-up a compressed stretcher and pulled his sedated friend onto it.

"I am going back," Leander said, his expression carried the full brunt of culpability for failing one of his men.

"You stay with Megaira and Hector; you will be safer with them." Safer. He looked with an uncertainty toward Dio as he spoke. The tranquilizer was temporary, only providing a short repose from the unknown future. Would it be enough time to get back to Thalassic and put Dio into a medical stasis to await a cure? He knew the answer. He had to believe otherwise though in order for hope to endure. Hope that Dio will again laugh his hearty bellow and be by his side in this harrowing aftermath.

"Take this for protection," he said, as he took her hand into his. "I found it back in the city after I first met you."

She looked down at what he had placed in her hand. The Fisherman's knife. Did he know what it meant to her, she wondered. Leander then took off his knife holster from around his leg and gave it to her to use with the Fisherman's knife.

"When I first saw the land after more than a year at sea I was hopeful. But then after seeing the destruction and the decay of the cities, seeing the dead piled in the streets, forgotten, and seeing the Chaots, we almost gave up. But then you appeared and gave us hope that we could survive on this land."

"There are moments that pass us by, soon to be forgotten. But some are defining," Leander continued. "Some break what was."

"Like the disease. And now having Dio bitten," she said. She could only guess what the soldiers went through—to have your entire life suddenly change and to know it would be something you can never return to.

"Yes. These moments can define the world. But you can define yourself. You keep going."

Leander hugged her one last time before he took his hand away from hers. In a wordless goodbye, he turned and left. She took one step forward as he disappeared with Dio into the forest, the air a soft breeze whispering nothings in her ears. Go to him. For this would be her last chance.

Then fate intervened: Megaira clasped her shoulder preventing her from following Leander. Her face burned of soiled anarchy at the loss of her comrade. Someone had to be blamed, someone to hold responsible. And it happened to be Nyx. "You did enough already. These were the same Chaots from the clearing, they followed you. They are raiding us, attacking us, to get at you. This is your fault, you should've listened to me and never returned. Let Leander go and pray we find the lab for Dio's sake—and yours."

All were out of earshot; only she heard the threat, knowing it was not baseless. Hollow was the two's amity, but the gun was not. A bullet marked for her flesh laid in the chamber, though Nyx did not plea for her life. Instead, she focused on what Megaira said about the Chaots for it went against reason. The Chaots were mindless, or so the Thalassicians supposed, but her conviction that they followed the soldiers, directed by a reason, contradicted any prior beliefs. The Chaots were led. They withheld the attack until the opportune moment, and Nyx believed that the strike coming when she was absent from the group was not a fluke. Then they withdrew after Dio was infected: this did not sound like an unrestrained frenzy, leaving her to wonder if the Pathfinder was behind it, wondering if his pack of Chaots was still near. Also if the soldiers were wrong about this aspect of Chaot behavior, what else could they be wrong about.

Megaira believed she had succeeded in making her point and proceeded to wrench her shoulder to pull her forwards. She was surprised Megaira had not yet riddled her with bullets considering her tone, but the soldier had to answer to Hector. If ever the large hulk was taken from the picture though, Nyx knew she would no longer be safe.

"Why we ever picked you up in the first place is beyond me," Megaira said. "We should have left you to be a feast for the infected, bitch."

"Why did you then? I did not want to be here."

"Just keep moving! I know you are not one of us! I always did and knew you were working for them to lead us to our own deaths!"

Them? The accusation itself was not extraordinary, for even she felt the insurmountable distance between herself and the other humans. And she could not forget the kinship she felt in the ways of the Chaots, the feeling she was home among those without restraint. But was it the Chaots Megaira spoke of?

"Quiet Megaira or I will lead you across the Styx myself!" A deep resonance interrupted as Hector plunged like an ox through the foliage back to the two, separating them by his body.

"You like her?" accusingly Megaira said, staring at Hector. "Is that it, is that why you protect her?"

"You know that you have my affection, Megaira," Hector stated, the tone distant. "However, Nyx is not the one responsible for Diomedes."

"I never had your affection or anything else of yours, Hector. You are a cold wall and that's it. And even if you cared for me in your own warped sense, guess what—you mean nothing to me. I just wanted someone, anyone, and you just happened to be the bastard I ended up with," Megaira said, turning on Hector. She continued in threat as her stare passed Hector and came to Nyx. "Watch her back is all I can say, because I will do what you can't. If I find the chance, it will be done with, and the girl will be no more,"

Hector conveyed no heartbreak as he stood unmoved between the two. His position unretracted, especially in consequence to Megaira's outburst. Too many comrades he had lost, too many hardships he had faced, to allow for an emotional attack to faze him. Wrath and woe strung together in Megaira, as she turned from the two. Her weapon clenched, she went to the rear to watch for Chaots, her words following her.

"I will go as far as the research station, for Diomedes sake. Then, it's me or her, Hector. And you know the only way to take her to the Thalassic should be dead, contained and prepped for experimentation. And if the prion is no longer active, as she claims, then we really have no use for her."

He said nothing in reaction to Megaira's words, rather he offered Nyx all she could ask for: a calming presence. Nyx wanted to comfort Hector as well, wondering if Megaira's sentiments hurt the stoic warrior. But truly nothing could be said, and any comfort offered would not be welcomed.

"Megaira is right, Hector," she spoke as Megaira disappeared from sight. Her voice did not contain sorrow but rather confirmation of what Megaira had accused her of. "If not for me, all would be saved. Dio would still be here."

Words held more truth than she knew how to convey.

"If not for you, we may be okay. Or we may all be dead. One can never predict what could have happened," Hector said.

"I disagree," she said. A breath. A pause. Emotionless eyes, but yet the depth of conviction reflected in them. "I was lost, you found me. Or did you? Am I the lamb you freed from the slaughter or rather the slaughter which came upon the lambs?"

Her voice solemn as she continued, not wishing to look upon him for fear of what might lay within him. Perhaps she would find what was never there before, and she would see a wish to confine her, to tame her. "I should leave before more die. I should leave before you die."

"If I die, it is my time. I will fight until then. I will not cross the Styx with trepidation, but rather with fearlessness through its water." Stopping his stride, he grabbed her arm to halt her in her wake. Grip powerful around Nyx's flesh, not to hurt but to make her understand and look at him rather than away. "If I die because of you, I will be honored."

"I cannot stay," she said, sadness sounded in her voice as she loosened Hector's hold and started walking away.

She had found herself in his eyes, in his soul. She saw no conflict of the desire to control her. Not to be caged nor captured. Unlike Leander who still did not understand, Hector did not wish to impose upon her. Yet it was impossible to compare the two; they were opposing forces in her mind. Leander aroused in her desire and impulses that she feared to indulge in. But Hector stirred understanding between them. Not lust nor romance, rather he contained a missing piece of her wayward soul. He had seen chaos, still was in its midst, yet honored rather than abhorred it.

Footfalls halted, a tremor upon her lips not wanting to be lost again. She would never know what would come of Leander if she left. Knowing that danger would always find the winds of lawlessness, and death would eventually end her bedlam.

Not turning from her fixation upon the birch trees ahead, she listened with a longing unbeknownst to all around. Hector's footsteps came up behind her. Stopping. She felt his hand rest on her shoulder in identification with her tribulation.

"I am too much risk to you," A whisper fell from her lips, though with a refusal to believe her own words. The voice of the sirens, holding ruination for all that she should touch. Why such thoughts, why was she haunted so? But she had to help Dio, and did not want to lose her ties to Hector and Leander.

"I accept it," Hector said. "And I will go beside you."

Chapter Fifteen: Telphousian

Two years previous: In search of command

From the fighting Telphousian came, tired of war. She fought, she saw the most vicious sides of humanity, and wanted it to be over.

She could easily leave the military, never again go on the battlefield, and live at peace. Gods knew her ability on the front lines was not the greatest for her aim was shaky under pressure. She would be glad never to fire another bullet again. But she wanted her just reward for fighting, and so Telphousian came to the Grand Master of the Bavarian Coalition himself.

"Tilphê, it is good to see you," Hyperion said, using her nickname to begin the conversation. But she knew the true meaning behind those friendly words: it is good to see her, dependent upon the reasons of her visit, that is. "How is the fight overseas against the Uprising? I have not seen very many encouraging reports ..."

"And that is why I come to you," she responded before Hyperion could finish. Not everyone could come to the Grand Master as she had; lucky for her, her connections ran deep through her family name. Her grandfather had been a respected member of the Bavarian Coalition, long before they had secured the power they now held. "I wish for reassignment to the Thalassic Undersea Colony."

Research based. Fighting would never occur there, even though it often served as a pivotal military intelligence location. Perfect for herself: never fire another bullet, especially considering that would be hazardous to do underwater, yet still be a pivotal authority in the government. But more so, she could escape her fears. Hide from them and never again be reminded of the chaos surrounding war.

"And I want title of Admiral, to be in command of the Thalassic," she finished.

This demand—yes demand, not simply a request—startled Hyperion as he took his time to reply.

"You know this is impossible. You are a Lieutenant—"

"—Lieutenant Commander, sir—"

"Whatever it may be, I cannot grant that much of an advancement. I can station you aboard the Thalassic, you have done your time fighting. Plus, I owe much to your grandfather. However, you will keep your current rank."

"I am capable of running the colony, Hyperion. Furthermore, I believe it is in your best interests that I be promoted," she said. "I know of the Bavarian Coalition, I know a select group runs the Coalition, and the one world government was formed in their best interests and not that of the people. Has it always been the Bavarian Coalition's objective to rule the world? Establishing a totalitarian world government, the New World Order, in order to dominate it."

"You are paranoid, Telphousian. The times of secret societies and conspiracy theories are over with."

"That is because they are now a reality. And you realize, given my namesake and grandfather, I am privy to documents to prove the world government's creation was not to establish a worldwide peace, but rather to serve its own self-motivating purposes. I understand this would not serve to destroy the world government, but I am sure you don't want more uprisings on your hands."

"Perceptive and demanding," Hyperion said after a long pause. After a longer pause still he added one more description. "And an extortionist at your best."

Telphousian smiled a hard wired smile for she knew she had won. And his next words confirmed this.

"Not full Admiral, not the head leader. But I will promote you to Rear Admiral of the Thalassic and you will be second in command. You will have to earn the rest of the silver stars on your own."

Two weeks previous: In the sea below

She never earned those stars; however, with the true Admiral surface side during her emergency quarantine of the Thalassic, she conveniently replaced him. Though the Thalassic held many political officials who had taken refuge aboard the undersea bunker, she was the highest military ranked official. And now, with the convenient use of martial law, she was the law.

Heels clacked down the circular corridor of the Thalassic. Two by two, pair by pair, the feet stepped in line. One pair belonged to the Admiral of Thalassic, Telphousian. The other pair belonged to her thorn, Leander. And though the steps were in line, the conversation, however, was everything but.

"It has been over a year, enough time has passed. We have to go surface side, for not only our sake but for those who may have survived the outbreak," Leander said

"Let's not discuss this," Telphousian replied, letting her hand brush Leander's arm. She let it linger there longer than appropriate among colleagues, smiling to herself as he pulled away. If he was going to make this difficult, all the better. They had years under here, and she had as much time as she chose to break him in. "Let's focus on something more realistic."

Leaning towards his neck, still keeping up with his gait, she let her breath caress his skin. Her hair of red fire lashed against his shoulder as she did so. A small delight to herself, even if her gesture was uninvited. "Be my side man, on and off duty, and I will make it worth your while. And maybe I will even approve this mission of yours."

He stopped. Here it is, she will finally get her wish.

"I am tired of this, Admiral. I am not about to sleep with you in order for you to do what is right."

But no; he disappoints. Blunt as ever, as well, as one passerby in the hall gave the two an uncertain lift of the brow. Let them talk, she was in command. If anyone stepped out of line, she could easily make them fish bait.

"Why won't you, Leander?" If he could be blunt, so could she.

He did not even answer; probably because he could not tell if she was serious or joking. Out of all of Thalassic, it was Leander she wanted. Perhaps because she followed the old saying of wanting what you cannot have. Unlike the other Thalassicians, he would not cave under her desires and power. And that, in and of itself, not only caused her to want him and hate him in the same breath.

But if he wanted her to be serious, she would. Though, she surmised, he would not like the answer.

"I already have discussed this with you: the outside is considered under quarantine until I say otherwise," she said, her voice monotone as she restated her rejection of going to the surface. "That means no one in and no one out."

Would he continue to be a thorn in her side? If only he could look past his need to be a hero, and see what he could accomplish under the Atlantic. Or if only a rat could come along, to help this lioness remove the thorn.

"If you see fit to reach higher than your captain status, and actually have some say in the political process," she continued, her tone growing sultry as she began walking again, Leander taking step alongside. "I have already proposed how to do so."

"You already know my answer to that," he said, but then he slowed in his step. Would this be it, her chance to claim him? "You may tell yourself you want me, but you don't. Whatever you feel toward me, is not real. It's a need to control things, to control me. You believe if I will be yours, then you can manipulate me. But trust me, this would not be the case."

And no. Not the chance. He was always the one to adhere to his ethics, and it sickened her. Maybe he was right, she thought, but did not really care. Either he would be by her side, or she would stand opposed to his efforts. She could not run the undersea colony with people questioning her authority, after all, she knew enough about mutiny on the seas as it were.

"Then you will stay down here, as all others are ordered to do. It is for our own good. I am the colony's leader and ..."

She was about to go on, but Leander interrupted: "And you should listen to the Thalassicians as our leader. All I am asking is for a small squadron to go surface side and investigate."

"Right now appeasing people is on the low list of priorities," she replied. Now was the time to pull rank and rid herself of the bother. "Foremost, I am not only your leader but I outrank you. I am the one who is Admiral; you will do as I order, without question."

She stopped this time, and stared at him. Not as a seductress, but as his commander.

He stopped as well, staring her right back as he called her out.

"This is not about who has the highest rank, it is about what is happening surface side, as well as the future of those onboard the

Thalassic. How long do you think we can hide down here?" he asked, persistent as always. He continued, knowing the truth behind her 'rank'. "But if you want to try pulling rank, Admiral, first ask yourself how you earned that rank."

"It is about who out ranks who." And Leander would just have to accept that. And if he does not learn his place, she would see to it he is stripped of all honor. She would find the rat to remove the thorn, and make an example out of his subordination when she does.

"What matters is that I am your commander," Telphousian said to Leander, turning into her quarters to dismiss his ambitious ideas. But before she slammed the door in his face, she left him with one piece of parting advice. "You are a soldier, you will obey."

Present: And through hell

"Someone has breached the moon pool, Admiral!"

"How is that possible?" Telphousian said in irritation at the cadet. No one should be able to bypass their security, after all an entire ocean protected them. But as she looked at the log she saw that the codes of Leander had been used to enter.

"I will handle this. Security come with me." She started down the hall to meet the offender. He and his squad had went against direct orders and broken quarantine. Now they were back, and she just had to pray that they did not inflict false hope of returning surface side in their ventures. The Thalassic was not ready. She was not ready.

The sight that met her solidified her control though. There was no hope that came to her sight. Leander was stabilizing a cot that had Diomedes on it. Dio seemed incapacitated and the others were no where to be found.

"You dare return after disobeying orders? And I see you bring risk to us all?"

"I bring Diomedes back, and he is sedated. I need him sequestered and put under medical stasis immediately to stop the infection," Leander said. "And Admiral, I accept any punishment you decide. But please, help Dio."

She knew what he would say next. That she owed it to Dio for what she had done to his family. How she had not granted permission for them to board, and therefore sentenced them to death. But was she not right? If she had let them come onto Thalassic who knew what would happen. Leander should be happy she allowed him back on board after that incident.

But he said nothing. He just remained silent and looked with a frigid certainty that she had no choice but to agree to his terms. It was either agree and help Dio, or face a rebellion from the crew that flanked her. She was their Admiral, but if she chose to turn her back on one of their own she would pay the consequences.

And if she chose to help, she could control the situation.

"Get Diomedes to the medical bay and send a waiting party to the shore for the other insubordinates," she said to two of the officers and then turned to Leander as she addressed the others. "And please escort the *former* captain to the brig."

As the sleeping giant of a man was pulled pass her, she looked down at him. She had never seen the disease of Chaos before now. Dio was no longer the man she remembered. Sleep did not bring a sweet meandering of sugar plums and dreamscapes but rather the sleep covered a beast. The slumber threatened to break, the monster would be awoken. She shivered at the sight of him, wondering if she had made the correct choice.

Chapter Sixteen

Hector, Megaira and Nyx walked through the night, not able to rest while the fate of Dio was ambiguous to them. What had happened during the Chaot raid was not mentioned. Emotions plagued Nyx, varied feelings running rampant throughout her. She felt such heartache for Leander and regret over Dio's fate tormented her.

Soon though kismet was upon them. The three came to their destination.

The research station stood before the triad, hidden in the tangles of the forest foliage and the dark of night. It retained the aura of being untouched by the outside. Vines had grown wild over its walls, encasing it. A disturbing sense of dread filled their senses, though the soldiers were too steeped in courage to allow the foreboding omens to stop their course. And so into the doors they plunged.

Heat pounded against her as she stepped through the entrance. Once this station was an inviting oasis from the summer sun's fervor, though now, without power, it became an oven. She wondered if it was a trap as she peered into the compound, and they would be cooked alive before they could find what they sought.

The soldiers hoped the key to the disease existed beneath the shadows. Did she want the same?

To save Dio, yes. But to save society? No.

She had no motivation to return to the norm or to the past, both of which she knew nothing about. Only her feelings allowed a recollection of her forgotten times. Primal emotions. And the only shimmer of past she recalled was one of pain. One of such control and limitation. Isolation and loneliness. Trapped. In a way, the absence of memories was a blessing.

If the soldiers did succeed in action and find the supposed end of Chaots, it would reset what was. Going back to the time before society fell would cause her to cease to exist, regressing to the illusory cage. She was a part of this life and this moment and had no desire to look back. Yes, the diseased dominated this world. But societal constraints dominated the previous one. Furthermore, fighting destiny would be in vain. You could not command the wind to remain idle nor wish the tides to rise, why then turn back the hands of time. Yet she followed.

Dark reigned in the belly of the beast. Guided only by their flashlights, the soldiers' hands traced the bowels of the research station. Searching over the desks, in hopes to retrieve … what exactly, she wondered. That sudden 'luck' strikes them and allows the soldiers to find vials filled with the cure—to bring good fortune to those afflicted, giving them a land of pink posies and faeries in which to live. Where unicorn's blood held immortality and their horns were carved from pure leprechaun gold. Such flukes do not happen; serendipity was a word unknown to the world now.

Nevertheless, they continued looking despite the unlikelihood of discovery. Perhaps it was what humans needed and why the Thalassicians persisted. A shred of hope dangled before them that light would breach the abyss fallen on society. It was what Pandora had safeguarded despite her wrongs; it was the crutch humanity fell on in the face of horrors beyond their comprehension. And now it fueled the quest of the soldiers.

A crack sounded followed by a burst of color; in Hector's hand an emergency beacon rod glowed green. Luminescence filled the room, but emptiness now manifested a greater tenacity in the light. Though the emerald hue shone, nothing was revealed. All remained shrouded. The rooms maintained a sterility never found in nature. Stark dimensions of desks and walls drew perpendicular angles and cleanliness unbeknownst to Nyx before then. Though even in its peculiarity, it held a type of familiar recognition to her. Not of a home drenched in the scent of fresh baked cookies, but of a nightmare beckoning its remembrance.

The three searched. Computers were rummaged. Their hard drives were placed into their packs to bring to Thalassic in the prospect that some worthwhile knowledge could be conveyed from them. Laboratory upon laboratory, room upon room, all were unearthed. The research led to no triumphs; all experiments had failed. Despite this, their search continued. What else could they do other than go home. It was not an option; the soldiers could not return empty handed and Nyx had no home to go to.

"Nothing," Hector said, ceasing her thoughts. He looked upon the documents, sifting through them. His face displayed a somber realization that knew the only way to save Dio had begun to slip from his grasp. Cruel reality replaced their hopes.

"There has to be something. We did not come all this way to fail," Megaira grumbled in a voice more akin to a growl than articulated words. Nyx remained silent as she searched, knowing that even a whisper from her may set Megaira into fury. Megaira continued, her words said to console her own worries. "We have to find what they learned, we have to."

Hector said nothing as he opened another folder out of the stack. Though this time, he did not toss it aside.

"Nyx," he said, his voice containing an uncertainty she had never heard from him. He held out the folder; bare in contents except for several papers. Before she could look at it, Megaira came up behind Hector and wrenched the document away. Eyes scanned the paperwork. Her face changed as she read, not to confusion but to an anger so menacing, so uncontained.

"I knew it. She came here to destroy us!"

The document turned in her hands to show Nyx what the folder contained. It was as if looking to a mirror. A black and white faxed photo portrayed her dressed in sterile white. A number displayed around her neck, not of a prisoner, but of a patient, or more correctly, a lab rat.

An experiment. Below mathematical formulas were written; repeated letters amongst the numbers that she did not understand. But familiar in her tumultuous mind: Y. X. Variables. N. To the nth powers. Nyx. The personification of night, the goddess of darkness. The Heiress of Chaos. A name stemming not from these, but from scientific formulas.

"What does it mean, Judas?" Megaira questioned. Round the campfire they had spoken of monsters and heroes, Judas being the monster in Christianity. And now to Megaira, Nyx was the Judas of their own myth.

"Why did you not tell us you were a part of this?" Anger flourished in her words.

With her memory lost, Nyx could not remember. Nor did she wish to. No words came in response, but she turned to run. A click rang out as the safety was removed from Megaira's gun. It caused Nyx to abruptly stop, knowing the sound that would follow. She yearned to flee, but she did not wish death to come of it.

Megaira moved toward the entrance of the doorway, using her body and weapon to block Nyx's only path of escape. As she took a step towards her, her foot knocked into something, but her gaze remained on Megaira. Sweat brushed upon her flesh, as the heat sweltered around her; strands of hair hung down her face, eyes shimmered intensity despite everything come to pass.

Click.

The noise flooded the air, not a gunshot but the dismantled safety of Hector's gun. He aimed his firearm, freeing himself from hesitation. Eyes a placid steel: the calm before the storm. Ready to release his victim from the mortal coil of men, though his aim did not follow Megaira's path to focus on Nyx. Instead, it was on his comrade.

"You will take aim off her now." Not a request, a command growled from between his lips.

"Are you crazy? She is behind this! Listen to what it says," Megaira said. She kept her gun pointed on Nyx as she adjusted the paper in her hand. Hector's aim did not waver from Megaira as she began to read; her voice out loud for all to hear.

"It has been merely months since the prion has struck this planet, but already our population has succumbed to the plague. The contagion originated overseas in the Mediterranean due to the initial attack, and has grown into a pandemic due to subsequent attacks worldwide and our inability to quarantine the infection. It continues to become out of control, spreading rapidly. Death comes to some, the prion seeking the brain to destroy it. Unfortunately, most survive; however, not in a favorable light."

"We have few details at this time," she continued reading, "but we do know that the cerebrum is impaired and all higher functions degraded. The purpose of the host human is to attack others, and thereby propagate the disease. Uninhibited hunger, rage and lust left unchecked. The surviving infected do not suffer death, rather the fate of madness. Myself and a few others ..."

Megaira paused. Her composure and face bore the weight of a telling tale: the fate that had probably met with 'the others' and this scientist.

"... have come here in seclusion to find a cure to save our civilization. We hope to not face contamination in this shelter but instead find success. If not, *Homo sapiens* may face extinction, what we had before thought ourselves immune from."

Another of the folder's paper turned in Megaira's hand. Another documentation of what ensued in this laboratory, written perhaps weeks, perhaps days, after the first.

"Setbacks are many within our measured time. But finally a breakthrough. We received the included fax from outside Intel: from someone named Glaucus. Not only does it confirm the presence of other survivors grouped together, but we heralded the faxed information as the key to stop this monstrosity."

"The equations and genetic code delivered with the photograph confirm that she is the origin of the prion; she naturally deviates from the human genome to be something else. Within her lays a previously undiscovered prion that either sporadically mutated or by familial inheritance came to be. From what we can tell, Patient Zero demonstrates no apparent signs of the disease; she serves as its creator and host in a near symbiotic relationship. The prion itself was procured from the host for use as a bioweapon and subsequently released."

As Megaira continued her voice was not the only low drum that captivated the three's ears. Noises from outside began the chorus to the tale, banging the walls. The id cometh to destroy.

"Update. We still believe the prion of Patient Zero to be a mutated form, but the origins are clearer. It seems to have many similarities to CWD, the Chronic Wasting Disease that has been previously contained in deer and elk in some areas of North America. Unlike other prions, this disease has yet to be found in the human population, however initial studies demonstrated the potential it has to cross species and infect primates. Unlike Kuru and CJD, the misfolded prions of the lesser known CWD are also found in salvia, urine and feces, causing the infection to be more virulent."

"Despite this discovery, we did not have enough time to use the genome sent to us of Patient Zero to find a vaccine, if even there was one to be found. This facility's security was breached. I now am the sole survivor amongst the scientists stationed here; I fear though my exposure will be imminent. My fate is one doomed to become the monster that now stalks this planet. To prevent this, I take my life in hopes that it will save my soul. If ever this is read, bode well. For we did not."

A hush fell from the listeners as Megaira ended the speech. The final thoughts of the researcher prevailed. Only the banging from outside could be heard amidst the exhalation of the three. Nyx's gaze turned downcast, as she looked to the ground. What her step had knocked into moments ago lay obscured by shadows, but now she saw. The writer's body, unmoved from the suicide she had just witnessed through Megaira's voice. The head stared upward. Eyes wide though empty sockets looked up at her. Would this become her own fate as well, as told by the pen of the scientist: to live as Patient Zero, a vector to the disease. To carry it and never be rid of it, lest she commit suicide as the scientist did.

Henceforth, the death of a species stained forever on her soul—but also the rise of a new race. A new race of the unrestrained, of those unbridled by moral implications. The Chaots. The wild. Evolution from one species to the next, the fit surviving.

Without word, she looked back to the armored soldiers. They would kill her if they realized what was bound to happen if she continued to survive among them. Among those they had sworn to protect. If she were the vector, the host, the originator of this contagion, they would never be rid of the pestilence until they were rid of her.

Megaira's motives were clear. But Hector? Would duty now overshadow all else—to protect a species or to protect her.

Hector did not move. Questioning whether life or death would be her fate, perhaps this was what ran through his mind. Or maybe, she thought, the decision was already made and instead he now contemplated only the method in which he would kill her, whether a death willingly and swiftly by his bullet or a struggle against the inevitability of her demise. She took one pace backwards, away from the soldiers not knowing what threat they posed.

Megaira's finger rested on the trigger. Nyx looked through the weapon's chamber to her impending death. Megaira's finger prepared to squeeze, her glare of the maniacal illustrating what she perceived to be honor.

"Stop," Hector said, roused to action. His gun lifted once more directed at Megaira, and not toward Nyx.

Megaira eye's fixed unto him, forcing him to confront her certainty. "You heard it, Hector. Do not allow your feelings for her to interfere with your duty, to protect our own. Kill her."

Their quarrel continued, commands given and denied between the soldiers. Nyx could make no move with Megaira's gun on her, and so stood, a deer in headlights, wondering exactly how these two would solve their altercation. Weapons pointed on all, trigger friendly fingers, the Chaots surrounding the compound as their feast fought amongst themselves.

"She is one of us now," Hector responded. "I will protect her."

A definite answer.

But not the right answer, at least not to Megaira.

She did not move her aim off of Nyx. But the focus on one enemy did not mean the disappearance of another. Noises echoed throughout the laboratory. Steps. Unearthly grunts. Yet nothing could be done to prepare to fight or for defense while the internal conflict still played out.

"They are coming. Megaira cease your aim and help me," Hector said through clenched teeth.

"No, we take care of—" A gun fired, interrupting Megaira. The shot rang within her ears. Nyx froze waiting for the pain to come. Was she dead? Did the hallowed soul come for her spirit, ending the reign of the wild and bringing only the bleak definitive of death?

But it was not she who bled.

Hector had shot a Chaot who had come up from behind Megaira. It had fell, bleeding near the rotting scientist. He had saved Meg, but still her aim remained on Nyx.

"Meg! Move away!" Hector yelled, again shooting the Chaots who were coming up from behind her. He shot a second; it fell. But then Megaira turned to face the third Chaot right as Hector fired again.

It was not the Chaot who fell. Rather, Megaira had unexpectedly put herself between Hector and the Chaot. The bullet had found her chest. Blood trickled down the sides of her mouth before spilling with even more tenacity, draining her life.

Hector's face grew blank, emotions drained. A comrade fell at his feet because of his actions. Not only a comrade, but his lover. As with all sorrow, he tried to bury it deep. Right now, the threat of Chaots forcing entry into the research lab needed his full attention and he had to get to Meg, to stop the blood loss.

The third Chaot focused on Megaira, and was about to attack her body when Hector sent his last bullet into its head. It fell dead on top of Megaira.

Hector rushed to her and knelt beside her. He pushed off the Chaot, lifting Megaira into his arms.

"Stay with me," he murmured into her ear. Nyx came to their side, putting pressure on the wound to stop the bleeding. But there was too much.

"We should of stayed ... I didn't want to lose you ..."

"I'm here. You will never lose me. I will find you in the next life if I need to. But do not go. Not now."

He continued speaking softly to her, though Megaira could no longer hear him. "Not now. Not from my hand."

Her power was now limp. Death claimed the trooper of the Underwater. Now of the Underworld.

"I cannot leave her. I need to bury her," Hector said to Nyx but before she could respond, the walls started to fall apart, the sound of the gunfire inciting more of the Chaots. The living id began to swarm within the research compound. Cries of insanity, thirst for flesh, intensifying in the Chaots as their prey came in eye shot. Mouths raving as if Hector and Nyx had already become their feast.

"Go Nyx. Now."

Positioning himself between her and the overflowing monstrosity, he reloaded and took aim. No bullets strayed in aggression from his weapon, but precise explosions dropped the diseased with each click. Hector protected the sole thing that was in his charge, as the body count began to rise. His duty was no longer to fight for Thalassic, no more to be a soldier for the people. He had killed one of his own. An accident. But Nyx knew it was one he could never forgive himself for. And so all he could do would be to continue to fight, even if his fate was to join Megaira. He even wished for this end, feeling the weight of her heavy over his shoulders.

And in this he would find the resolve to bring the titans to their feet.

"No Hector. I cannot leave you."

"Now."

The word left his mouth with such fortitude that it roused the spirit of the wind within her. She had to go—his solemn word spoke—or they both would die. And though unsaid, she knew that if she left, she took the curse with her. Only then would he have the chance to escape this massacre. Hector would survive without her by his side. If she stayed, both of them would be doomed. Or so she had to tell herself, had to believe, in order to turn away from the warrior. Turn and run.

From behind she heard the raging firefight continued. She became deafened by the screams of many in torment. Death was coming. And now the roles were switched as she neared the outside. It was she who escaped the binds of Hades, but uncertain whether she should chance a look behind. She prayed that her Orpheus would be only steps behind her, ready to lead the way out of the underworld. That he would be in her wake, alive. A look back, seeking Hector.

Nothing.

She had lost him as once the forlorn poet had lost Eurydice.

Frozen to the world, adrift again in the winds, she ran from the room. Never to return to the serenity of the soldiers, her anchor was lost. At first she followed the green light of the beacon rod down the familiar path they had come down. But she saw movement, heard shuffles and the hungry groans of Chaots swarming toward the commotion behind her. She diverted and stepped into a corridor that they had not explored yet. Dark surrounded her as she stepped quietly in the hall in hopes it would lead away from the Chaots and towards the outside. Her heartbeat was fast and loud to her, mimicking the gun shot over and over again, an echo that would not end as it beat into her ears. She had left the flashlight behind in the rush, but hoped that her eyes would adjust soon.

She heard a breath. Hard and sharp, it cut through the far away screams. It was close, only a few feet away. In the pitch dark she could not see anything, and so could only stop and hope that it had not noticed her. She wished her heart would quiet, foolishly for surely the sound of it was only magnified to her. Another breath, this time though it was closer to her.

Another.

And as the fourth breath came she lunged forward, and slammed against the figure. They both fell, she on top of it. It struggled, trying to bite and grab her. She held it back, using her weight to subdue it. Teeth came forward again, then realizing the futility of its position, the Chaot began to shriek. Nyx brought her head down, crashing her skull against its.

Everything went black, even more so than the black of the corridor. But she struggled to stay conscious, falling to the side of the Chaot and laying on the hard tile. The hit must have knocked out the Chaot, for it lay motionless besides her.

Get up. It took all her effort, but she knew that the sounds may attract more. She stood unsteadily, and continued on. As she turned a corner, she saw some light and came to a room with a window to the outside where the break of dawn could be seen. She looked through, and saw Chaots everywhere. But they were moving toward the entrance to the research station, about twenty feet away. She silently opened it, and slipped out of its narrow crevice.

She began to run through the ferns that seemed as tentacles wrapping around her legs. Thoughts flooded her mind as she continued running through the forests and into the swamp. Her kinship with the Chaots was understood in basic science, not as she thought it would be. She fantasized that mystical, esoteric and primal philosophies explained her affinity with the Chaots. To have her spiritual realities replaced by simple biological mechanics tore at her deeply. But what dug deeper, tearing her apart, was a voice:

If I die because of you, I will be honored.

Hector had said this once. But she did not bring honor, only damnation. She had lost Hector, unsure if he lived or died. There was no honor in that. Even if indirectly, she had made Dio into something that no longer bore resemblance to the cheerful bloke. Leander left. Megaira was killed because of her. She caused the Armageddon; all died because of what she was.

She ran on alongside such thoughts. She ran on until her energy finally escaped her and she fell to the mire.

The mud swallowed her; the breeze yielding to the murky depths surrounding her. She wished to stay there and become one with the swamp, to forever lay and not again face what would come. The swamp of sorrows, of sadness, that consumes the hearts of the brave. Surrender, it whispers. Her heart heavy, all she could do was plea silently, yes. Take me. End my struggle.

The Pathfinder looked out, watching. Even as a Chaot himself, he was responsible for the raids on the humans. He orchestrated her demise— not from life, but from the final strands of humanity that surrounded her. Of the soldiers, of her own humanity, making her his own. Recognition came to him as he looked at her. Recognition of a life forgotten, and of the origins of his life now.

Chapter Seventeen: The Pathfinder

Three years previous: In the skies above

"Hook up!" shouted Jason.

The call boomed from the Jumpmaster's voice, reverberating through the aircraft. The elite team of paratroopers heard Jason even above the wind. During the intermittent silence between his calls, the noise swallowed them in the metal shell of the plane as if being sucked through a vortex.

"Check Static Lines!"

No pitch, no resonance, just a monotone yell. He showed no emotion, just an overriding control over the situation. Sweat dripped down his forehead. Nerves maybe, though mainly due to the sweltering compact oven of the drop plane. It was small in order to go undetected. No comfort. A smile hitched his mouth. Sure, must have been made that way to deter any last minute cold feet in the men. To jump from the metal conductor was all they wanted at about this moment, even considering what it was they jumped into.

Enemy territory, occupied by the Uprising.

They would go into virgin land, in order to assess the layout and pave the way for the rest. Identify safe landing sites, ideal approaches, and areas to circumvent. To cut the way; they were the metamorphic machete carving the path. The first to face danger. The first to shape the unknown into the known.

"Check Equipment!"

Whatever they faced below though, he mused, it was better than being cooked alive in this craft.

"Sound off, equipment checked!" Many voices in one unison rang out in response. His boys have done him well and would continue to do so in flight and on the ground.

"I blaze the way to far-flung goals—" Jason called out, and as soon as the last word left his mouth the others of his platoon called in a resounding unity.

"Behind, before, above the foe's front line!"

"And beyond," he added as the plane slowed to drop speed. Three Minutes. He opened the door. The blast of air swelled within the innards of the plane, calling for the soldiers to jump into its freedom.

Huh, cooked alive. Hope that that was not what waited for them if caught.

The one minute reference point passed, and he called the same. He continued sweating, despite the cool air now being shuffled among the fully geared paratroopers.

"This is it, live together, but we do not die alone. Die together, while carving the enemy's tombstone," he said. "Got it?"

"Yes sir!"

The thirty second reference point passed.

"Stand-by!"

The tension of those thirty seconds passed faster—and yet at the same time slower—than anything he had experienced. His life was for one purpose: go in first, carve the path for the rest. Live ahead of it all, live ahead of the fear.

"Go! Go! Go!"

He would jump last. Knife clearly defined on his lower calf, if anything should happen to his brothers-in-arm, such as a faulty chute, he would have to be the last to be able to dive to them through the air.

They jumped. So did he.

The blast of cool shot up around him. The metal surface was replaced with nothing. Sweat steamed from his face, as he looked out through night vision goggles to account for all of his platoon. The parachutes pulled open in sync; olive clouds amidst the green glare. All accounted for. All ready for the war below.

They were called the Pathfinders, they would fulfill their namesake and lead the rest to victory.

Over one year previous: On the sea below

Rising smoke circled Jason's head from his cigar. No longer over enemy lines, he stood aboard the Destroyer ship looking over the fleet of the

Scipian across the Atlantic. Fresh from the frontline, his aircraft had landed here to refuel supplies. He also had supplemental orders: Determine the research being done aboard, specifically the hazard versus performance ratio. The Bavarian Coalition had decided to use Commander Triton's biological research, and needed to be assured it would meet their needs and end the Uprising. Not a far jump for Jason: from assessing the situation of the foe to now the supposed friend. What he found out was that the friend was by far the worst of the two threats.

The bio-agent was war-worthy, yes. It was dangerous. Unethical, even, he thought as he walked down the stairway to the ship's laboratory. He stopped in front of one room and looked through the polycarbonate glass cell to view the confined female subject. Nevertheless, the questionable ethics did not make him waiver. This was war, and the Bavarian Coalition needed to fight against the insurgency. But the contagion that the head of the Scipian, Triton, procured for wide-scale use was more than a simple bioweapon that could be contained in attack. It was unmanageable. It would bring the entire world in danger, and not just their enemies. Hence, he could not deem the research consequence worthy.

He squinted through the puffed fog as he looked out toward the woman before him. Dressed in white, behind an impenetrable glass. She glared out as he looked at her, as if she could escape her cage. Despite the conditions, she was willful to the end.

He was not supposed to be here. Hell, if that stopped him. Hell, if that was not part of his job description: go against restrictions. Go where no one else should.

Several clacks of footfalls on the hard ceramic floor echoed as someone came up beside him. He had no need to turn to see who it was, he knew the smell and breath of acidic evil anywhere. Instead, his gaze remained on the woman. As Triton approached to stand next to him, Jason could see the change in her. The fear that became present.

The other spoke to him; his voice was cunning. "She is intriguing, is she not?"

They both knew he was in a restricted area, that need not be said. They both also knew what would happen; but, that would come later.

"Not for the reason you see, Commander Triton."

"You see her on another level. Is that why you contacted your superiors to end this research?"

Hard, stern as ever, Jason did not allow the hidden threat to deter his confidence. The communication was classified, and if Triton knew of it there was the possibility that his message never got out.

"No, it is not. Your research jeopardizes civilization. If what you are working on ever breached the hull ..." he paused, knowing specifics would not have to be spelled out. Triton knew clear well what would happen. "I cannot allow you to continue. You should soon be receiving the orders to terminate your work."

"I chose you. A Pathfinder for the Army. I hoped that meant you could see beyond what others could not and be the first to support this world altering cure. But ... well, I am disappointed in you, *Pathfinder*. We intercepted your message."

A cough came from Jason through the smoke, not of uncertain surprise but of confirmation. Realization, and undoubted confirmation.

He saw the woman looking at them and listening, curious of the two despite her situation. But also if felt as if the fear he had saw when Triton came was now directed at him. That she feared for him, not for herself.

"I cannot condone these experiments," Jason replied as he put the cigar in his mouth for one last drag. Scars painted his face from the wars he had survived. He did not have the typical soldier build, for his shorter stature put him at five foot six. It was best for the jump to be small, he joked, less likely that enemy fire would land on you. One would never guess his size looking at him, for height would go ignored as his eyes glowed as if fresh from the forger. And now he looked at Triton, the fire clear. "This work will end."

"We intercepted your message," Triton repeated, the tone the same; the expression the same. "And we terminated it. Your superiors will not receive word, our research will not stop."

Two armed guards stepped out from the hall at Triton's words, and stood to protect the Commander though Jason knew Triton did not need protection. He knew the man's background: Naval Special Warfare Command Unit, highly respected among his peers, many battles under his belt. Older now, but he could see he was still a force to be respected. Jason knew what would come, but was powerless to stop it. Even so, he fought. The cigar fell from his hands. Grabbing his weapon, he fired at Triton.

No bullet discharged. The leader of the Scipian did not fall.

"Did you truly believe it would be that easy, Pathfinder?" Triton laughed, as two of his guards grabbed hold of Jason. The gun itself had never left his side, even in sleep, for it to be robbed of its bullets. Except at the check point boarding the Destroyer ... did Triton plan this that far in advance? Even before Jason had decided that the research was not safe?

However, he was not about to make it easy for Triton either. Pivoting backwards to make the guards first unbalanced, he swooped his arms out from in front to behind their heads as they fell forward. They struggled to keep hold of him, though he did not need them to let go for his plan to succeed. His hands now in back of each head, he used their momentum against them as he crashed their skulls together. They dropped, one hitting the door lever hard as he fell. But as they did so Jason felt a stab to his body. Triton brought the metal point of a needle to his side as he was distracted, piercing through his clothes and into his flesh and pumped the liquid into his bloodstream.

He sank. His mind still alert, but his body fell paralyzed. The cigar was on the ground near him, smoke still rising. Triton stepped on it, crushing the tobacco and smothering the smoke underneath.

"I am sorry. But you should have never undermined my operation."

Triton looked on from above. Jason felt nothing, not even the cold floor underneath his cheek that was smashed against it. He could only hear and see as if a powerless bystander from inside a shell he no longer had control of ... and one he feared he would never again have control of.

"Though you do have it right. I do not make a weapon to help end the war. I make one to begin a new kind of one. With exposure to the Drakōn mund prion that we procured, the prefrontal cortex will not die, it will transform. Death of the Uprising will not come as the Bavarian Coalition wanted; instead, the contagion will fuel the Uprising's cause and end the one world government's regime."

Triton leaned over him, another syringe held tightly between pinched fingers. The liquid inside red. The hand that held it gloved. No emotions splashed on his face, only cold eyes looking through a blank stare of scientific separation.

Jason could guess what it was and what Triton meant to do. He did not plea or threaten him. He accepted fate.

"Unlike the pathogen that was constructed, which needed to be in vapor form, you will be able to experience it unmodified. Pure."

The metal syringe sunk into his neck. The red injected into his own bloodstream, leaving the container only with a tinge of what was left. His limbs may have been immobilized, his movements limited, but pain still came. He felt blood trickle down his face. Down his nose. His eyes watered of red tears. His last sight was of the woman forcing herself against the door that had been compromised during the fight. Trying to reach him.

It felt as if he stood again on the plane before the jump. What lay down this road was unknown, but he would face it—even embrace it— and come out leading the rest. He was the one ordered to always go first. And now he was the first to be transformed by this pathogen.

Even though tranquilized, the torture he had previously faced was nothing compared to this. The only thing he could compare the pain to was an antiquated reference: the mummification process of the Egyptians. The hook sliding within the nasal cavity, the rod pressing against the brain, hooking it and yanking it out. This was what it must have felt like if the process was done alive, and surely a few misdiagnosed souls had underwent it in ancient times. Having their brain scrambled and then ripped out alive. Only that could define the pain he felt.

His body convulsed. His mind tore away as if a witness to his transformation. Though still everything was seen through a red glare, reminding him it was not over. Triton took several steps back, wishing to part himself from the risk of contamination, though not from the scene. Scientific curiosity? No, that was not it. Something else haunted Triton's eyes. The woman had wrapped her arms around him, and it felt like a parting embrace of who he was once and a beginning to who he became.

Pain still. But now it drained, though ever present.

Now the chaos came.

Images of his past he grasped to, of his platoon standing beside him, of the jump. Of them conquering uncharted territory, and leading the rest forward. As if grains of sand, they slipped, sifting through his clasped fists.

I never surrender, though I be the last. Though I be the first.

One year previous: And through hell

Static.

It came in interludes. Realization, lapses—horror. Blood over his hands. No, not his, not now. He was still aboard the ship, he felt the sway below his feet. But no longer locked in a cell. How long had he been caged away? Weeks ... months ... years? Time seemed an inescapable prison in itself, but when walls and solitude are added it became insurmountable. Yet here he was, finally free.

A body lay in his grasp, intestines strewn down his lips in feast.

He continued. He could not stop.

He was hungry. Hunger that could never be satisfied.

Screams abounded from around. Shots fired. He ran to the gunfire, ripping the gun away and then trying to do the same with the arm that had welded it. First it would not tear away. He pulled. Again pulled, pushing the figure down and standing on it as he tugged on the arm.

Ribs cracked beneath his stance. Blood poured from the mouth. The arm still in his grip as he pulled.

He looked at it. Recognition shimmered. Was it the same as his? He looked from the appendage to his own.

He clasped the almost lifeless fingers with his own, closing them into a fist.

Catch the sand that falls away. Plea the wind to come, to bring it back. Falling from the skies, falling from sanity.

One grain came back. One grain remained: You are the Pathfinder. You will lead.

He dropped the arm and looked out.

Two lay dead in his wake. But he needed to kill one more.

And then he would lead. As he had always done, as he had been trained before. As what ran through his bloodstream as potent as the contagion itself. He would lead.

Chapter Eighteen

The earth began to take Nyx.

Around all sides she felt the mud devouring her, bringing her to her origins to be reborn. Sinking, she looked away from the sky to the marsh. As all hope was about to be drowned, her gaze became lassoed by the hint of color vividly dancing before her. It appeared in transfixion against the background of gloom, the metaphor spoke of by the Fisherman: The Dragon's Mouth. The orchid, Arethusa.

The orchid's pink hues and purple shades inspired her. Against all odds it stood. Alone surrounded by the dismal. However, if it grew against an array of colorful blossoms, its own singular beauty would be lost in oversight. It was vibrant partly because of its background, the forlorn despondency of the swamp. And yet it still bloomed.

She was alone now. Her only companion was desolation. Her spirit and strength could persist, particularly because of the morose that surrounded her. If society still reigned, she would be the malignancy, caged as the rat. But in this apocalypse, she bloomed. She could never be unrestricted among the soldiers; their steps dictated where she would step. Their words upon her ears would shape and mold her. Their sights would dominate her own. And that was not who she was.

As the sole orchid reached for the sky despite, and even because of, the bog, she did the same. Struggling at first to be released, she crawled from the suffocating mire.

She stood. She stripped off her defiled clothes. These were badges of society, embroiled with filth. She sought for release once more. Nude. Unencumbered. As on the beach, when the feeling on her flesh was the wind alone and not the tapestries of man. The savagery of her mind shimmered; almost inhuman in its quality. For she was 'something else' as in the scientist's prose. Not as the other humans were, but one uninhibited. One who was wild. One who was free. Even more so than the Chaots, for the disease did not control her, it did not infect her. Rather, it was her own biology. It was who she was, without influence.

Again she ran. Albeit, this time not with rage suppressing her footfalls and not with sorrow dampening her soul. Rather she ran simply to run. She ran to feel the wind against her skin and through her hair. The peregrine falcon found her and flew besides her. This time not to hunt, but simply to fly.

All that happened was a mirage of the thoughts, a reality that contained no real truth. It was in the mind where reality existed, transformed as we wish. And even in a thought, we can influence the heavens, in the quantum flux of the universe. And it was as she did, influence the heavens, influence the earth. Distant growls rang as melodies to her ears, those of the Chaots, those who had lost the essence of what it was to be human. As awe was found in a lion's roar, and a child's cry, it was now found in the unrepressed abandonment of the id. Her legacy.

The Chaots were no longer the undesired, for they were a part of her. They came to be because of what she was. The only words written by the researcher that haunted her: procured and subsequently released. By whom?

It did not matter now. Not when sorrow and freedom both tore in contrasting harmony within her soul.

Still she ran.

Running liberated her. Without stopping to catch her breath, she continued. Panting, she seemed to first die with exhaustion, then be reborn in her second wind. It was the only thing that clarified her mind with a precision of thought lacking both doubts and fears. Now she was bare, within and without. Her own abandon was what had saved her. Her own abandon was what damned her and all of humanity.

Chapter Nineteen

If not for her quick and unpredictable gait, the Chaots in the marshlands would have surrounded her. Running wild kept Nyx from being torn limb by limb by the lions of misfortune. Though they could not infect her because she was the carrier, they could still ravage her. The Chaots would not care that she was their creator. But one cannot catch the uncatchable—until it stops.

And finally, she did stop.

She approached an inlet of water, signaling hope that the ocean was close. The inlet also provided a cove for fishing. Hunger lurked as the shadowed meal darted beneath the rapids. Hunger akin to when she had first walked along the beach; hunger that, in light of her origins, stood for interpretation as much more than the simple need for a meal.

Breaking a branch above, she fashioned it into a spear by sharpening the edge with her knife. She smiled as she did so, remembering the

Fisherman, her muse in times such as these. Bringing her feet into the running waters, a chill crossed her spine while welcoming the revitalizing depth. She lowered herself and began to hunt among the fish. Did the Fisherman anticipate that his wisdom would be necessary in these moments. Not only had his words offered advice in fishing, his guidance often spread to realms beyond the hunt. She needed him, more than he knew. More than even she could have predicted.

Especially now, for a Chaot was closing in around her unannounced, hunting in his own right. What she would never know was that others waited to see the outcome. The Chaots who had survived the encounter with the soldiers watched in the cover of the trees. And their leader, the bronze-eyed Pathfinder, stood among them. His eyes pierced the forest, looking out to observe.

Underwater, she was unconcerned about what happened above. The current of the cove mimicked the winds as they invigorated her. The fish at first fled, but she presented no threat and they became unheedful of her. In that moment she lashed out, the spear piercing the scales in an unforgiving attack. She had neither the luxury of enjoying her victory nor savoring her meal, for as soon as she struck, so did the Chaot.

Swift splashes interrupting the currents sent all the fish scattering. The brutal charge of the Chaot caused her to drop the spear. Emerging for a breath, she paused only for a second as she saw what disturbed the waters. Only one Chaot attacker, but she could not underestimate his threat. The infected male was tall and muscular. She went under again in hopes to retrieve her spear from the bottom in order to attack.

She grabbed the submerged branch that formed her weapon. As she retrieved it, the Chaot attacked again under the water. He sank his teeth into her calf. Tremors of agony stabbed her; she dropped the spear in reaction and pried the Chaot from her. His bite loosened, and he distanced himself, preparing for another assault. She would not wait. The innocence and fear that hindered her in the caves dissipated; the abyss no longer frightened her. She knew who she was, the maker of the beast. And the creator can also destroy.

She kicked the Chaot's forehead, stopping the oncoming attack. His mouth opened in a momentary shock, releasing oxygen and thereby changing his motive from attacking to getting back to the surface to replenish his air. This gave her a crucial break. Swimming down, she grabbed her spear once more and turned to the Chaot. With fury he was diving down again. He did not meet his prey though, rather he encountered a predator. Nyx rammed the spear forth to hit the oncoming hulk, using his momentum against him. It impaled his eye and entered his skull. Instantaneously, the Chaot met death.

Red tinted the cove's water as she swam to the surface.

The Pathfinder smiled from his perch above. Nyx proved worthy, and would serve well besides him. But before his claim could be made, the others came.

In the last moments after her kill, Nyx remembered pulling herself to the marsh's shore. Her calf bleeding from the assault. A dart flew from the distance, implanting itself in her side. A blurred haze replaced the acute pain. Black rolled across her sight, but before all went numb she saw the shadowed figures emerge from the forest. They came upon all sides of her sedated form, lifting her body from the marshes.

Fighting unconsciousness, she saw the silhouette of the ones who took her. Even though sounds exploded around her, each gunshot refrained from touching her. Everything was dreamlike, as the veiled men engaged in battle with a small number of Chaots. But it was not a battle to the death, but one to capture her and then to flee.

Before the darkness encased her mind, she saw her captors. She did not see the familiar faces of the Thalassic soldiers nor the decrepit stares of Chaots. Instead the features were expressionless, covered in black armor and respirators that hid their entire faces. She saw only eyeless, expressionless stares looking toward her.

Then there was nothing.

Nyx opened her eyes, letting in the light. Stark blank walls decorated with only a mirror surrounded her. Dressed in loose-fitting white pants and tunic, the only other cloth on her was a bandage wrapped around the Chaot's bite on her leg. Several people clothed in biological protective suits hovered in the room. They did not even look human, but simply an extension of the medical devices around her. A suited man stood near, checking the vitals marked on the machine besides her. He said nothing to the waking subject, rather he regarded her as a thing, jotting down notes before walking outside the room with the others.

For now, her only company: her own reflection. She had never seen herself, other than the ripples the waves offered her of a distorted image. But now a mirror embedded in the wall cast back a clear portrait to her.

She wrinkled her nose to see the response. The two dimensional depiction wrinkled its nose as well. She remembered the myth of Echo, who had been trapped and restricted to be only a voice resounding what she heard and nothing else. And now Nyx stared at another, trapped as well, only able to echo the images placed before it.

She tried to get up, to leave this room of white. But as she moved, she found herself tethered to the small cot with padded chains. The range of movement only allowed her to sit and lie.

The door locked and secured. The air trapped and inert. The ventilation self-contained in sterilization and purification. No wind came from within, nor from without of the room.

When one catches the wind in a jug and cork, it is no longer the wind. It ceases to exist.

Her soul screamed in desolation, but outwardly she remained silent. Her phobias surfaced in the confining walls. Not solely in the tangible but in memories. Not memories of the specific, but of familiarity. Though she would not let this be the end—she would not surrender to the whims of others. She coveted only the capricious impulses of her own hand and not in this prison of another's will.

She will fight. Timing though will dictate her rebellion.

Hours passed. Only the phlegmatic beep of the surrounding apparatus sounded. In her sight the barren walls stood, decorated by the impassive. The mirror brought slight animation to the cell in its light reflections. One could not even envision if it were day or night. No window enlightened her, no understanding of the outside let in. But feel ... she opened herself up to discern slight undulations. They rocked in rise and fall all around.

Before she could question the origin of the shifts, a loudspeaker echoed a monotone voice. Words without the face of humanity arose. Though the initial phrase held concern in meaning, it was with disdain in proclamation. "Alone in the woods? That is not safe considering what we have invested in you."

"Allow me to welcome you home to the Scipian," he continued. "Do you remember me? I am Commander Triton." The voice shaped a place: The Scipian, and seized a name: Triton. Yet the voice was merely a faceless ghost to her, playing god while hiding without spine enough to face her. "Tell me what you have done, for surely you did not succeed in what we set you out to do."

What did he set me out to do, she wondered, uncertain of the meaning behind his words. She could not remember having been here, but she could guess it was the same place that used her—those who had procured the prion. That had created the weapon which brutalized the world. These people must have taken the photograph of her found in the laboratory.

"When I first laid eyes on you, I knew that you held the answers," his voice, though still arrogant had sorrow in it. "Your genetics and what was dormant within you was an unstoppable prion. Perfect in every way. What we call Drakōn mund. What gave rise to the Chaots."

He spoke of her perfection, not as human but as an inanimate tool.

"Why am I not like them?" she asked, though was unsure if she spoke of the Chaots or the humans.

"Our scientists discovered that the prion is not fully dormant in your mind. Sections of your brain are under its infliction. You were spared from the full ramifications visible in the others, possibly since you have been exposed to the prion since in the womb and so your brain adapted, creating neural pathways that typically are not present," he answered. "And it could be an adaptation of the prion, to facilitate its propagation and form a symbiotic relationship with you."

To have your deepest, clandestine questions of your soul ripped from you and answered, left Nyx silent. She had never spoken to anyone of her affinity for the Chaots. It was as if Triton dared to look too deep, raping her conscience as the folder's contents had. All her questions were answered in such simplicity. Yet hints of truth still offered the romantic. He confirmed what the research compound had unearthed. She spawned the new race, the new era. The goddess, the creator of the Chaots, lay within her, chained by her remaining humanity. If that would shatter, what would be left?

Triton also reasserted her part, pivotal to the genocide of a species. She brought the downfall of humanity. She was responsible for the fall of society and the death of many. How did she feel because of that? How could she feel? It was difficult to find the remorse. The scope was so grand and she was far removed from it. She could not feel sorrow for the deaths of those she never met, a society that she had never known. And even more so for a society who had abhorred her.

"You would bring about the demise of a corrupt government, of a corrupt people."

"Why?" A question formed from puzzlement of how one would wish to devastate his own kind, though she said it not in horror but in curiosity. She spoke toward the mirror, the sole response her own reflection. Was there even another beyond the glass, or was it to hallucinations she spoke? The question asked to Triton, to herself, to everyone. To no one.

"Ha! Why you ask?" he laughed, though as he continued his tone grew contemplative, as if she were a collaborator rather than a prisoner. "Would you not? To end the rules that another made, to end a society that is fundamentally flawed, to be able to start again and bring freedom rather than unrealized enslavement."

She could not disagree with his rationale, but despite him fulfilling his goals she still heard sadness. She felt the depths of his reasoning extended deeper than what he said. But she understood the surface of what he said. For even she would fight to destroy any rules imposed on her. Maybe this made her evil as he. The face from behind the mirror spoke, but yet the voice was not the ultimate foe. For it was her blood that had damned humanity, an antagonist to herself, written as if in a fantasy. In her death, salvation could be found. In her life, the living were condemned.

All she could do now was let him talk, let him tell of his plans. Coil in silence as he did. Wait. And when the time dictates, then he will perish as the rest of them had.

"However, if your prion, the Drakōn mund, worked as we expected, the attack would be self-contained. We did not expect the Chaots to survive this long. It was suppose to be a massive decimation. But not of everyone, just enough to get people to question the one world government. To fuel the Uprising's goals so we would have a chance."

"The Chaots were expected to live long enough to fulfill the Uprising's goal, to show the world of the Bavarian's cruelty, but then die off," Triton said though his voice faltered. "As with nature, we learned it is unpredictable. And nature always finds a way to prolong and propagate."

A weapon too virulent for containment. The uninhibited could not be inhibited.

"You though, were unneeded after the era of Chaos began. Until recently."

Nyx sat in silence, letting him continue his story. Though, all the while she scanned the room. The enclosure shrank at every moment that passed.

"Recently the last remnants of the Bavarian Coalition, an undersea establishment of Thalassic, came to the surface. I cannot have them bring the one world government back, for all of this would be in vain. It is impossible to infiltrate them because of their secure location under the Atlantic. The only way would be from the inside. This is why we decided to again put you to use."

"A walking time bomb. They would not be able to understand the threat you posed, for you function as a, more or less, capable human. And you would not be wary of your role, for we gave you a memory blocker. Once inside, sooner or later you were bound to scratch one's hand, contaminate some food or what not, and then no more Thalassic. That is another trait your prion has over Kuru and Mad Cow. It is virulent and unforgiving in its transmission. Just like CWD, the Chronic Wasting Disorder, from where it's origins were traced. Even your salvia has the infectious prion within it."

"Yet you did not go into their society. This time, however, we will see."

This time. Again they planned to send her from the dragon's mouth, a flame entrenched soul to inflict her danger to all. A Trojan horse, the innocence of her persona hiding the devastating finale of the aquatic society. And again her memories would most likely be erased, damned to lose all that she was. Though without the anchors of the past, she could again live in the moment. But she did not want that. For it would not be her choice to forgo the recollections of her friendships. Her fate would not be in her hands. Rather it was as if she was a puppet, a maddened scientist as her puppeteer. She would not allow Triton to pull the strings; she would sever them even if it meant to cut her own thread of life rather than allow the Fates to do so.

But guarded and secure, she could do nothing away from the faceless eyes that discerned her every movement.

"Why do this?" she asked. But he did not answer. In the silence was an emptiness that answered.

Chapter Twenty: Triton

Fifteen years previous: In the asylum

Glaucus, a young boy of six, walked besides his dad, hand in hand, to see his mother. Blonde hair framed his rosy cheeks, red from the autumn chill. Every few months he would make the walk down the paths encircled by the pines, each time he would tremble in their shadowy confines. But not this time. He was older, he told himself, time to part with his childish ways.

He made his fingers into an imaginary pistol, and shot within the gloom to scare away the nightmares.

On the hill in front of him, there stood a mansion. More pines surrounded the somber palace, even larger than those who stood guard on the path, serving to mark its age in their gigantic presence, and serving to be targets for his pretend bullets. Built probably around the same time as the trees were planted, the mansion stood in crippling senescence. The dark windows and haunting architecture spoke silently of the tragedy that happened behind those walls: of the insane who resided within and the torture they underwent to cure them from madness.

He hesitated on the stone steps leading up to the mansion's entry. Titans must be guests here, considering the doors lofty appearance, the young boy mused. He wondered if his gun would be able to take them down as well. Convincing himself that he could, he took one step and then another. The door seemed to eat his father who walked in first, Glaucus's hand slipped from his.

Into the mouth to see the insane. His mother. His face wrinkled at the thought, uncertain if he should free his mom from the mansion's mouth, or if he should shoot at her as he had at the pines.

His dad stopped to talk with a nurse about seeing his mother. Glaucus slipped away as he did, his concentration elsewhere as it always was. No one noticed the little boy, no one knew of his getaway. His only companion were snippets of their conversation coming to him as he walked the halls.

"What are the chances Glaucus will inherit his mother's condition?"

The boy walked, listening only partially to the adult conversation. He was glad to get away from his father's watchful presence, his attention being elsewhere. Now he could test his bravery in the inside of this hell hole.

"Because it is an autosomal recessive inheritance and the father was not a carrier, he will be a carrier, but will not develop the disease," the nurse answered. "Your wife was a rare case, having both her parents as carriers. However ..."

Soon the boy was out of sight, but still the conversation echoed in whispers to his ears. He stood on tip-toes to look in the locked rooms that lined the halls. Men sitting in corners, looking at nothing. A woman around his mom's age banging her head against a wall.

"However?" his dad said, urging for the nurse to continue.

"Well, I can't say much due to patient privileges. Also, I'm not a doctor ..."

The little boy stopped at one room. His fingers touched the door's small window to stabilize his tip-toe. He peered in to see a girl near his own age, but maybe a little older than he. The room only had a few fixtures including a bed, sink and toilet, and also had a couple books scattered on the hard tile floor. One had a colorful picture of the Greek gods gracing the cover. One was a children's book.

"Please, this conversation is between us. I just want what is best for my son."

"Okay. I guess I can say that sometimes our knowledge of inheritance and onset of mental disorders is incomplete. For instance, there was a woman—completely normal. However, she became pregnant and it must have triggered something. She went insane and even had to be quarantined due to her aggression."

His father was silent. A pause. What sounded like a hand in a pocket, crumbling of crisp dollars being exchanged. Then the nurse began to continue. Though Glaucus's focus remained on the girl locked behind the door, sealed away in the dismal depths of the converted mansion.

"She died, but we managed to save the child inside her. The strange thing is her daughter is in here now. There was no one left to care for her, nor give her the care she needs. She does not have the insanity of her mother, but still, she is not quite right. All her life has been in semi-quarantine. The doctors and nurses here avoid her, almost as if superstitious. She is, whether it be genetics, our fear or the long term isolation ..."

The caged girl had dark willful hair. Luminous eyes. She looked up from the children's book that was sprawled in front of her and met Glaucus's stare.

" ... like nothing from the ordinary."

Glaucus looked to the book—Where the Wild Things Are. He smiled; he read that book and always thought it to be so bizarre, so unlikely. He always preferred Madeline, even if it was a book about a girl. Raised away from a mother, like himself, and with courage.

The tone of the nurse changed, as if trying to cover her loose lips with a shrug and change of subject. "Not to worry you, just to let you know that we never know how these things will be inherited. We never know what is out there. But I shouldn't of said anything. Your case is not the same; you have nothing to worry about."

Contrived pistol ready, Glaucus brought his fingers into a gun form. He aimed at the girl behind the window pane door. Pressed his thumb down to his elongated fingers, and fired. The little girl looked back, bemused and curious of the other's gesture.

"Interesting. Thank you for your help."

Suddenly uncertain of his action to shoot, and perhaps afraid that his pretend bullet had no effect, Glaucus ran from the caged girl, down the halls, back to reality. But they did not go to see his mom yet. His father had him in tow and walked straight to the office that had the word 'Director' on it. His dad seemed like that calm before the storm you always hear about in movies. And so Glaucus stayed silent, not wanting to get caught in that riptide.

"You have a young girl here without cause?" his dad said to the man who went from an angry red to a flustered pink when he must have realized who his dad spoke of.

"Ah, you speak of Patient Zero. I am sorry but I cannot discuss ..."

"Do you know who I am?" his dad said as he threw down some ids and clearances. The Director of the Asylum fumbled over them, and fell into his chair, defeated looking.

"Commander Triton. Please accept my apologies. I am not responsible for this case. I inherited it. All I know is something got swept under the rugs, some deaths of a patient, a civilian, and doctor. The patient had given birth here, but killed her husband and the doctor in a fit of rage before dying herself due to complications of child birth. The only survivor was the newborn, who we quarantined. She does not have a birth certificate or name for the head of the asylum did not want a paper trail. It is not my fault. Please, do not bring me before the Coalition."

"I will not. But I will take the girl and all the files you have on her and on her parents," his dad said.

"Fine ... fine. It is your problem now, but I warn you nothing good will come from her. She is cursed."

"She is a girl," his dad replied, his tone carried such contempt towards the director's superstition.

Who was this girl, Glaucus wondered, silently in awe of his dad's authority over the man. Was it the one from the cage he was watching? Are they taking her home? Perhaps she can be his new friend now, he thought happily.

Six years previous: Through the swamps

Triton had brought the girl from the Asylum to the Scipian all those years ago. The Scipian was the fleet under his command, and it was the only safe place he could think to bring her after running the tests on her blood and the samples taken from her parents. He had discovered both parents had a variant of CWD, chronic wasting disease, which had never been reported in humans before. The girl had a mutated form of this prion, and he did not know whether she was exposed to it in utero or somehow 'inherited' it from one or both of her parents.

He needed to run more tests to learn more and perhaps help her. All he could do for her comfort was provide her with an extensive education and many books, but he had to isolate her due to the transmittable and infectious nature of the prion.

At least he hoped that the books could bring her an assemblance of freedom, yet he knew that the characters lives were even more restricted than her own. For the characters within each book were trapped between the covers. Forced to live the one life, over and over again. But she could read many and have many lives, even if not free to live her own.

When he had first heard of the girl, he had thought her situation was a fated key to unlock and reverse his wife's collapse. But it was not. Nothing could now help his wife. But maybe he could still help the girl, to somehow isolate the prion and study it further, to see how it interacted with its host. Maybe there would be answers to neutralizing it so she could live a life outside quarantine. But this was not the only thing on his mind for he had a son that he was raising alone and he had learned the Bavarian Coalition's true ambitions.

Now, he and Glaucus trudged through the swamp. Glaucus swinging at each mosquito that took a bite from him, his face held a scornful teenage expression of having to be dragged along by his father.

"Why can't you just go to a flower shop, like a normal person?" He said, sweat dripping down his face as he waved away another blood sucker.

"It is for your mom."

"Dad ... she would not even be able to tell the difference—" but Glaucus held his tongue knowing better before he finished that statement. All the memories that were of his mother were from the asylum, so Triton could not blame him for not understanding why this was important to him. Why the woman who was Triton's wife, would always be his wife in his eyes, despite the disease that now hides much of the person he once knew.

They walked in quiet some more, through the swamplands, searching for the last gift he would ever give his love. Before her deterioration, she had such passions. One of those passion was to photograph flowers, but in her pictures she loved to include greys and gloom as the backdrop. She had said that you could not appreciate the beauty if it was all sunshine. It was through the hardship, that true beauty was found and could be fully appreciated. And why Glaucus and Triton now trudged along in the swamps: to find true beauty amongst the gloom to give his wife.

And to tell his son why it would be the last thing they would give her.

"Glaucus. Your mother ... well, there is nothing we can do as you know. The doctors believe it is time to let go," he said.

He did not want this. He could not lose the one thing in his life that had brought him meaning. Now life seemed like a mimicry. Nothing mattered, and it felt like he was wandering aimlessly without purpose. Even though she was not entirely the same, he had her. He knew she was somewhere inside. Now though, he would have nothing left to hold on to.

"I know Dad. I've seen how she is getting. It's for the best."

Anger ... no it was not anger. It was sadness, was it not, Triton wondered. Sadness filled him with hearing his son's sentiment for it was *not* for the best. None of this was for the best.

"I wish you knew her like I did. I can't tell anymore the memories of a few decades ago versus the memories of yesterday. They seem the same in my mind. Are they not the same? They are all just the past, and the time I impose on those memories is so arbitrary. She is still ..."

What was it he was trying to say? For he knew he sounded crazy. But it was strange how reality was shaped. It was based off of memories but yet what are memories if not just random sparks from neurons. They are not real. And when he loses her, would she even be real anymore, he thought as he stopped walking. ... As he felt himself give up.

"Hey Dad," Glaucus said, a look of confusion crossing his face. He did not understand. He could not. But the confusion was replaced by a confident smile. Glaucus wanted to make his father happy, despite all else. "Let's find this orchid. If it will make mom happy, it is worth these mosquito bites."

Two years previous: The calm before

Word came out among the Bavarian Coalition of a possible bio-agent the Scipian was working with. Now the head of the Coalition, Grand Master Hyperion, sat before him.

Triton clasped his hands together as he looked out from behind his desk. No pictures mounted it. Of course he had family. But Glaucus was now a young man and stationed with him aboard the Scipian's flagship. And his wife ... He could not think about her and stay focused, for without her an emptiness had come within him.

"I know you may harbor resentment. Your honorary removal from the Navy was unfortunate but necessary. The death of a loved one would be quite a blow to any person," Hyperion said.

Triton narrowed his eyes. He understood that Hyperion knew the true reasons of his removal. Not shell shock, but rather rebellion. Triton discovered the truth behind the Bavarian Coalition, to become a power headed by the elite, and fought to expose it. However, Hyperion believed that this dog was now chained. He was not though. Triton had not abandoned those ambitions and instead they had only served to grow more extreme. What Hyperion did not know was he now spoke to the originator and leader of the Uprising. Of course, if his thoughts became words, surely Hyperion would no longer be asking for his help and instead demanding his head.

If only Hyperion knew what would come from the help he asked for.

"All under the bridge. I was an idealist back then; I understand your decision to remove my position. I am just grateful to still be involved with the Bavarian Coalition, even to this lesser extent."

"As you know," Hyperion replied, "the Uprising has been difficult for us to contain. People we can deal with. Ideas we can not. We worry that the disobedience will spread. The nonsense of no governmental involvement in the affairs of the populace goes against what we have built. To finally have the world under our lead as the New World Order and now to have that threatened by a handful of revolutionaries is unacceptable."

"And so you turn to me?" Triton said.

"Yes," Hyperion answered. It was as if his voice played the puppeteer, pulling the strings in a macabre performance. But Triton knew otherwise. "I know the Scipian is in possession of a bio-agent that could exterminate sections of the population in self-contained attacks. Thus the resources and buildings would be preserved, and the viciousness of battle would be easy to cover. We can tell the people it was a natural epidemic. No need to make martyrs of the rebels. And the ideas of self-governing freedoms will be quieted."

The Bavarian Coalition requested a quiet epidemic. He knew he would be forced to comply. However, he would give them something they could not keep quiet, and that would fuel the end of the one world government. It would be extreme, but sometimes radical measures are needed when faced against an otherwise unconquerable adversary. He would give them a weapon that could not be ignored and that would expose the Bavarian Coalition for what they truly were.

"As I am sure your informants have advised you," Triton said, "the bio-agent will be ready soon. The Drakōn mund prion is a perfect weapon."

He spoke of perfection. He knew perfection was something unattainable, for everything had flaws. Beauty is found through imperfections, and for those who do not understand this, satisfaction could never be attained. He learned this through his wife, and he loved her despite and because of everything she had become.

"Tell me about what you have discovered," Hyperion said, and Triton continued explaining the weapon that was discovered within the girl.

"Unlike its close epidemiology to New Guinea's Kuru and variant CJD, it does not have long incubation periods. The period between exposure and symptoms needs to be brief in order to cross the line from dangerous disease to military weaponry. It also presents something new: our enemy will never see what is coming."

So ironic considering who spoke, Triton mused to himself.

"Biological warfare normally centers around viruses, bacteria, fungi and toxins, but a prion would be unexpected. The prion disease never loses toxicity and spreads like a virus. Prions are extraordinary as weapons for unlike the others, they take what humans already contain and use it against them. PrP, cellular prion proteins, exists in all of us. Once a prion disease, which is a misfolded PrP protein, is introduced into the host it will cause a cycle of the other proteins misfolding. The diseased prion basically teaches our healthy PrP proteins how to misfold. And death will come to your opposition."

"Good, and so the Uprising will silently fall. I will send my best to check on your research in the coming months," Hyperion said.

All the cards came down, all the pieces he had lined up even before he realized he was playing. His goal changed from helping the girl to helping society break its chains from the totalitarian world government. He hated that innocents may die, but that was the price of freedom. The Bavarian Coalition would be exposed and the people would fight against them. The path to liberty would be revealed. Even if that path was paved by way of corpses. For you cannot have beauty without the gloom.

One year previous: And through hell

Water crashed against the hull of the Destroyer, though it was not the only thing that crashed against the ship. People. In droves they came, in small boats fleeing the scattered islands of Maine. They thought the islands would provide sanctuary from the outbreak. They were wrong.

Now they hailed the last remnant of protection, the fleet of the Scipian, which stood in the sea as if it were an array of islands in of itself. At first, in a civilized manner they requested entry. Denied, they began to act as if they were already the Chaots, ramming the ships, clawing at them to board. The siege of the seafaring castle had begun.

"Take us further out!" The command was hollered from the side of the Destroyer, followed by gunfire. Each shot landed in flesh, or in water. The ones that hit their targets served to pluck the humans from the ship as if they were no more than blood sucking ticks. And they would be if boarded; the fleet was at maximum capacity, six thousand people. Anymore would only serve to drain them of their resources.

"Don't hit the hull!" Another shout, showing more concern toward the ship itself than another human.

Triton walked to the starboard side of the ship. He dared a look down between his gunmen. Children, the elderly, people of every race, age, and sex, all trying to climb aboard to their salvation, using ladders and throwing grappling hooks. They did not help each other. In a frenzy they used what they could to try to breech the hull, standing on whatever —and whoever—they could. He knew that what he had done, and what he was doing now by not allowing them aboard, would haunt him. But the chasm between humanity and the Chaots did not seem all that great when he looked down to see the desperation of those trying to board.

Situated along the ships' edge stood a barricade of his followers. They traced the ship's edge looking out over the railing. Every man and every woman that could fit along the ship's circumference aimed a rifle over the side, assuring no one could breach their castle.

Every person, that is, except one.

"This is not right," Glaucus said over the gunfire. He flanked the side of Triton, anger rose as if he were a Spartan besides the Persian King. "Take those aboard who you can. We can find safety for them on another island, further from shore."

"You know of the risk of infection," Triton said to his son. "It would not be saving them, but damning us all."

He looked over to his son. Glaucus was his humanity. Though they both struggled with the past, Glaucus had somehow managed to come out unscathed and willing to see the good in people. All Triton could see was the deaths. His parents, his wife. His brothers in arms. But Glaucus allowed him to see life another way whenever he looked at the man who shared his wife's features.

"Let them board," Glaucus said. His tone changed from anger to reason, the low drum of his voice matching the engine of the ship.

"Very well. Come to the bridge and we will discuss this," Triton responded. Perhaps he was acting unreasonably about the risk and should allow the rescue of these people. Of course proper quarantine procedures would have to be put in place, he could leave that up to Glaucus.

"There is one more thing I need to discuss with you," Glaucus said as the two climbed the stairway towards the bridge. "I sent information on Patient Zero to a research laboratory on the mainland. I hoped the information would help them find a cure."

"I know," Triton said. There was nothing that came and went off this ship that he was not aware of. He had saw the information his son sent and allowed its passage. He knew they would not find a cure, for the Scipian would have found it if there was one. However, he did not want to squelch the hope that Glaucus held on to that they would.

Glaucus paused, as if registering that Triton was not upset over what he had done. Did he think of me as a monster, Triton wondered. Have I fallen so irreversibly?

"That brings me to Patient Zero," Glaucus continued. "She is imprisoned here, but I believe she should be no longer. She has served the Scipian's purpose. Grant her freedom."

"And allow her to walk among us, infecting us?"

"There are preventative measures we could take. If she were aware of the ways of transmission, she could prevent them."

"You are as the mythos behind your namesake," Triton responded, shaking his head. "Glaucus: the sea god who fell in love with the beautiful nymph Scylla. Despite his love, his actions brought about her doom, transforming her into a monster who destroyed many."

He continued, pausing at the door to look back at Glaucus, "I know you act for the sake of others, but your rights will only bring about wrongs."

"I wanted to ask, Dad, is she the one from the asylum who you took in?"

"You remember that?" Triton asked, seeing an almost boy-like wonder in his son. He had wanted to help the girl, but no matter the intentions, the outcome was something he would have to live with.

Opening the door, he allowed Glaucus to proceed first. Though he regretted it the instant he walked in.

Three sides of the bridge were windowed, the blue sea was all that could be seen. No havoc existed outside, only the heavens and the deep blue realm of Poseidon. But the ocean's charm did not captured his eyes, rather the Pathfinder, Jason, stole his sight. The Chaot of his own creation jumped on Glaucus, teeth ripping into his throat.

Triton swung a closed fist, connecting with the Chaot's jaw, throwing him off of Glaucus. Jason staggered back several feet, and continued to withdraw to out the window. Triton neglected to see the Chaot's atypical behavior, retreat rather than attack. The only thing he could focus on was his entire life pour away as the blood flooded from his son's body.

Triton propped Glaucus up in his arms. It was too late, the bite severed the main artery and he was bleeding out. Triton's hands were now soaked red with the blood of his only tie to this earth. A question struggled to be answered behind Triton's rising anger: was it indeed Jason who had killed him, or rather Triton himself for making Jason into what he was?

It was impossible how Jason acted, Triton tried to reason. Chaots know no vengeance, harbored no memories. Yet he swore that a shimmer of recognition lay in his eyes, and swore that a smile elated the Pathfinder's lips as he attacked.

He sat speechless. Jason took one last look at Triton, as if to say that now they are even, before escaping out the window and down the bridge's tower. He had escaped his cell aboard the ship in the pandemonium, had waited until he could kill the one shred of humanity left in Triton, the same fate as Triton had bestowed on the Pathfinder.

He had nothing. Even if society would renew, Glaucus would not be apart of it and be forgotten. That, he thought, was the one thing everyone desired. To not be forgotten. Death was not itself feared, but rather being consigned to oblivion was. That you did nothing, effected nothing, was nothing. And so he made a vow to the fallen. He would not be nothing nor allow Glaucus's death to be nothing, he thought as he took his son's hand in his once more and for the last time.

Chapter Twenty-One

Walls surrounded Nyx, obstructing her view. The repression of confinement was more atrocious compared to even the Chaots themselves. At least the Chaots were tangible. She could run. She could fight. But here she was alone, locked in a cage with the key thrown away. The claustrophobia of oppression was now her enemy. This she had to fight.

She lay awake, fastened to the bed, starring wide at the ceiling above. She wished her thoughts could pierce through the material and again see the sky. The path that waited here was a loop, bringing her back to the shores without memory. Maybe the Fisherman would be there again, to carve her path to deliverance. And this time, she may succeed and bring Hades himself to Thalassic. Hell then would rule in the land of the living and into the water's depths.

She could not let that happen, and she knew why.

Leander.

One answer to that simple question. All else remained dubious, but she knew his heart still beat. If it had stopped, her own heart would have crumbled. She believed such, even if it was only a sentimental fairytale. But if she could lie to herself that indeed he lived, it somehow made it easier to get through this predicament. Somehow it would not be farfetched that she could again be a wayfarer in her steps alongside Leander, and not a captive in the Scipian, not a pawn to the Kings.

"Tomorrow will be the day."

The voice spoke through the speaker, sifting through her consciousness as if it did not belong to a human form. He used her, but eventually she would have been unleashed even without his intrusion. Surely it would have happened, unhurried in its own time. In the end the Chaots would spring forth from the kin of chaos, from Nyx, and be the next era of humanity. Blank slates heralded no mercy, for evolution was a force that beckoned the tabula rasa of humankind to be crushed under the force of nature's dissonance.

However, he was the one responsible for her imprisonment, the one who used her for his own ambitions. She looked at what she believed to be a pseudo mirror, wondering with what ease the glass would break and if Triton was standing behind it. Then she could expose him to what he longed for others, but not for himself.

As if reading her mind, he said, "I would not want you to worry; I am well protected from what lives in you."

They were so similar, and yet so different. Both desired a change from the status quo, but both disagreed on intention and inevitable destination of humanity. Both had dragons curled behind their masks of humanity—monsters ready to strike. Nyx's was a part of her, beyond her control, the Drakōn mund inherent in her blood. But Triton forged his own evil, and soon it would be clear the true nature of the beast.

"What lives in me will live. You are unable to tame what is meant to be," she said.

"I lost everything. I will not lose you."

She did not understand what he meant, but perhaps that was why he caged her, she thought. But even caged she remained willful, though how long would it take for her to be a mere echo of what she once was? As the beasts in zoos are just a mirror of their former selves, her fate could be this as well.

Oh Hector, she thought, why are you not here to put a bullet in me as I swore to you? Though what I abhor is much different than what you do. I do not fear the fate of the Chaot; I fear the fate these humans impose.

She closed her eyes, imagining her future. In the age of beasts, elders would no longer reign. Only the strong. Only the warriors. Considering most laws were set due to the inclination of elders, she began to yearn for natural selection to interfere. Triton should be dead, and all of his kind who were decrepit, caught in the ways of the past.

Nature will find a way.

She opened her eyes with a newfound strength. Although he acted under the pretense of controlling her, he would understand that she had rebellion within her. This would be difficult for him to curtail. If and when she dominated, all would be lost for him.

She had hope. It was what the soldiers clung to, and what she now embodied. In her sights were the walls, but in her heart a spirit remained, unsettled by control. Caged. But not for long. Not forever. She would fight to be free and no man-made walls would stop her.

A smile tugged at her lips, as the thoughts of such fury sketched inside her mind. Hubris brought many down before, greater kings than he. Will Zeus's vengeance bring tragedy to Triton as well? Let the god's hand take no mercy, let Chaos's daughter again run in the winds so wild.

"I did not mean for this," Triton said, breaking her expectations that he would speak with arrogance. "Everything fell apart. The Bavarian Coalition targeted more areas than I and my intel knew they would, causing the prion to be world wide. The prion itself was more virulent than imagined and we were not able to control it."

"And what was your true intention?" she asked, wondering what the truth was behind this dream of an utopian society. That was the flag he railed those of the Scipian under, but was it just a means to the end.

"I admit. I wanted chaos to come. I wanted such aftermath that forced the people to act rather than be complacent. It was the only way I could make them see their prison, which was otherwise invisible to them. The only way I could give them hope. Something I could not give to my wife," he added quietly before continuing. "Something I can now no longer give to my son. The loss destroyed me, but I rose. And humans will rise in the end."

"You will fall," she said. "Despite your idealism, humanity already crumbled. It already fell to pieces."

The breakdown of society clear, for no longer did morals triumph even in those not infected. It was a time of the wild through and through. But he claimed too much, and the time of the wild would be hers alone.

"I know. I was responsible. And the only thing I can do is try to make amends, to rebuild," he said.

"But it did not fall by your doing, Triton. It was I." It was she. She spoke to infuriate the leader of the Scipians, but as those words left her mouth she released the haunting truth of them. She was responsible for the cessation of society. Soon to become the decimation of a species. She knew what she should feel. But sorrow did not come. No woe. Who was the monster then between the two? "Humanity will not rise again. The Chaots will."

"They are an evolutionary dead-end though," he responded.

She remembered the baby in the arms of the Chaot. Nature will find a way. And indeed, it had. "It can be inherited. Do not lie to yourself, Triton."

He paused, doubt replacing his certainty. "A non-mendelian, non-genetically encoded trait. If your prion follows an unconventional pattern of Darwinian evolution ..."

"Our team had believed the Drakōn mund to be an acquired prion only. But there are genetic prions. There is a gene in our DNA that codes for the creation of PrP. If the disease could change that gene itself and cause mutated or misfolded PrP to be created, then this could pass on genetically," Triton said. The realization that the world could permanently be altered passed through his voice as he spoke.

271

"A new species will rise," she said, "and you will not be able to stop it."

Triton did not leave but still sat behind the one way mirror. Looking at her, studying her every move. He had lost his wife to madness, lost his son due to his own actions, and was now losing himself. But as he looked at her he wondered if he indeed thought of her as a daughter? In some sense an extension of Glaucus, for his son's last words were of freeing her. And he had cared for her for a large part of her life, since he had found her in the asylum. He sat, unable to move away from such a paragon, such a weapon that she devastated all that she touched, but could she be a savior as well?

Time elapsed. Nyx was alone now. The weight of imprisonment charred upon her mind. What would she give to run again within the swamps. To feel the mud sink underneath her footfalls, ever compressing but never-lasting in their allure. To let the breeze sweep her hair in its temperamental caress, pulling her to where it desired. But the air held stale, the walls a prison.

She heard a melody pulsing against the walls, lulling her to sleep. The rest allowed a release from her introspection, and brought her to a time of innocence as she dreamed.

Days fell away to bring her back to the waterfalls. "Then live," Leander whispered as the time diverged to an alternate reality. Steps down a path not taken. The screams from the camp did not interrupt the two, which once brought their ultimate separation. Rather, Leander leaned close, letting his hand travel through her wayward hair. His breath sent such sweet caresses to her skin. Lips met. Souls intertwined.

And she found more than lust. Something deeper. Something unexpected. It was love. The kiss subtle against her lips, and in it she found what she always ran toward but never could grasp.

"Leander," a confused murmur left her mouth, not understanding what it was between them.

"Do not question," her own words repeated to her but from his lips, "do not be anything but here."

But I am not here. The rigid surface of the examining table that served as her bed seemed to chew upon her dreams, bringing reality to what should be fantasy.

"Why did you leave me?"

A question asked of what had not occurred in her dreams. Time was skewed within sleep; though, Leander answered as if knowing exactly what she meant. "Because I love you. And though you always doubted it, I do know you. And that is why I left. I knew you enough to understand that I could never have you. I could never kiss you."

"Kiss me again. Have me now," she answered in defiance.

His smile lightened her dream at such a request, his hand again to her hair. But rather than the first time he had met her in the town, his fingers did not tie her unkempt hair to calm but instead took a strand and brought it forth—misplaced. His gesture made her move forward to feel his lips against hers.

He did know her. And though she wished to deny it, she loved him.

Closing her eyes, she leaned back to feel his mouth stray from her lips and go along her chin down to her neck. His hands fell upon her form. As passions rose under his touch, everything changed. No longer a sweet caress of warmth but of agony. Teeth closed in around her flesh, as excruciation flooded her system. Her eyes opened beholding not Leander, but another. It was what sprung forth from her blood. Chaos.

The Chaot barred his teeth, grinning in self-repulsion, her blood trailing down along his skin.

"No one else but I."

No one else would ever know her except chaos itself in all its dire nature.

No one else ...

She awakened, struggling to forgo the dream. A contrasting medley of passionate fear played in her mind. Nyx longed again to be asleep in order to be with Leander, but was too afraid to close her eyes once more.

Something was different though. So much the same: a racket of beeps emanated from the monitors. The walls stood as perpetual guards. The mirror reflection was of herself in this sterile room. But the shackles around her wrists—not locked. The door—no longer the green beacon blinked subtly as a tell tale sign of its security. No light.

She did not question why. She wasted no time, knowing they would soon discover this fluke. Her stare went subconsciously to the mirror, wondering if Triton sat behind her reflection, cruelly watching the farce in rebuttal to her defiance. But why risk the chance that she would contaminate the Scipian's fleet? She stepped from the metal bed, her bare feet touching the floor as she walked across it to the door. And opened it.

Chapter Twenty-Two

Nyx walked through the unlocked door and into the hall. A hiss sounded. She jumped as a decontamination shower pounded down onto her. It was not meant for loose clothes but rather the suits, and the chemicals stung her skin and lungs. She shut her eyes, hoping to save them from the irritation, and ran to the far side.

Searching for an exit, she reached blindly forward. She clasped the handle at the far end of the hall and pulled it, not knowing if this too would be unlocked. The door opened. She retreated from the spray and to a room that contained supplies. Biohazard suits that were used by the medicinal crew lay arranged along the wall with various sterilizing supplies. It was where they suited up before exposing themselves to her; as if aliens, so separate they were from her.

Another room. Showers burst as she entered; fear that the stringent would again come dissipated as water instead of chemicals sprayed. A mist filled the air, soothing her. For moments she stayed under its stream, letting it take away all that was behind her. The caustic chemicals. The imprisonment. The cell. The past.

The water dripped down her face, the medical johnny became soaked and clung to each curve of her body. But she could not linger, so she moved forth and opened the final door.

A corridor welcomed her. But what more was the breeze. Distant, but present. She followed it, running barefoot over the rigid floors. Dashing left and right, she did not hesitate in the path of the wind that guided her to freedom. The steps she took were strange, as if her body swayed back and forth, oscillations beneath her feet. Could it be an earthquake? The alarm started blazing. Red lights flickered in emergency as if lava surging forth in response to her question. Sounds thundered around her.

Footfalls resounding from the guards came closer and closer. She came to the end of the hall and stepped out. Dark skies greeted her. Trees, sands, even buildings were absent from view. Instead, the nighttime ocean stretched out before her. It pounded in cascades against the steel hull of the surrounding ships and the ship she now stood upon: the Scipian's fleet.

She could no longer run ... could she?

A shot from behind her answered. The bullet whistled by as the men surrounded her. It roused her to action, running forth to jump into the tempestuous seas below rather than be trapped again.

"No!" A familiar voice called out.

The command did not come from the direction of the gunfire, but elsewhere. Nyx was not sure if it was directed at her, or to the men behind her to stand down and stop firing. She recognized the voice, as if from an echo of long ago. But she could not grasp its source. Not only the voice but what she was doing. Running along this deck, looking for freedom. She remembered for moments how she halted before, and how she was determined to have no pause this time. But like awakening to a dream, her memories slipped away forgotten but her resolution remained.

She jumped from the Destroyer. Plunged into the seas below.

Waves collapsed over her head, sucking her down into the depths. Bullets hit the churning waters near to her, ricocheting the sea into a frothing broth. Their target never to be found. A cacophony played around her of waves and ammo, but down below was the quiet, ne'er ending reclusiveness of the abyss.

The tides pulled her down toward the elysian fields of the netherworld. Charybdis dwelled below, the whirlpools of the creature capturing her in their down-pull. Though the need to live drove her to kick up and away. The instinct found in all the living beings; the unbreakable and tenacious will to survive and not surrender to the bearer of dark tidings. Her head broke the surface, but only for a mere second as a wave forced her down, refusing her air. Again she tried, again to fail. Caught in the sea's anarchic torrent; the ocean tossed her asunder as a ragged doll forced into submission. However, her conviction prevailed. Her strokes forced her upwards to break the surface.

She caught sight of the ships grey against the thundering skies. A riptide drove the runaway to safety, taking her out of the enemy's view. The current transformed from a curse beating her downward to a blessing, having facilitated her escape from the bars of the floating prison.

But land was not in sight in the dark, and the storm showed no signs of abating. She only saw a translucent line between the blackness of night and of the ocean. Even the stars did not mark a separation between air and water as their reflections danced upon the rising waves. Did she even swim through the water, but rather the sky? Each hand coming down in stroke to touch the small lights of another world, rippling them into eternity.

Predators feed at night within the waves.

A ghostly reminder of what swam below. Predators ravaged the sea; their hunger akin to her own that night on the shores with the Fisherman.

"Grant me safe voyage," she whispered, but as the waves arched around her, guided by the wind, she quieted in her pray for she no longer yearned for the sands of the shore.

Tranquility within the storm. As one finds wonders in the tempestuous clash of lightning and magic in the tornado swirls, she could only admire the sea's perilous strength. She could not refuse. This was life. Each moment spent in safety's harbor would become forgotten in the grand scope. The mundane and predictable are lost to the memories. What created life were the moments of jeopardy and change.

The moments when we leave the nest, spreading wings for the first time to face danger.

Not to hide. Not to exist.

Not even to run.

But to live.

And life was clearest when the obscurities of death become unmasked.

The waves took her away from all comforts, painting her with a vulnerability that she allowed herself as part of the sea's great energy. The persistent, unfettered ocean itself granted reason, shedding light to life's mysteries. It left her stripped of strength and humanity, but complete and stronger than ever.

She did not know how long the wrath of winds and seas came, but finally it rested. The storm ebbed. The waves quieted, leaving her alone in the stillness. Kicking, energy almost drained, Nyx knew she could not live forever in the ocean's breadth, however it was desired for there always seemed to be others, surrounding her at every turn.

Except here and now.

Silence sung to her. Freedom flowed within the salt-filled sea. One place still on the planet where one could lose themselves: away from humanity and society, what little was left of it.

The dark sky fought for dominion as rays of light pierced it from the horizon. The battle ensued on the sky and sea. Stars divided the wave's crescents, speared by light from Helios' hand. Soon the nightscape lost the battle to the sun, as the perpetual war between day and night was bound to play the conflict eternally. Her eyes, red with the salt, looked over the new dawn in search of land. Cumulus clouds accumulated in the west, the sight of land beneath their shadows. A welcome sight to her, especially with no ship in her view to circumvent her getaway. Maybe while guided by the storm, they had crashed into the outcroppings of rock. A pipe dream, but one could hope.

Triton and those of the Scipian deemed what was best for her, imposing their will upon her. How she wished to forget them, but not the wisdom. The Drakōn mund lived inside her. It proved she was not an outsider, but an accomplice to the era that now unfolded. She was the cause of it all. Either she could scorn herself or embody who she was. She chose the latter.

A confidence in her stroke, she swam toward the shore. She needed solid ground though, no matter her wish to forever swim in the unwavering release. Not simply in the sea, but in life. All this time she sought to be unrestrained, unconfined by the very aspect of living. Though the definition of life was in opposition to absolute freedom: the soul confined within the body. Sustenance and shelter a necessity in order to avoid death's prison.

All this time she had been looking for something that could never be achieved. Pushing away the people she cared for most.

Hector.

Leander.

The latter name whispered out loud, the winds echoing her feelings toward him. Her dreams of the night before danced in her mind. She never wished for love, viewing it as a cage built by emotion. Now though, that cage hinged open.

Just another reason for her to swim faster, to break the tides and find where Leander had gone—if he was still alive. If.

The call of the peregrine falcon signaled land was near. He circled overhead. She wondered if he could see her, if he realized he became her soul. He was boundless by even gravity. His freedom allowed the rest of her to walk earthbound, restricted but free. All she needed was to look up, see the falcon, and lift to the heavens. He was her guide, her guardian, her spirit.

Almost to the shore. It would not come soon enough, even under the watchful eye of the falcon. Something grazed her leg, stopping her in her tracks. The movement felt sensual, though desire did not come. A chill did. The streamlined shadow below her highlighted by the rising sun depicted a clear profile; the predator she had once warned the Fisherman of now hunted her. A shortfin mako shark swam in the water depths.

The Fisherman had told her to blend to nature, to become one with the wild. She followed his words, remaining calm. She moved her hand underwater to the bandage that wrapped her calf and made sure it was secure. But then again she felt the shark brush against her. The metallic skin felt like sandpaper, grating her hand. Her presence lured it to turn and come again. Though she hoped it would not attack and knew the shark could only be met with its own tributes: strength and curiosity. If it sensed the vulnerable, it would strike.

But sound broke her composure.

Yelling from the shore.

The deep sound distracted her. Her body trembled along the fin of the passing mako. Her breath quickened and deviated from the surroundings as she wondered who called out. Within this falter, came the wrath.

The shark's body under her turned from his course; the departure from the norm of the ocean now clear. Parting the sea, the shark came as a raptor in pursuit. Instinctually she moved in order to avoid the more brutal force of the shark's jaws. The teeth barely grazed into the skin of her calf; one predator's mark replacing another's. Only a muffled scream pierced her lips before the waters covered her face in the downward pull of the predator.

Your life in another's hands, whether it be a lover or demon, human or Chaot, falcon or shark, brings you closer to them. But she would fight for their roles to be reversed. Escape being the prey by becoming a predator. Act bold. Fearless. She tried not to panic as the shark pulled her, for that would mean her death. He had a superficial hold on her body, teeth scarcely breaking her skin. The mako's teeth were not serrated; they did not cut into her flesh so much as grasped her, and in that she found the advantage. She attacked, plunging her hand to the beady eyes: bloodlust alongside beauty looking at her in the black orbs. The mako did not rely on the nictitating membrane, hence its unprotected eyes were left victim to her fingers as she jabbed him. Blood sprouted from the sockets causing the shark's body to grow rigid, skewed within a sharp pain. Its clasp over her body loosened, and the serpentine creature doubled over in agony. Its tail coiled back, whipping out and the jaws released her.

Swimming up, she broke the surface and breathed. Was it over, she thought looking for a sign of the mako. Life relied upon imperfection. Evolution needed it. But what happened when imperfection became perfection? The mako shark had evolved from its predecessors one hundred million years ago, even before the great white sharks appeared, which may of even spawned from the mako shark. For millions of years of evolution to be deflected by a singular attack was not likely.

She saw the dark figure again, darting underneath, signaling the fight was not over, it would not retreat without a true test of abilities. Stalking not with its blinded sight but now with its electrosensory perception, it swam toward her. Born in the womb to attack, now outside the shark allowed the sense to lead him to its victim, each of her movements causing electric impulses, signaling location to the carnivore.

Kicking outward, she struck the nose of the shark. Its course changed away. Seeing the retreating form skid within the depths again, she began to swim to the shore. Exhaustion was making her strokes heavy. But she had to swim, for who knew when the mako would make the next round of attack. The water blurred around her, consuming her. She saw nothing. She heard nothing. Silence only below in the waters. Only a blackness threatening to encompass her life. Lost within the darkness, the light no more. She fought against this, trying to keep her head above the water.

Freedom does not come with death.

Rather it is the most oppressive prison that one could face.

Chapter Twenty-Three

Skin, salty and wet. Nyx no longer felt the waves; rather, she lay on the grit of the sand. She felt pounding on her chest. A device covered her lips, pumping the needed oxygen. Water plunged up through her mouth, pouring to her side. Fresh air filled her lungs.

The Fisherman stood before her.

He had swum in a fury through the sea after having called for her, dividing it as Poseidon himself could never have done in order to get to her in time. Such fear had risen from him, concern that a bullet had hit her or that the sea's fury would drown her. But the storm ebbed quickly and he had seen her. But he also saw the shark's fin behind her. He felt as if he were separated from her by limitless miles. Each stroke served to lessen the distance, but not by enough as he saw her begin to sink in a wave of blue.

He dove, swimming underneath the crashing tides. Luck served him, as his hand circled round her body and pulled her up. The shark lurked to the side, only having temporary retreated to wait for its prey to weaken. Breaking the surface, trying to pose her chin up to divert the ocean waves from her mouth, he fastened a life preserver around her. And then he saw the shark coming. Without remorse, without restriction, fighting for its meal against the perceived competitor. The Fisherman reached for his blade. It would not be the mundane and unchallenging that came to clash against him. The shark served as a true match for him, unlike the fish of the shore.

Instinct ruled them both, instinct to attack, instinct to protect, instinct to hunt.

The shark abruptly pivoted in its path, turning away from the two, and thrusted its crescent-shaped caudal fins side to side. The propulsion rammed into him, parting him from Nyx. Then, the mako turned back, its dorsal fin parting the waters, heading straight toward him.

Staying vertical in the waters, the Fisherman rotated out of the shark's path just before contact. To the side of the mako, he reached out and jerked his hand into its long gill slits as it passed. He dug deep into the sensitive flaps, tearing into them. The shark spasmed, throwing him off. It turned to attack again; still vertical, he grasped onto the shark's head. It could not bite, for its nose was in the way, preventing it from wrapping the jaws around him. All it could do was whip itself in the waters, trying to get loose from the Fisherman's death grip.

This time, he used his hand holding the dagger in his attack. This time, he would not go for the gills.

He plunged the blade into the predator's skull, into its brain, killing it.

Indeed there were predators in these waters, and he was the most fierce of all.

Now the Fisherman kneeled near Nyx on the beach. His skin was dusted with salt from the ocean, water droplets fell from his bare shoulders. Her focus cleared. She saw the Fisherman, a mirage, an oasis in the desert. Was he there, she questioned, or a figment of her fevered imagination. She strayed back within the black, not of death but sleep. In the arms of Morpheus, the god of sleep and dreams, she drifted as the Fisherman assessed and treated her wounds before carrying her to the shade.

"Don't leave me," she said. A plea to his shadow as she slipped in and out of consciousness. Through her sleep, she felt the calloused hand press periodically against her forehead as if to check her temperature. Sharp pains came as nightmares as he stitched the bite. And through her dreams, she reached up, searching to find her savior. The Fisherman's hand enveloped her own, as silence brought her back to an undisturbed rest. Yet as she fell deeper within the dreamscape, chaos reclaimed its interrupted hold on her mind. Haunting her, calling her, deriding her.

Her dream transpired as reality. She was the key to society's end. Drakōn mund spilled from her blood. The Dragon's wrath unleashed. She was the beginning to the realm of chaos.

Darkness reigned. The Chaots came.

Nyx awoke with a start, breaking the nightscape of her dreams. Sweat dripped down from her forehead. She called for the Fisherman and reached for his presence.

But only the waves resounded in response; only the ocean breeze reached back to her outstretched hand.

"Fisherman," she called again. Fisherman, his true name unknown to her. She knew it was pointless though, he had left. The only trace that he had been there was the new bandage wrapped around her leg. The hospital gown replaced with a black shirt and combat pants. The Fisherman's knife and holster that Leander had given her was by her side. That she also sat in the shade and not drowned in the abyss testified to the presence of the enigmatic figure.

The pines reached forth to the skies, untouched by the disease that had eroded the human race. But it was what stood fearless within their branches that caught her attention: the peregrine falcon.

From its perch she saw its enduring gaze upon her, a quiet guardian watching over her.

"I thought I would find you here."

Hector. His voice came through the underbrush, his figure dense against the leaves that clung to him. The sound made the falcon fly off, going higher to the top of a white spruce tree. Hector emerged from the forests, dirt covered, though his eyes shone through. A smile broke her misgivings, as she limped across the beach to reach the one she had presumed dead. But before she could throw herself into his embrace, she stopped. She looked at him as if seeing him for the first time.

"But how?" she asked.

How are you alive? How did you find me? So many questions in one.

"I came to the shores that you first spoke of when we found you, in hopes you would do the same. Back to where you said you first began to remember. I fought death to come here, to come back for you."

"Where did you go after ..."

The sentence left incomplete. She did not need to speak it for it to be understood. After the scientific compound, after the Chaots attacked and destroyed the safety of the group. After the death of Megaira.

"The Chaots may be nasty, but hell if I would give up without a good fight. But when I got out I could find no trace of you, so I was going to go back to the Thalassic to find Leander, to see the situation for myself, to see Dio. But I was stopped by one of Thalassic's waiting party, who were sent shoreside to escort us back down. I was warned of the circumstances. Diomedes is dead."

He stopped and looked at her. She saw the wars reflected in his face, the fights he had endured. And the frightening prospect that the next fight would be his last. And the next fight was clear, it would not be against the Chaots, but his own kind.

"Leander is imprisoned. Soon he will face death as well if his sentence is carried out. He faces execution for going against orders, mutiny, and endangering life aboard the Thalassic."

She stood silent, faced with two crippling losses at once. Dio gone to the netherworld, and Leander fated to join him. Execution was severe, though in the end of times, as in the beginning of times, the uncompromising sentence outweighed the risk of continued mutiny.

"The guard on watch warned that I would be placed under arrest if I entered Thalassic. He was ordered to do so on sight of me, but his loyalty to me outweighed the current government. I could not risk imprisonment, yet, for I did not know your fate. I needed to make sure you were safe, Nyx. I ..."

His voice faltered, broken between his allegiance to his captain and his wish to ensure her safety. Rather than have him struggle between the two, she spoke. "We will go. We will save him."

"But I cannot put you at risk." He crossed the distance between them and placed his hand upon her arm. In his actions were the love of a father, of a brother, and of a friend. Unconditional and protective.

"You will not be. I will put myself at risk," Nyx said.

A smile lifted his lower lip in a roguish arch, as if knowing that despite his wish to safeguard her, she was self-ruling to the point of no return. It was almost as if he expected her answer. Trouble would lay ahead and she welcomed it with him at her side.

"So be it," he said. "We will leave at dusk and enter the Thalassic."

Placing her hand over his, she at first felt his body stiffened, but soon he relaxed under her touch.

"I am sorry about Megaira," she whispered, not knowing what else to say.

"I am too."

Chapter Twenty-Four

The day was clear and sunny. The ocean lulled a false sense of serenity. Hector and Nyx sat on the rocky outcroppings near the shore. They ate wild blueberries. No fish though, for they could not start a fire and risk exposing their location to the Chaots, the Scipian, or the Thalassicians. She heard the ruffle of feathers in the pines, assuring her that the falcon still looked over them and perhaps in wait for another treat.

The only other sound was Hector's voice, a resonating undertone carrying plans and strategies. Planning precautions of going down to Thalassic by way of the submersible stationed near the shore. He warned of the waiting party that guarded the sub and spoke of the leadership of the Thalassic under the self-proclaimed Admiral Telphousian. Telphousian had taken the title in the aftermath of the War, claiming that society needed a ranking leader to continue efficiency.

After strategies were discussed, Nyx spoke of what happened aboard the flagship of the Scipian. She repeated what Triton had claimed, all the mysteries of life erased by his words, her last sentiment striking her one concern: "Am I free if this mutation structures who I am and I pose a risk?"

"There is a saying: In the sky, there is no distinction of east and west; people create distinctions out of their own minds and then believe them to be true. Nyx, it is a distinction you see between yourself and your genes. But as with the sky, there is no division. Your genetics do not dictate who you are, rather they are you. As for the risk, just be wary for now."

That there was no distinction seemed at odds with the Mythos: the distinction between Mount Olympus, Hades and the Elysian fields were clear. Gods and humans. Distinctions were what ruled a hierarchy. And even beyond the mythos, many aspects of society had distinctions. "Where did you hear that?" she asked.

"In Greece, in Kalambaka," Hector said.

"Tell me about that time," she said, knowing he needed to tell someone. He needed to go to the Thalassic free from the burden of his past.

"I was serving the Bavarian Coalition, the one world government. People praised their unity. Finally they believed global peace could be achieved. I didn't see it that way though. Of course, I saw a lot more than the civilians did. Firsthand, I saw the price for this unification."

"What did we fight for?" he continued. "The stated rationale was to secure the one world government. Supposedly, one government that encompassed the world would end wars and disputes. It would redistribute wealth. It would homogenize society. It would put total control into the Bavarian Coalition's hands. Wrong or right ... that was not for me to question. My duty was to my squadron."

"Our initial assignment was to protect Central Europe; there I understood the war. The Uprising in that area not only desired independence from the world government, but they were extremists. They fought for dominion. Their war cries still resound in my sleep, followed by cries and screams as bombs detonated."

A pause. The death, the brutality left unspoken. He continued as if he had never hesitated in his retelling, but Nyx could see the memories stained in his face. The war.

"I was later reassigned to Kalambaka, Greece. Our government wanted to strike at the heart of the Uprising's rebellion, at the ideas that had shaped such an outcry. They could not risk another rebellion forming because of the Uprising's ideas. I arrived in Kalambaka ready to die for the Bavarian Coalition, as any soldier should. But what I found changed me, and it was there I learned the wisdom of the priests. I thought they were naive to the situation, but now that I look back, maybe it was I that did not understand."

"I was there for the initial outbreak of the disease," he said, his voice conveyed so much more. The unsaid hardship played out in Nyx's mind over what occurred. His squadron. The Chaots. His difficulty in leaving those who he fought besides. "At the same time the World Government bombed Kalambaka, they also proceeded with similar biological attacks throughout the world to pinpoint different cells of the Uprising and destroy the entirety of it in one go. They did not anticipate the consequence: the Chaots."

"I was brought to the Thalassic in order to give a firsthand account of the initial repercussions. The Thalassic was originally used for scientific development; however, with the onset of biological warfare it was used as a secure underwater bunker. Before I could return surface side to fight, the chaos peaked, causing the undersea colony to quarantine themselves from the outside. And you know the rest."

"Often, I wonder about the priests of Meteora. Did they survive up on the pillars? I like to believe so. But I now know what the priest there meant, Nyx. I have found my place. I know what will come. And I need you to understand that it is with all my heart that I give myself to it."

Hector had sounded as if he had prepared to die. She could not understand, nor accept, that.

"Hector. I told you to stay away," an armed guard warned as Hector and Nyx approached. Wariness in his voice could be heard through the respirator, signaling that the encounter would not go well. There were three guards against only Hector and her.

"I know," Hector said. "And I am sorry."

But sorry for what, he did not say as he moved forward before the watchman had time to react. Hector brought his elbow across his face. The guard went down. Hector took his weapon as he fell, and aimed it on the other two before they could ready themselves. His reflexes surprised Nyx. She knew she should not be, after all he not only trained in combat but had been in battle many times. These three guards seemed green, and were all too quick to relinquish their weapons to Hector without hesitation.

Hector checked the unconscious guard over, though his aim never wavered.

"Rope?" he asked. One guard removed his backpack, and obeying Hector's command, kicked it over to Nyx. She rummaged through it, finding the rope. Hector moved up besides her, giving her one of the guard's guns. At least he had showed her the basics. So she held the aim on the three as Hector restrained them with the rope. However, given enough time they could free themselves. He then motioned toward her to come by his side and together they crossed the dock and entered the compact submersible.

Once inside, Hector began programming the coordinates to Thalassic. Then he had her memorize a map of the Thalassic, including the basics of using the submersible, from radar to initiation of the autopilot. Her heart crumpled, almost unwilling to listen to the latter. She did not want to believe any possibilities of Hector not returning with her. But she watched in order to learn.

Underwater, the feel of the breeze and music of the waves were lost. Instead only the emptiness of this place persisted; a void of sensation, cutting her off from the world. Some might feel safe from the Chaots, so insulated and protected. The Chaots could not penetrate these walls of steel, nor get pass the unfathomable depth of the ocean. But for Nyx, it was a transport to a society she was neither accepted by nor desired to be a part of.

Hector must have seen her uneasiness as the waters split to allow them to traverse the deep sea, and moved to her side. A sound mind was necessary in order to defeat the odds. Neither fear nor insecurity would provide them with the edge they needed to rescue Leander from the underwater cell.

"This is the easy part, going into the below and the hell that will stand before us. All our strength will be needed to face the climb back above the ground. All our fortitude will be needed to get back to the skies."

She gave a nod in response, knowing he was right. She could not lose her wits now when Leander needed her. She could not lose him, as they had lost Diomedes.

Through the circular windows, she viewed the small fish slipping by and the larger ones that baited them. Life then gave way to darkness as the water lost the blue sparkle. The only light came from the submersible's beams, and in it the sand floor emerged. But soon from the black, came light so extensive. It was as if they found the bed of the rising sun, its place beneath the waves, where it rested before springing upwards to break the sea and bring the dawn.

The light came from the Thalassic. She looked out of the submersible to see an extensive collaboration of man-made edges and lines. Tunnels spiraled across her view, going in and out of larger compounds with the lights visible from the outside. The complex formed a labyrinth of interconnecting tunnels adjoining pods. The pods of residence, of work, of communal gatherings, all came to form one organism, the colony under the sea. Most visible was a greenhouse that cultivated sea vegetation, the massive uv lights dispensing life-abiding energy for the plants. The collaboration of the domed civilization against the perpetual night seascape was awe-inspiring.

"The Thalassic is what is left of civilization that we know of. All contained essentially in the Underworld. What irony becomes of humanity's fate," Hector said though did not join her to look out upon his home. Or did his home now become what was behind enemy's lines for him, she wondered.

The sub soared through the sea as the falcon may have crossed the skies above, but without the grace and beauty of the winged predator. It lurched forward and underneath the Thalassic toward the docking port before traveling upward. The hull consumed the sub into its underbelly, as if a marsupial welcoming home a wayward offspring. Water dripped away at the emerging sub as it came to a halt within the moon-pool in the docking port.

Hector held the gun he had confiscated from the guard. He stood on one side of the circular door as the submersible aligned its exit with the egress bridge connecting to the emerging vessel. He looked toward Nyx, as if trying to drown out all second thoughts of bringing her down here. She hid to the side of the door to await his signal. What lay outside the door would be war, she realized. In moments it would come crashing upon them with no relief.

Chapter Twenty-Five

The hatch of the sub opened. Hector jumped out and grabbed the first crew member he could. He pressed the stainless barrel to the crewman's temple as he looked through unyielding eyes at those who may have been his friends.

"Back off. I come for Cap'n Leander," he growled, "and will leave once I have him."

Nyx stayed behind as planned, still in the shadows of the submersible. She wished to do something but knew her role was simply to find and release Leander when Hector gave the signal.

The crew circled and readied their weapons, aiming them at the dissident soldier, but not firing. They were not trained for war but for research. They knew that Hector had the tactical advantage. His bullet would go through their crew-mate's brain if he fired. Conversely, they did not have a direct shot and if the bullets ricocheted, they could possibly damage the Thalassic.

One woman stood away from the rest, hands palm forward as if waving the white flag to Hector. Shoulder length red hair framed a face that was pale; not by nature but reflecting the lack of sunshine inside the shell of their compound. Her expression glistened with feigned kindness as she approached. Her clothes were colored as the crew around her, dark navy slacks and shirt bearing the insignia of stripes down one arm. The stripes identified her as the Admiral, Telphousian.

"We will not allow Leander to leave. We must have the basics of society in place or face the consequence of falling into chaos ourselves as the surface dwellers have. The sentence must be carried out; he will pay for his crimes." As Telphousian spoke her voice did not waver, despite having to face the renegade threat. "You yourself must face our judges for your own crimes. Disarm, Hector, and do not allow this disruption of the Thalassic to continue. Do not jeopardize all that we have worked for. You are a soldier, not an insurgent."

"Leander is only guilty of desiring humankind to move forth, rather than wither beneath the scourge of the ocean. We should not live in fear, for in that fear those above will be damned and we will flicker out like a dying flame. Maybe you should question your own motivations, Tilphê," Hector said to the Admiral. Endeared to her, as her name left his lips. Though when she had proclaimed leadership, when she had solitarily announced what was necessary to preserve humanity, she emerged as a changed creature. He had now lost her, it was in his voice, and what stood before him no longer bore resemblance to his friend. "Question if the true reason you imprison Leander is for the safety of the crew, or if his punishment stems from his rejection of you and your fear that others will question your claim of leadership."

"Do not dare question my own motivations, Hector. Look what you have brought to the others," Telphousian said, taking one step closer to Hector. From the shadowed sub, Nyx saw a mixed look of surprise and anger on her face. It was clear Telphousian did not expect him to know of such personal rationale that motivated her decisions.

"Consider what Leander's lofty convictions brought. The death of Diomedes. Disloyalty towards the Thalassic. And the risk of infection to us all," Telphousian said. Nyx knew what the Admiral said had truth, but Hector's only response was to press the barrel more firmly against the crewman's head.

"We are society's last hope," Telphousian continued. "Let us prosper under the seas, blooming above only after the threat of the Chaots destroy themselves." Her voice filled with disregard to any who did not bear the Thalassic emblem. But to Tilphê it was not disregard, she believed herself to be justified.

"The Chaots are humans," Hector said. His response opposed the Admiral's detached idea of the Chaots. She was unconcerned about the victims and whatever hope they might have. She did not care to even look for any other groups of survivors.

"Surely if there is a chance to save them or any survivors, we should try," Hector continued. "And even if you do not believe it is worth it to do so, the Chaots will not simply die. We will perish however, waiting for them to."

Telphousian took another assured step toward Hector. Her complete attention on the warrior, as he had planned for. She did not believe any other was aboard the sub, and Hector was at the center of the Thalassicians' attention.

"Go Nyx. Now," Hector said. His stance remained resolute, as he roused the next part of his strategy.

The Admiral's assurance wavered. She was no longer in control of the situation. The uncertainty to whom Hector called to came to an end as Nyx slipped by and ran. The presence of the outsider confounded Telphousian, incredulous that a human unaccounted for could even be alive. Nyx ran forth, using the moment's diversion to get past the leader of the Thalassic and head toward the barricades. The other crew dared not move to follow, as Hector pushed his captive down. In one precipitated movement, he reached for Telphousian and grabbed her as a hostage in replacement. And what happened after that Nyx did not know as she ran down the unfamiliar corridors of the familiar map, leaving Hector behind her.

Startling several members of the crew as she passed, appearing as a strange nymph, Nyx sprinted through the Thalassic halls. The crew wondered if she were real or a hallucination. They viewed her as one would seeing visages of mermaids spring to life before their eyes: a mermaid was more likely to be seen below the sea than a fabled survivor of the Armageddon. Should they trust their eyes, or blame the sight on cabin fever? But before decisiveness came to their actions, she was gone.

The detention center came to view. Her stomach fluttered partly in exhaustion from the sprint, but mostly in anticipation of if Hector's plan would work. She could find Leander. The three of them could soon be safe back above the water. But what if they were too late ... what if Leander already faced his sentence of execution? However, her fears alleviated as she came to the cells.

Behind the bars was Leander.

"Nyx." Her name left his lips, as if a forgotten dream sprung to reality. He came to the bars, gripping the metal as if not trusting himself to stand.

With voiceless haste she grabbed the keys that Hector spoke of, pushed them into the lock and turned.

The jail door opened. And there was Leander, free. Hers.

His disbelief was as tangible as the crew she had passed, but he moved with resolved single-mindedness out of the cell and towards her, taking her in his arms.

"Nyx ..." his voice now faltered as if all his hopes and desires had been fulfilled having her in his arms once more. His hands moved to cup her chin, wanting to speak of his objections at her risk in coming here, but unable to. All that was in his eyes was complete and unrivaled joy to see her again.

"I could not leave you. I had to come," she whispered in response to the unsaid protest. Her words stumbled over each other, for all she could think of was being in his arms and having his warmth envelope her.

"I should have never left you. I ..." Leander said. It was as if he could see within her soul, hear what she had not spoken. Complete her thoughts. But before he could finish his heart's confession, Leander moved his lips to hers. He knew words could never encapsulate the entirety of what he felt towards her. Only in the sharing of souls, in a kiss, could that be done. And in his kiss he brought to light all of his love toward her, finalizing his fate.

Chapter Twenty-Six

A kiss.

Leander's lips tender on her own, a gentleness Nyx had never experienced. Love kindled so much so that she became lost in his arms.

Many say that in a kiss, souls touch. Those who said that were right. Nyx's and Leander's souls touched, and he took a piece of her that would forever change him.

They parted.

She looked to him, her face changing from that of desire to regret. Sadness crept over her. The clouds of desire began to recede leaving her to forever grasp for the moment that had passed.

"No ..." a whisper realizing what she had done.

A thorn defends the rose, harming only those who would steal the blossom. A proverb of ancient times, sprung to life through her.

Leander wondered why she would say such, for he had thought their feelings were realized in the kiss. He loved her, she him. But in the midst of his silent concern, something stirred within. For unbeknownst to him, her kiss bared the poison of the latent disease.

Red flooded within his eyes. No longer the chestnut hue remained vibrant as the Drakōn mund brought havoc to his brain. Watching the change occur, watching how the essence of humanity degraded into chaos, she froze but then held him tighter wishing she could stop this. There was nothing she could do. Blood began to run from Leander's nose and mouth as the frontal lobe became a ruin of devastation. The human essence destroyed. His hands grasped the sides of his head. An abrupt scream echoed from his contorted mouth, as he fell to his knees in her embrace as the transformation commenced.

If only she could go back in time for mere moments and change their fates. To go back before when nothing mattered other than having his warmth and touch near her. But as she held him and pressed her face into his shoulder, she felt his convulsions taper. His hand reached up. The arm was covered in the red of his own blood, and rather than seeking her in comfort it grasped forward erratically. The movements mirrored the Chaot. The resounding scream in his voice was no longer human, it was no longer Leander. She did not want to leave him, but forced herself to unravel her arms from around him. She took a step back retreating to the cell that she had just freed him from. And that freedom damned him, as it had with her. Pulling the cell's door close, she locked herself inside and withdrew until her back hit the furthest wall. She dropped down, her sight never leaving her love.

What she had done. What she had lost.

"Leander," Nyx whispered as Leander found his footing and took a cumbersome step to her. Hand reached through the bars, as if to pull her to him and finish the kiss. Though this time without compassion; this time without the tender caress.

She closed her eyes shut in hopes that her guilt would disappear. She had betrayed the one who had promised to stand by her. She had damned Leander with a kiss. The one who wished to know what it was to be uninhibited, now was forever so.

"I am so sorry."

Such simple words, a breadth unfathomable. She said it not to the gods residing above, but to Leander. For only he could grant her the forgiveness she needed. However, her absolution was now forever lost in his insanity.

Guards ran in alert to the prison break, but what they came against was not expected. Through her closed eyes she saw nothing, only the darkness which obscured so much—but not enough as screams came forth. What was now Leander held no mercy to the security of Thalassic as he sunk his teeth into the guards' flesh, rousing the disease to awaken where before it had missed. Cries of agony. Inhuman screeching. All came forth as Drakōn mund propagated itself, and delivered the Scipian's ambition to the underwater.

Thalassic was no longer untouched.

What seemed like hours passed. The explosive ring of bullets filled the air. The concern of the hull being breached by stray bullets no longer took precedence as the crew faced their worst nightmare. The disease spread, rampant within the Thalassic, fulfilling Triton's hope to destroy the last bit of opposing civilization. Thalassic could have threatened his goal of unequivocal rule over the new land, but now it was being decimated into the fate of the land dwellers. Nyx was simply a tool and she had fulfilled her use.

The guilt of destroying Leander consumed her. Leander was the first. Her first true victim; the first one directly infected by her, that she knew of. Did she make him into her own marionette, her genetics melding him into the chaos she desired? She grasped unto some hope that a direct transmission of the prion would have alternate effects. That somehow it could grant Leander some freedom of self, rather than the destruction of all that he was. She sat behind the prison bars, watching the hands of the newly formed Chaots reach through and try to grab her as their feast. A few had given up the fruitless endeavor and ventured off into the underwater colony, spreading the chaos, bringing the plague to the rest.

But Leander and one other stayed close to her. Their skin was not decomposed as the Chaots on land. Only the trail of fresh blood from the nose and eyes told the tale of what they were. No longer did their eyes shine with sagacity or hope; instead they fell prey to the same passionate chasm-less void as the other Chaots.

One Chaot, dressed in the navy hues of the Thalassicians, reached his arm further through the bars reaching for her. His shirt began to tear and fresh blood spurned from the metal that he pushed against. A futile task, but nevertheless she shrunk away from his actions. Leander paced back and forth, every so often rattling the bars of the cage with such hateful longing for her that she almost succumbed. She gave him this fate, now she wished to share in the consequences. She had the key, she could open the cell and go to him. Whatever would come, would come.

He sensed this. He stopped his strides and reached through the bars to beckon her.

She stepped forward. Her hand went out to touch what had become of Leander. Her hopes fleeting, yet persistent, that he had not completely perished under the disease.

Gunfire intervened. An aerosol explosion of red liquid and flesh splashed against her. Terror came as she thought she had lost him, in soul as well as body. But as she wiped the crimson from her face, she saw him alive. The victim was not Leander. Though, the second Chaot was reduced to a heap besides the cell; tremors animated his body in sporadic aftershocks of life. Leander turned to face the bullet's discharger.

Hector.

"Stand down, captain," he said, aiming his firearm toward his friend, his next target.

Leander took a step; Hector's words had no meaning for him. Even if they had, he would have continued undeterred because of the uncontrollable hunger outweighing any sense of reason.

"Leander," Hector said, "you can fight this! You are stronger than this!"

But nothing could escape the plague that was unleashed.

Closing the distance, Leander took another step. Hector could no longer safely wait, the remorse that flooded him spoke volumes of what he would be forced to do. His finger again found the trigger. But he did not press down. He did not disperse the bullet and instead, Hector's aim lowered decisively. His fellow soldiers from Kalambaka. Megaira. He could not do it again, it was destroying him.

Relief passed for a moment in Nyx at Hector's resolve to not kill him. She wanted Leander to live, despite the prion that now absorbed him. It was still Leander before her. Hector knew this, she believed, and he would rather die than kill his comrade as he had done many times before. Yet it was kill or be killed, and Leander made his move. Jaws upturned in a deadly smile, Leander began his attack on Hector. Though he had mercy, the Chaot had none. Hector accepted his choice, and prepared for death by the hands of his captain.

But Leander stopped. Pain stole his features as he trembled in one last spasm of life.

And then he fell.

As Leander struck the ground in defeat, Nyx's figure remained standing in his wake. The open jail cell behind her. The Fisherman's knife in her hands, covered with blood. A sorrow that would never waver penetrated her own heart. She saved Hector, but at what cost? She kneeled besides her fallen love, taking Leander's hand in hers.

Fighting regret that filled his emotions, Hector steadied himself. She had just saved him, and now he had to save her.

"The Thalassic is comprised. We have to go now."

He reached out for her. Part of her died with Leander. But part of her desired only to avenge his death, and she knew how. She knew who had set her loose upon society, who had devised her slaughter of the Thalassic. They would pay, as she had.

Letting go of Leander's hand, Nyx watched as it fell to his side. His hand had still been warm, and now only the cold air pressed against her palm.

Love lost, by the lovers own hand.

Nyx and Hector ran through the complex of halls away from the prison and towards the submersible. Zigzag turns wove them through the maze to their destination. Chaos erupted in the corridor mirroring the fate that was on the verge of consuming the Thalassic. Nothing could stop the tides of the ocean. Some Thalassicians underwent the change. Blood sprouted from their noses; their hands grasped their temples as if they could stop the invasion. In some, the transformation was already complete. They blocked the two's way back to the sub. But before they could trap them, Hector tried a door. Locked.

He lifted his foot and rammed it against the middle of it. Under the pressure, the lock gave way and door opened. Safe harbor.

The room was dark. Hector's focus remained near the door, in case intruders were to enter. His gun ready to shoot. Nyx looked around into the shadows. At first nothing except a green light flashed in her eyes. Shadows flashed on and off as the light did. She could only wish they would awaken from their static reflection, and crawl along the floors to take her. Take her to the underworld ... to Leander. Would she find the captain she had met in the seacoast town, or would it be the Chaot that had replaced his personality, thriving in the afterlife?

"Find an alternate exit," Hector commanded, his concentration focused on the door they had came in through, ready to kill anything that followed.

She walked further into the room, her eyes adjusting to the dark. The opportunity of retreat did not appear, only a body in stasis.

Diomedes.

Death had not taken him. Truth replaced the lies. Hector had been given the wrong information, for Dio was there. The equipment to the side testified to his life, as the faint green pulse throbbed on the monitor, recording his heartbeat. Tubes and wires ran along his body, fluids continually poured into his veins. Some to keep him alive while inert, some to keep him immobile. The Thalassic had kept Dio alive, but not for the reasons Leander hoped. They had kept him alive as a Chaot. Their goal seemed solely to study their enemy, not to cure Dio. The equipment attested to that.

Hatred simmered in Nyx to see Dio in this state. She began pulling the wires out of him. She would not allow him to remain an experiment, a lab rat as she had once been.

Without the sedative to keep him in suspended animation, Dio began to stir. His mouth opened as his breathing quickened; eyes rolled under his lids as if persecuted by nightmares. One finger twitched, followed by the whole arm. That was when Hector took notice, and aimed his gun toward his comrade.

"The priests I spoke of, their advice," Hector started and for the first time she heard indecision in his voice. He could not face another death of a friend. "I don't want to give myself to this—killing my friends. Where am I to stand ... what do I give my heart to ... when everyone I know is dead."

Nyx walked between Hector and Dio. Reaching up, she put her hand on the barrel of the gun. Her weight pivoted it downward, the aim no longer on Diomedes.

"You are a warrior, yes, but not simply a killer. And you stand nowhere, Hector. You run," Nyx said. "You found what you sought upon the peaks of Meteora, and it was not a person or place. It was the journey. Give your heart to that, for it will never die."

"Leave him, Hector," she continued, "We did as much as we could for Dio. He is no longer a research subject but as a Chaot he can at least attain vengeance against those who had kept him here."

The same vengeance she hoped to attain with those who had held her. Those who had stripped her of everything, of Leander.

Dio began to move, urging Hector to make a decision.

"Then let us run together, Nyx," he said, the sadness in his voice mirroring her own. "Let the journey lead us."

Without an alternate exit, they had to go back the way they came. Hector opened the door. As he did, Nyx took one last look toward Dio, struggling to sit, struggling to stand. Soon the drug would completely wear off and he would be a Chaot in the fullest sense of the term. Chaos will follow him. Retribution will come.

"Now Nyx." Hector took her arm and they began to run down the corridor of the underwater compound. The Thalassicians who had begun transformation before they went into the room, had now fully metamorphosed into Chaots. In erratic precision they ran after the two as Hector and Nyx came into the hallways. The few became many as the scent of life caught the senses of those undergoing the change, and the many became too much thus hindering their escape. But it was not the Chaots who proved to be their undoing.

Several unexpected and unexposed Thalassicians stood at the end of the hall as Nyx and Hector turned a corner. Bullets poured in frenzied waves down the halls as they saw the two. Fear governed their actions. Not fear of the tangible, but the fear that came only in the irrepressible terror of nightmares.

Fear directed toward the Chaots. It had been festering under the water, toward the unknown threat, and now in the gun fire it reached its ultimatum. And the fear towards the Chaots now directly became toward Hector and Nyx as the bullets came to them.

Seeing the incoming rounds, she moved in front of Hector, her form as a shield to protect him. But it was too late.

His hand reached down. It pressed against the blood that spilled from his abdomen.

"No, we can still make it. We can still escape," Nyx said as she tried to pull his weight over her shoulder. He allowed her at first, stumbling by her side in several hindered steps. The Chaots began to gain on them. Hector fired his gun toward the incoming enemy with Nyx as his crutch, but soon the fiery blasts were replaced by hollow clicks as his ammunition ran out. The Thalassicians who were shooting had turn and run. Hector tried to reload, but only had time to load one cartridge before the Chaots came upon them. Fire came again, but it could only ebb the wave so much. Hands grasped Nyx as she fought to keep Hector standing and achieve escape. Hector fought the beasts with his free hand, tearing their arms from Nyx despite the pain burning within his torso.

One bit down on Hector. Teeth bore within flesh. Hector knocked the butt of the gun into the Chaot's face, freeing himself from the death latch. Freedom would be short lived though, as another death latch ascended: the prion.

He held the gun out for Nyx to take it.

"One bullet."

"No, I won't. Come with me, please!" At first she grabbed his arm, not wanting to leave him. She could not suffer another loss, and needed him to be besides her. But Hector pushed her away from him. His expression spoke volumes, and left no room for discussion.

"Your oath, Nyx. Remember."

She looked at him, into his eyes that she once thought were an unbreakable wall. The wall did not fall, but instead had opened to allow her in. He had trusted her. He had believed in her. As she did with him. A drip of blood began to fall from his nose, signaling the prion had began its destruction. A wordless goodbye passed between them, as she took the gun and fired.

Turning away so she did not have to see his body hit the ground, and the Chaots descended upon his lifeless form, she ran. She did not turn back. Unlike Orpheus and Eurydice, she knew she had lost him even if she did not glance behind her. Only her need for vengeance fueled her escape, for she had lost all else. She had to live long enough to bring ruin to what had destroyed all whom she had loved.

Anger filled her soul like flesh moldering in the swampy marshes. Oh, if she could kill, if she could feel Death's hand cover her own and allow her to bring the end to those she despised. Sorrow lashed in her heart for those she had lost. Anger fermented deeper still. Did pure evil reside in these thoughts of revenge? Yet she could not rid the hatred from her soul, even if it condemned her.

How she did hate them. Not the Chaots, for another was responsible. The Chaots were puppets on strings. It was those aboard the Scipian's fleet. It was Triton. They would have to answer for what they had begun, they were the harbinger of her hate. Now animosity burned in her soul, leaving a taint forever in its wake. And it was not simply toward those of the Scipian, but towards herself.

The innocent façade of Nyx was a mirror, her surface reflective of what stood near it. But underneath? Underneath lay much more: layers of enmity that were in truth darker than the most barbaric killer. Smile and display the niceties in reflection, but at the core that smile is imitation for no happiness was inside. Look beneath and the stench of contempt beckoned to be released, unrelenting if ever to touch the light of day.

Come close, and I shall push you off the cliff. Turn, and I will bring the blade down, rendering you forever lost in eternity. Now, those of the Scipian were safe. But soon they would die. In her blood, a monster that slept, now awakened. A killer released by them, only to turn and bite its maker.

She arrived at the wet room with the submersible craft. Evil churned, humanity was lost. All she wished now was to get to the sub, to find the Scipian.

But someone stood in her way.

Nyx came to a halt as a gun clicked before her. The safety of the revolver was disarmed, and Admiral Telphousian pointed it at Nyx. The Admiral stood, red hair displaced, her face full of rage. The wrath boiling inside Telphousian did not stem from the disease, for she was not yet infected. Two Chaots who were chasing Nyx came up from behind and into sight. She took her aim off Nyx and fired at the Chaots; it took three shots to down the two. The Chaots fell leaving Telphousian alone with Nyx, alone with her need for requital.

"You are responsible! You brought this to us!"

Telphousian's eyes shone as she took several steps toward Nyx. Her weapon displayed her intent as the aim returned to on her.

"I tried to protect my people," she continued. "I tried to harbor them in the safety of the Thalassic. And now all is lost and it is because of you!"

A shot rang out in the room; the whistle of the bullet sounded in Nyx's left ear. It missed, embedding itself in the hull of the Thalassic rather than her forehead. Sparks flew from the impact. Several wires collapsed; splinters and shards ricocheted around her.

The Admiral snared in discontent as she brought her second hand up to steady the firearm.

"This time I will not miss. This time I will bring you the retribution you deserve!"

"I did not intend for any of this," Nyx said, calm in the face of fire, unconcerned by death after all that had transpired. She deserved it, for all who had trusted her and all who had died because of it. "But what you see before you ..."

Was a part of her. Though most abhorred the transformation, in its own way it was chaotically beautiful. She was their mother. The genesis spawned from her, and she could not provide repentance for what had become of the Thalassic. The death of Leander and Hector ... yes. But not the rise of the Chaots.

" ... is evolution," Nyx continued. "I released those souls that were living with such restraint under you. Under the imposed restrictions of your society. I liberated them from their prisons."

Two more shots rang out, one after the other. But they came in anger and disbelief as Telphousian listened to what she perceived as the raving of a lunatic. One bullet flew past Nyx, finding itself in the hull of the underwater compound once more. The other grazed her cheek. She took a step toward the submersible in the moon pool. Fear alongside anger sketched in Telphousian; Nyx would use that to her advantage. No longer wayward in her path, Nyx stood, a determined woman accepting her mantle. She had lost all the humanity that had kept her balanced—Leander, Hector. Stripped of the two, only chaos remained.

"I will free you. From your role, from all your duty. Imagine living rather than trapped in this skeleton of society. You cling to the past. Look around you to what is present. Embrace it," Nyx said.

The Admiral's face crumpled under the vivid crimson locks in unwilling reluctance. It had been so long since the sun had brought warmth to her skin or the breezes could catch the fiery hair. But embedded in her was the responsibility to her crew and the obligations to maintain whatever shred of civilization remained. But Nyx had begun to crumble the walls around Telphousian, as the prion manifested within the Thalassic. The crew was no more. Civilization unraveled. All that remained was the Admiral's own self as an obstacle to liberation.

Nyx spoke again: "Kill me and end me. But the real enemy would continue above and we will both lose. Join me, come to the surface to breathe fresh air and to find your vengeance. Rid yourself of this coffin."

"Die Bitch," responded Telphousian in a solemn hiss.

She aimed the weapon to Nyx and fired. This time she would not miss. But the weapon clicked, empty of ammunition. Nyx tilted her head in a curious testament, a smile gracing her lips at the sudden twist of fate. No longer the target, she made way to the submersible. She took one glance back at Telphousian before boarding. She saw shadows behind the Admiral; the Chaots advancing to claim their dictator. Diomedes in the lead.

"Stay then. And join the others in their fate."

Nyx entered and swung the sub's hatch shut, locking out all sounds from the outside. She did not hear the screams as the Chaots grabbed Telphousian; she did not see the blood that came from their carnage. Any pang of guilt was secondary to all else that had come, and all that waited to come.

Chapter Twenty-Seven: Diomedes

Days prior: In the forests above

"Look at those two lovebirds," Dio said as he watched Leander dive into the water. Leander wished to save Nyx, though it was clear that the waters did not threaten her life. Dio did not say such, he just laughed as concern overtook his friend in his response to help her. Who was he to stop such attraction?

A smile crossed his mouth in memory of when he was in love. Love, now long lost. He touched a blooming flower to the side. His wife always smelled of fresh flowers, and that smell now permeated the air as he watched Leander swim to Nyx. He saw an echo of his own relationship, the difference though was clear. He had courted his wife immediately, pronouncing his love at first sight. Leander, however, was too worried he would lose Nyx, impeding his chance to ever be with her. If only Leander could let go of his hesitation.

And Dio knew what it stemmed from.

The scenes fresh, for never would they wear: the scenes from a year ago aboard Thalassic. The monitor that displayed his family's death. His daughter's transformation into a Chaot, Leander's attempts to save her. Trying to save what never could be, and hence was doomed to fail. Did he blame Leander? At first, it was hard not to. He distanced himself from his friend. But he saw how hard the captain punished himself, and understood that his pain almost matched his own as a father. Almost. And not only did he see Leander's undecipherable pain over his failure to protect Cassie, but also the person who was indeed responsible for his family's fate. Telphousian. If Admiral Telphousian allowed his family quick access to the moon pool, they could have quarantined his mother. Then his wife and daughter would never have been infected.

Only if. He could not remind himself of the past or it would drown him. Instead, he could find his family as if with him still. He walked alone through the forests, leaving the lovers to themselves. He found his wife through the rustle of leaves besides him, her embrace in the wind, her voice in the songbirds. Her scent in a flower.

The interlude of peace splintered as a new sound, new scent, new sight emerged. Bronze eyes looked out between the bark, catching Diomedes in their forge. He froze. One second hesitation too long. The firearm came to Dio's hand, finger pressed on the trigger even before reaching their target. Sound blasted as bullets punched holes in the birch's white bark, yet missing their mark. The Pathfinder, leader of the Chaots, came forth and attacked.

Dio fell, soundless in the racket of his comrade's gunfire. The flowering blossom crushed beneath his weight.

Minutes before: In the waters below

Hibernation. Diomedes laid dormant on the research tables of the underworld, of Thalassic. No inner clock would awaken him. Unlike true hibernation, his sleep was perpetual. Nightmares replaced the sweet dreams. Spring greens would not be the reward. Hell was what waited.

All that could be felt, was. All the agony boiled within him, overspilling in waves until finally he surrendered to it. Hours ... days ... time had no meaning anymore, leaving the present an uncertain enigma. But as he submitted to a ceaseless slumber, something awoke him. Nyx tore the wires from him, freeing him from the anesthesia induced sleep. He saw her standing over him. In blurred vision ... blurred thought. He could not call out to her.

Where was he? What had happened?

Where was his daughter ... Dio grasped out, reaching for her but his arms encircled only air. The fragility of fatherhood broke in his empty embrace, the death of his daughter remembered. Did love easily slip through fingers, fingers that soon would rot in decay? Cassie ... he breathed the word, but his brain so confused in the torture, that he could not find the meaning behind it.

The moment of sanity dissipated as soon as it had breached his mind. The glimpse of his daughter, or her metamorphosis, emptied from his thoughts. Now it was pain again, encumbering every second of his life and drowning out all else.

He wrestled the bed sheets, the wires that had been pulled from his skin, but he could not understand where he was, or what had happened. It was dark. He was alone, not only in solitude of body, but of mind. Not simply the passing of a moment, but of the finality of isolation. He rose, stumbling to the door.

Open. He could not focus on what was on the other side, nor the reasoning to leave the room, all he knew was he must. Driven by instincts, he knew he must feed. Who was he now? So many would say a monster, a beast. A creature who had no place among the living. Light from the hallways filled his senses as he stepped through. Primal emotions unearthed as the clouded illumination came upon his eyes; it became too much stimuli, too early from his awakened cocoon. Hands came to his lids, scratching his own skin as if to stop the light from invading his senses. Blood streamed down his caramel face, tears of red stained his features. He wanted darkness, not the light. Perhaps it was a monster he had become.

Hatred came in waves within his misery. Memories came and went. Of those he had lost. Of his daughter. Of his wife. He had no refined cage of society to inhibit these emotions, nor to direct them into any coherency. They collided within his mind, images of his lost kin, images of the one responsible. Hair of fire. Eyes black without soul. No words, no names, no thoughts or reason, only images, rage, and now the drive to allow the emotions to materialize.

Suffer. Agony. Pain.

Opposing all thought that was left in his mind, opposing all who he was, the id ruled. But did it indeed oppose, for it was always a part of him. The disease did not create something new, it solely tore away the restrictions of the mind, leaving who we truly are. And who was he? Either an animal limited by the governing canon or one who wishes to feel the primal environment. One who has been stripped of what they had evolved to be, one who wants to return to it.

He was trapped between Chaot and human, sleeping in a coma induced by the Thalassicians not as one or the other but both. Both limited and limitless, the boundaries blurred as he walked. Pandemonium surrounded each step; yells and screams from the afflicted and their victims filled the air. He ignored it all. He walked through it, as a daydream, oblivious to it all.

Take arms against a sea of troubles, his conscious called, as he wandered the halls in a wakened slumber. And by opposing them, end them. End the one whose inaction killed the ones you loved. Yet to end her life, he would end himself. The agony shaped him, the unfulfilled turmoil, without it ... would leave him without. Adrift. Meaningless.

Each step became heavy, each step called to his ancestors. There is no good or evil, is there?

He tore at his face again, this time not due to the blinding light. Instead, he tore at the mask of evil he now bore. Trying to get it off. Trying, failing, stepping again down the hall. Screaming now as pain grew forth. Not pain of the body, but of the soul. His mouth wrenched open in a shattering uproar. No humanity held in his cry. No mercy would be found.

The flowers of his memory, his wife's scent, were lost. The sweet smell was that of rotted decay. The decay became the desired, as he grabbed a person, breaking through the haze into reality. Human or Chaot, he did not know, did not care. He lifted him, and brought him against the hull of the Thalassic. Again and again, he rammed him. Face bent, eyes gorged, Diomedes looked at him. And smiled.

Again he rammed the male into the wall. Laughter intertwined with screams, both came from Dio as his victim died due to his rage.

He held him to the steel. Drop by drop he watched his victim bleed.

He would kill the flaming haired woman, the Admiral of Thalassic. But now, vengeance sought refuge in his mind as he watched the blood, drowning out all else in its hypnotic spill.

Disgust pervaded the refuge. He dropped the body. It fell limp, disfigured. A hollow shell of what once walked down the halls. He cried, falling to his knees. Grabbing the weight of broken bone and torn skin in his embrace, he held it close. Just flesh, he thought, trying to distance himself. Flesh that needed to be sheared from the wearers. He began to feed. Bites between his cries echoed the halls.

Brutality imprisoned his mind, the images of his daughter faded through the famished bites. Memories shrouded beneath his mind's metamorphosis. The images of the past, of his wife and daughter, disappeared. Only the vision of red remained. Only the one subject to his hatred. Death edged close as his brain succumbed to the full weight of the Drakōn mund. The disease persisted and twisted his thoughts, leaving nothing of love. He would soon travel to the netherworld of the souls, yet he had no soul.

And so he returns, to the living. Soulless. A Chaot to the fullest.

Awakened from his humanity, from the scaffolds of pain, freed from death itself, the eyes of the Chaot opened. His lips turned in a sardonic twist, as the flood of memories left him barren. Barren, with the need to fill, with the need to gouge himself on other life in order to satisfy the hunger. The glory of a mind wasted away into insanity, non compos mentis.

Even the insane can come to be more.

His eyes adjusted to the light, sight blurred by the red that ran down his face. Everyone looked like the red-head of his wrath, everyone who he saw he grabbed, shredding them underneath his strength. Biting them, killing them, transforming them, it did not matter. It felt good as he indulged in the long withheld urges.

The purity of animalistic rage silenced for one clear thought: he was not human. Not civil for a civilization, not wise as the genus classified. Still, blood coursed through him, giving him life. And now pain served to remind him of that life. Pain imposed on others, and on himself, invigorated his soulless mind. With the prion's hand, Diomedes tore away all of the denotations of humanity.

And through hell

Red poured. More and more, over Diomedes and along his wake. Trailing him as he walked through the shadows, through the underworld to his fate. Others followed, deeming him as the Alpha after seeing his carnage. To the moon pool they walked. Once, the moon pool could have been the saving oasis to allow his family inside the Thalassic. Now, it would serve to damn the one who had sealed their fate.

Telphousian. His wanderings seemed like the misdirected ambles of the insane, for even he knew not where he went. But the whispers of who he once was guided him to her.

Red hair of fire, left behind from the coals of the wanderer. Tilphê. Her name meant unclean waters, filled with larvae. And he was Apollo, he would vanquish her. A god, disguised as a beast.

He came to her. He took her in his arms.

Was she crying? Tears came down. Tears of remorse for what she had taken from him. No, no regret shimmered behind the red strands. The tears mourned herself, tears scared of what he would do.

Mouth opened as if to speak, as if to grant her contrition.

A growl rang through the dark throat, the black void surrounded by white. The teeth came down to her forehead. He pressed his mouth closed, the severe opposite of a kiss; flesh tore from Tilphê as she pulled away screaming. Blood spurted as a rainfall. He came again.

And again.

And again.

Chapter Twenty-Eight

Moonlight pierced the window of the submersible as it lashed out above the waves. Nyx unlatched the top hatch, letting the ocean breezes drown out the heartache. She had one goal and she could not allow the pain of losing Hector and Leander to blind her fortitude. Now that her objective was in sight she had to move without indecision.

She had used the sub's radar to bring her near the location of the Scipian's fleet and focused her path to the flagship. Now she faced the task of boarding the Destroyer without detection; stealth and speed were necessary. The night granted the cover of darkness and she could board in its veil. Standing on the outer shell of the sub, Nyx pulled the cord of the escape raft. It bulged with air taking float upon the crevices of the ocean. Fastening the compact motor to its inflatable shell, she placed it on the low setting to ebb the noise upon arrival.

The reflection of starlight danced along the metal hull of the Destroyer as the ship floated towards it. The ship itself was daunting in its appearance and to her knowledge held the last fragment of humanity in this world—those responsible for the apocalypse.

The raft reached the side of the vessel and near the anchor's cord. Grabbing hold of the metal cable, Nyx tethered her raft. She climbed along the chain, until the deck came into view.

The first person was the hardest, after that it all began to blur. The first though ... that was the one that etched itself into her memory. A man dressed in uniform, cigar between his lips as he eased over the edge of the vessel. Fumes rose from around him, a calming tap of his fingers rattled on the rail as he enjoyed his smoke. She moved in attack. Coming up from behind the gentleman, she sank her teeth deep into his shoulder. As she once wished to do with the raw fish that was caught with the Fisherman; as she had seen the Chaots do. Hot, thick blood poured between her lips. Her feast pulled away as the man brought a surprised fist to the girl. She fell near him; her hand came up to wipe away the trail of blood along her chin.

At first the crew man just stood astonished. Then he started to move with purpose, wanting to destroy her. But his pace slowed. The knowledge of what had happened sunk in, his damnation written in his face. He was bitten by what he assumed was a Chaot. Before he could react, he began to change. Blood discharged from every cavity on his face. His ears, his tear ducts, his nose. An unearthly rumble came to his lips as he fell to his knees before Nyx. Hands went to his temple as he screamed for mercy. It was as if he bowed to her, his creator—his new god.

After several uninterrupted, perpetual seconds, the screaming stopped. He looked up from his genuflect and stared upon Nyx, the vessels of his eyes throbbing red. He was about to attack her, but noises came from behind causing an interruption. Several crew members had hurried to the commotion, becoming their new targets.

He attacked. Nyx attacked by his side. A siren calling, surrendering all to death in her wake.

And the transformation had begun.

The second apocalypse. The phoenix will rise from the flames. The Chaots time has come.

Over the Scipian's ship, clouds grew dark and dry thunder punctuated by lighting echoed through the sky. On board the maelstrom continued, the disease spreading through those who had facilitated its widespread entry to the world. Those aboard had believed they could harness the power of chaos and use it for their own ends. However, you could never tame a wild beast, and it now turned to bite the hand of its proclaimed yet false maker. Some changed, their frontal lobe altered under the convergence with the disease. Others died.

Through the mayhem, Nyx began her search. She needed to be assured that one person would suffer: Triton. Triton, the one who had procured the prion, the one who had used her as a weapon against the Thalassic and all humanity.

Screams chorused her hunt. She walked, no longer untouched by memory and tragedy but as a predator in search of her prey. Where was he, she hoped he was aboard this lone Destroyer but perhaps he stayed with the bulk of the fleet. She struggled with the impending defeat of her purpose, though knowing it would not be a lingering defeat. She would find the other ships, she would find him.

But then another found her.

The Fisherman.

Nyx stood, wondering if he was the figment that she imagined him to be. Her guide, her savior, her anchor to humankind and to her journey. He looked at her and the blood that ran down her mouth. She wasn't sure if he knew all along what she was, the harbinger of the disease, and what seeing her now brought to his thoughts. But he said nothing, he led her silently as if untouched by the chaos surrounding them. They came to a door and he turned to her with the key in his hand.

"I asked you once if you came from the dragon's mouth to devastate or bloom. But it was not a choice between them. I see now you have done both," the Fisherman said.

"Why are you here?" Nyx questioned. Was he even there? She was still not sure whether he was fantasy or reality. Two things were definite: he was her guide, he had the key.

"Soon you will have your answers. But promise me you will find peace behind those doors. I unlocked the room you were contained in once before. Now it is your turn to unlock the barrier in your path. Finish what you came here for."

It had been the Fisherman who had unchained her and unlocked the doors when she was captured last; it was he who had allowed for her escape from the Scipian. Her fingers wrapped around the metal before putting it in the keyhole. It turned; the door opened. She stepped in to face Triton.

But no one was there. She turned to see if the Fisherman knew where he had went to, but the Fisherman said nothing. He walked pass her to the desk. He sat down behind it.

"No. It can't be you," she said, not willing to admit her hatred was to be focused on her protector and guide.

"I am sorry I used you." Sincerity was in the Fisherman's voice. In Triton's voice. "I used a voice changer when I spoke to you over the intercom aboard the Scipian. I did not want to shatter what we spoke of on the beach for you."

"My son's last words were of freeing you and I fulfilled them," he continued. "I am sorry it took me so long to get here."

Nyx said nothing in reply; instead, she focused on him, trying to understand that he was both the good of her life and the evil.

"I let you go on the beach, half wishing for you to take down what remained of the Bavarian Coalition: the Thalassic. That was the original plan, and I was there to make sure you crossed their path. But I also hoped that instead you would carve your own destiny. I let you go again aboard the Scipian, wishing the same. But I also knew that it would not only be the Thalassic, but the Scipian, that would be affected ... whether it be in destruction or salvation ... or both."

Still silence came her response. Blood streaked her features, her hair stained with red, the line between human and Chaot, good and evil, blurred in her as well in the Fisherman. Though the dichotomy that she represented did not favor the humans.

"You are not one of them, Nyx," he said. Did he believe his own words? "You do not belong behind locked doors. I regret so much. However, you should regret nothing."

With ease, she could turn him into a Chaot. To take away his intellect to see what really laid underneath it all. Or she could kill him. But she could do neither. He had been her captor, and for that she hated him. But he was also the Fisherman, the one who freed her, who taught her and saved her. It almost felt he had always been her teacher, her mentor, her guide—even within her forgotten life.

"But in the end I destroyed Thalassic and my friends," she said.

"Maybe at the heart of it both Thalassic and the Scipian, the Bavarian Coalition and Uprising, were remnants of a dying age and not meant to continue. Maybe civilization is at its end and now it is time for a new era. Or maybe there is hope somewhere, but just not in the corrupted hearts of those that fell to ashes under your touch."

"Even if that new era is the Chaots?" she questioned, looking toward the Fisherman. Though she now knew his name, he symbolized an enigma that would always remain a puzzle to her even as he sat before her.

"Society, at its core, is self destructing to begin with. Corruption. Apathy. Most of us forgot how to live. I forgot," the Fisherman said.

Silence followed. She waited for him to explain more, however he offered nothing.

"Come with me," she said to the Fisherman. She wanted him to. To be by his side, for he was a hunter. Like Hector had been, his soul that of a wandering predator which would never succumb.

He looked at her, the confusion clear. He had expected death from her.

"I have my own path now, separate from yours," he said.

Nyx had killed both Leander and Hector. The pain in her heart struck deeply as she thought of them. If the Fisherman did follow her, she would be his undoing as well. She could not suffer through the heartbreak that came when she walked besides those she did not belong with.

"Be safe, Arethusa," he said, calling her by the orchid he had once compared her too. As he said the flower's name, she saw a sadness and lost pass within his gaze.

"You too, Fisherman," she said, calling him by the endearing epithet even though she now knew his true name. For his true name brought hatred to her heart, and she did not wish to feel that.

The Fisherman nodded; farewells left unsaid as she walked out of the room. But an implied sentiment was exchanged, one he had said days ago. Back upon the beach, the Fisherman had left her with one piece of wisdom: That life is driven by death and madness. Despite these horrors, there stands one thing. A trace of hope withstands the environment that destroys all else. The orchid Arethusa grows and even flourishes in these impenetrable swamps. It is a piece of lasting dignity where no other can be found. Can she be the Arethusa and bloom even within the devastation?

And now he let her go again. She stepped out and returned to the pandemonium unleashed on the ship. This time though she understood the guidance he had given her when they first met.

She would bloom as the orchid did. She would destroy as the swamp did.

Triton watched as she turned and left. He was alone. This had always been the state of things for when was the last time he could remember he was not? And now he knew that he had lost, and it was not now that he had been defeated. It was when his son died. When his wife died. He had focused on death as an equalizer, but what did that give him now, he wondered.

He closed his eyes and thought of the last time he was truly not alone:

The sun felt warm, but the ocean breeze brought a chilled contrast. Sand caught in the wind came across his notes and books, and he rashly brushed it away, annoyed at the inconvenience of trying to study at the beach. But then he heard laughter. He looked up for a moment from his notes and saw the silhouette of his wife and son back when he was just a baby. The orange soaked sky was a backdrop to them playing on the shore. The glee that came from Glaucus's chubby pursed lips matched the happiness in his own smile. His wife waved at him, then motioned for her husband to join them.

He had to finish up though. He smiled and waved back but then focused once more on his notes.

How he wish he had joined them then.

Hours before daybreak, the night was at its darkest. Promises of a new dawn lingered with the knowledge that the sun would soon rise. Nyx brought oars in and out of the water in stride as she headed toward the shore. Behind her a distant glimpse of the Scipian's Destroyer rode the horizon. Fires rose in a vivid orange and red. Screams of chaos played out a distant symphony of the bedlam.

Another stronghold of humanity fell.

The moon shone over her and lit her way to the shore. Back to the beginning. Herself and the sea. Even the peregrine falcon circled above.

If only the Fisherman could be with her too.

Chapter Twenty-Nine: The Fisherman

There is one thing that is real. One thing which holds no bounds and brings life. One thing that never ceases to bring us awe. One thing that lets us know we are alive.

The fight.

The battle raged forth, man against sea.

Each wave slammed against the ship, spraying water on the deck and on the Fisherman. Fisherman, ha, if Nyx were still besides him he may be renamed the Sailor man.

No, he told himself, you hunt not simply sail. And now you hunt for safe ground. For survivors. He wondered if Nyx would be by the Chaot's side when he returned. Would he be forced to oppose the one he both damned and saved?

Or would the fate of the Earth no longer be a battleground between humans and Chaots: the Chaots replacing mankind. Himself, the only one left, an old man on the sea, the last one of his kind. If that were to be, then he would accept his days. Perhaps he was more similar to the Glaucus myth than he claimed his son was. If the Earth fell in darkness as Scylla did in the myth, he would still be devoted to her for evermore. He would still fish by the shore, a fisherman over all else.

Another wave crashed against his boat. Lightning clapped, thunder bellowed. He could not tell if it rained, or if the water pouring down was simply the sea in its ire. He neared the shore, in hopes the gods would allow his passage, but would it be for monsters or heroes whom they sided with? He knew he was the monster in this myth, but hoped to find his redemption. No. His actions were unforgivable. He knew that. But he would still search for penance.

However, it seemed that the gods allied against him as his ship became beaten by the iron clad fists of the sea. Waves were as walls, colliding violently into the wooden hull of his sailboat. He stayed on deck, securing lines, steering the sail himself when all else failed. One wave boomed. It lifted from the sea to form a claw over his boat, coming down and taking him in its stead. It knocked him off his feet, and pulled him to the deadly waters. He dug his hands into the planks, skidding cross the surface. He fought to stay onboard; he grabbed the railing before all was lost.

Lightning struck the mast. Zeus joined Poseidon in this travesty. Flames rose, the explosion tore his grip from the rail and pulled him overboard into the ever tempestuous sea.

Now it was he alone against the gods. No ship, no solid ground to stand on. As Odysseus, the sea threatened to break him. He swam, bringing one arm over another in stroke, reaching as far ahead as possible, before bringing his arm back, carving through the water as if he were a sculptor, and it stone. Waves turned him to and fro, battling him down.

The Fisherman felt the flush of rapids around his body; a pull downward in a tidal whirl. Weighted to the bottom by the waves, it took him to the abyss.

He would not wait to see if he emerged as the Greek sea god Glaucus did, torn of his mortal coil to live within the ocean's depths.

Fight rose in his body as he sunk. But no more was the fight against Triton, or against a world turned sour, but now against the brutality of the ocean waves. Swimming upward, he opposed nature itself to again breathe in air. From the sea he came, the warrior rises.

He endured. He won. Not the final battle, but he won a small token for humankind: Hope. Hope that despite the odds, humans could prevail once more.

To the shores he came, coughing to spew the water forth from his lungs. Hands grasped into the wet sand, grasping the earth between clenched fists. He was home. The battle with the sea tore his clothes from him; and now he felt the wind against his bare chest. He understood what Nyx had always knew, what it was to feel free. His hands left the sand. He stood, steadying his feet. He looked out. Vision clouded, but it came to a sight bringing forth such muted harmony.

Land.

Not only land.

Survivors.

Chapter Thirty

Sand boundlessly reached out over the expanse in front of Nyx. It was as it had been in the beginning, but so much more. Each step planted itself in the seashore, leaving a print that would not last. The winds, the tide, time, would see to that. The breeze caressed her skin; the salt of the air touched her lips. And the daybreak heralded new possibilities to come with the new day.

The Fisherman was gone, off to the oceans from which he had came. Leander's heart and Hector's spirit burrowed into hers, never to be forgotten and always missed. They were a weight, but not simply that. They had become a beacon of hope to her.

The peregrine falcon flew above in the clear skies, following her path. She smiled up at her familiar and in response it called, resembling thunder from the heavens.

This time the destination of her travels was not unseen. Her desires were not unknown; her past not a clouded image. She walked towards a future. She walked with a past. She walked to face the last string of old, in order to begin anew.

Chaots stood on the rocky shores ahead, watching Nyx step toward them. In front and center, stood the leader Jason, the Pathfinder. He stood silhouetted by the hue of the sea and the timeless sands. His skin was a copper shimmer in the sunlight, beautiful as a sculpture yet to be fashioned in the rock. She saw the final design in the uncarved masterpiece and understood now the order beneath the chaos.

Eyes colored in red and black, passion and violence, life and death, stared out from the gathering of Chaots. They did not attack; they accepted her as one of their own. Nyx joined by the side of the Pathfinder. His hand came out to her and traced down her arm, in wordless acceptance of his new queen.

She smiled. Reaching down to the holster Leander had given her, she took what was inside. And then she sliced the Fisherman's knife across the Pathfinder's neck.

He fell to the sand, dead. Surprise tarnished his lifeless eyes, but aside the surprise was the realization that he had indeed found the queen of the Chaots. But she stood alone.

Bringing her hand to his throat, she soaked her hands in the Pathfinder's blood. She brought her fingertips up to her forehead and painted the red down cross her features, down to her chin. A warrior now exposed underneath. She looked out at the Chaots.

Would they attack?

No.

They bowed. Harsh, uncivil, and callous were their genuflect, but it signaled that she was now their leader. Kill the old and become the new, as in the days before the constrictive rules of society.

Would she stay? Would she be the new Pathfinder of the Chaots—their creator and guide? Or did fate call for her to continue the walk down the shores of time, to see what lay ahead?

The sun proclaimed mastery by her side, as it burned down on the sands, burning what once was, and now ready for her to choose. Ready for the new era to begin.

Epilogue

Years Ago

"I have one!" she said, lopsided smile plastered on her lips as she looked toward him in excitement. It's funny how something that should be so boring was instead turned enjoyable, just by her smile. He looked at her, but only for a moment, before his gaze rested on the curving roads ahead of them. The interlocking branches of the canopy created a natural tunnel for the road and shade for the two of them on their journey.

"Let's hear it," he said, knowing this game was pretty lame, but at least it passed the time. Now in New York, though definitely not the city people imagine when they hear that state's name. Instead they were in upper New York, where trees dominated, rather than the concrete of the city's jungle.

"Ok. What is one thing that you found out about me after we moved in?"

"Well," he said after a moment thinking about the question. "It definitely has to be the way you use toothpaste. What kind of barbarian squeezes it right in the middle of the tube?"

"You're such a savage," he continued. "If I knew what I was getting into ..." He laughed as he spoke, looking out of the corner of his eye at his girlfriend's reaction. "How about me?"

He saw her look up to the sky as if racking her brain for the perfect comeback, looking up at the canopy of leaves around them. Sunlight broke through the crevices of the trees, lighting up her face as she spoke to him. "Oh I know——"

But he never got the chance to hear the rest. He slammed on the brakes, but too late.

The car slammed to a stop. Her vision was blurred, her heart pumping as if the adrenaline was readying her body for fight or flight.

"Are you ok," her boyfriend frantically asked. She felt his hand on her shoulder and that brought her back to the present.

"Yes, are you?" She said and he nodded that he was fine. Looking to the street she saw a crumbled body of brown fur. Quickly she got out of the car and ran to the small deer. It was a baby, a fawn. Blood spotted the fur aside the white splotches of youth.

It was not dead. Breath filled the chest, bringing it up and down in a hard labor. She kneeled beside the fawn, and stroked its fur in a gentle caress. Trying to calm the deer, she whispered to it how everything will be ok.

"He's still alive," she said as he approached her. But it was not said in hope of a better life. They both knew it was too hurt to survive. They both knew that they had to end its suffering.

She watched as he took a jagged rock. Told her to look away. She brought her hand up to her face and covered her eyes. She heard the sound. The crunch. The death. She kept her face covered until she felt his hand reach to her chin and turned her to face him. "I'm going to move the body away from the road so no one hits him again."

He wiped away the tears from her face; the deer's blood smudged her cheeks as he did so. Then he moved back to the deer and she followed. One moment can define a lifetime. One moment can set all else in motion. One moment can be the last, she thought as he lifted and carried the deer's body to the overgrown ferns on the side of the road. He picked one flower and gave it to her. Such beauty to signify such horror. Why did flowers become an offering to the dead? Such contrast to the rot that will come. The emptiness that the reaper's hand takes away. Did they show that something with beauty can still spring from the ground, where below worms eat away at carcasses? That death in turn brings life and hardship sparks light.

As if reading her mind, her boyfriend circled his hand in her own, careful not to crush the flower that he had given her. "I wish I saw him."

She had seen the deer though.

That was the weird part about it, the part that she could not separate fact from fiction. She remembered the sun hitting her eyes, so she had shaded them and looked toward the road. The deer was standing there, but not as one would expect. It was not startled, like a deer caught in literal headlights, but it looked as if rot and emptiness had already come even before the car hit it. Was it just a foretelling of what would be, she wondered, or was she mistaken.

Letting her hand fall from his, she placed the flower on the deer. She did not want to look up at the fawn's head, for the image plastered in her mind, painted by the sounds of the rock crushing the skull was enough. Instead, she focused on the splotched pattern on brown and white of its body. It seemed frail, not just because it was young. Was the fawn's mother close by, would it look for its baby all of her life without knowing what had happened?

Again they drove through the natural gateway of green but now quietly. No smile escaped her lips, no laughter filled the car. He felt terrible. He should have seen the deer and swerved around it. The fawn's mangled body played second fiddle to the image of its skull. The sound it made as he brought the rock to the deer's head. The feeling of it break under his hit. And the feel of how it weighed like nothing as he picked up its lifeless body to move it from the road. She must hate him.

But suddenly she broke the silence and broke his preconceptions.

"After I moved in with you," she said, continuing the conversation they had before the accident, "I found out what a big heart you have. And how your love was without end, so much so, that I stopped looking for the horizon. I found out how much I loved you back."

Her voice washed away the darkness that had shaded his thoughts and brought the beauty of the surrounding and of her back to him.

Hitting the deer was a defining moment. One that could bring tragedy, yet he wanted to change it into something else. He took the ring from his pocket.

"I have been waiting for a perfect moment for the last few months," he said. "But I haven't found one yet. I know, this is far from a perfect moment ... probably the opposite of one. But maybe it is in life's imperfect moments that we grow the most, that causes the most change and the most clarity. For I know now that not only do I want you in my life, but you are my life."

He hoped she would say yes. He hoped that their path would intertwine into eternity.

He looked over at his wife, concern marking his features as he swept away a stray hair from her face. So much had happened since he had proposed to her on the roads of New York. They had married. She had gotten pregnant. However, the past few months of her pregnancy had been difficult. Tremors had started. Odd behavior changes. At first the doctors blamed it on the hormones of pregnancy. Then on a virus or bacteria. Give it time, it will pass, they said. She took antibiotics and other drugs, however worried that they would affect their baby, but knowing that they had to stop this downward spiral.

When those did not work, the doctors began to think it was a mental disorder triggered by the pregnancy. And when she got worse, they had her committed to a mental health institute where she could get the care she needed. He just hoped that once they had the baby she would get better. But now he had started having the same tremors.

He hid them from her. He did not want to add to the stress she was going through. He had to be strong for her.

This isn't going to be forever. He had to believe that, and the idea that one day he would be standing next to her again. The sun lighting up her hair as she looked at him, again like how she used to, again with the love they shared for each other. Yet every moment that future seemed more distant, as a new one became clear. She was slipping away from him and he was powerless to stop it. And now, with the tremors, he was following her decline. Following her footsteps away. Not even the hopes of the baby could bring peace. He stood, letting his hand fall from hers. He hated seeing her like this, chained to the bed. It was said to prevent any self-harm, but he knew it was not just 'self-harm' that it was there to stop. She was burning up, she screamed in pain and anguish.

"Someone help. Please we need a doctor. We need to go to the hospital," he shouted, pleading to deaf ears.

Pain came in waves. These last months it felt as if she was lost at sea, further and further from the coasts she was pulled. She tried so hard to stop it. To grab any lines her husband threw her way, to pull herself back. But despite her efforts she drifted further. And now the child inside her was coming as she herself was caught in a final and deadly riptide.

"I love you," she whispered to her husband, as tears came to her eyes. But not the sweet saltiness ran down her face, as the smell of iron taunted her demise. She screamed again, struggling against the padded straps that weighed her down. Hearing parts of conversations, her husband frantic. The doctor working.

She felt the straps being released from around her wrists. It must have been her husband, no longer wanting her to struggle against the chains that held her down. But release her it did, as the sea of her dreams turned dark and dragged her mind down into its unending abyss.

A baby cried. She felt blood stream down her legs. Too much. She felt her husband's touch along her forehead. It made her momentarily remember when he had taken her face in his hands on the road in New York. Had wiped away her tears. Then even that moment was lost from her mind.

She had to get away. Had to run from this confinement. She tried. Tried to leave.

The doctor was in her way. She wanted to escape, to force herself pass him and away. She clawed at his face in attack. His hands came up in defense and wrapped around her throat choking her.

Gasping for air, struggling against him. But suddenly her struggle ended. The strangulation stopped. Air again. Her husband had hit the doctor over the head to protect her. The doctor lay motionless now, and now her husband's arms came around her.

His touch was not like the doctors. He did not move in harm ... but still she acted. She felt his skin come to her mouth. The gush of his blood ran down her lips. *No.* Why? She could not stop. Life escaped her husband and came into her. Life escaped herself as the trauma grew into too much. Blood poured from her wounds of childbirth and she fell on the floor in her love's embrace, enclosed by red. Husband and wife now dead. Surrounded by the newborn's cries.

As the flower was to the deer. Now the baby was to them.

Acknowledgments

I started writing this book in April 2007, though I put publishing it on pause due to life circumstance and having the story grow more within my mind every year. I would like to thank Linda Bertrand, Spencer Beaver, and Paul Beaver who contributed to this book in the editing process. Thank you to Cristina Tănase for the beautiful cover design. A special thanks to TGC, especially Jenny Jones, where I found my inspiration initially. Finally, I am profoundly grateful to Eric Walker, Nicholas Borgen, and Mauricio Borgen, who have helped me during all of the years of writing and revising.